Praise for the Edgar® and Agatha award–nominated Gaslight Mysteries

"Tantalizing."
—Catherine Coulter, #1 *New York Times* bestselling author of *The End Game*

"This long-lasting series . . . has lost none of its interest or attraction. . . . Thompson has always vividly shown the life of the rich and the very poor of the city. . . . This is a strong tale, emotionally and historically, and a puzzling mystery."
—RT Book Reviews (4½ stars, top pick)

"Victoria Thompson shines. . . . Anne Perry and Caleb Carr fans, rejoice!"
—Tamar Myers, national bestselling author of *Tea with Jam and Dread*

"Fast-paced. . . . Another Victorian page-turner!"
—Robin Paige, national bestselling author of *Death on the Lizard*

"*Gangs of New York*, eat your heart out—this book is the real thing."
—*Mystery Scene*

"A fascinating window into a bygone era." —*Kirkus Reviews*

"Thompson vividly re-creates the gaslit world of old New York."
—*Publishers Weekly*

"Sarah Brandt makes an intriguing sleuth, and [Thompson's] Gaslight series is a consistent winner."
—*Booklist*

"Rewarding reading to fans of Rhys Bowen and Cordelia Frances Biddle."
—*Library Journal*

"With writing this good, I would recommend not missing a single Thompson tale."
—*Suspense Magazine*

MURDER ON PLEASANT AVENUE

A Gaslight Mystery

Victoria Thompson

BERKLEY PRIME CRIME
New York

BERKLEY PRIME CRIME
Published by Berkley
An imprint of Penguin Random House LLC
penguinrandomhouse.com

Copyright © 2020 by Victoria Thompson
Excerpt from *Murder on Wall Street* copyright © 2021 by Victoria Thompson
The Edgar® name is a registered service mark of the Mystery Writers of America, Inc.
Penguin Random House supports copyright. Copyright fuels creativity, encourages
diverse voices, promotes free speech, and creates a vibrant culture. Thank you for buying
an authorized edition of this book and for complying with copyright laws by not
reproducing, scanning, or distributing any part of it in any form without permission.
You are supporting writers and allowing Penguin Random House to continue to
publish books for every reader.

BERKLEY and the BERKLEY & B colophon are registered trademarks and BERKLEY
PRIME CRIME is a trademark of Penguin Random House LLC.

ISBN: 9781984805751

Berkley Prime Crime hardcover edition / April 2020
Berkley Prime Crime mass-market edition / February 2021

Printed in the United States of America
3   5   7   9   10   8   6   4   2

Cover art by Karen Chandler

This is a work of fiction. Names, characters, places, and incidents either are the product
of the author's imagination or are used fictitiously, and any resemblance to actual persons,
living or dead, business establishments, events, or locales is entirely coincidental.

To all my Italian ancestors who bravely left their homes and families, endured hardship, and overcame prejudices to build a new life for those of us who came after them

I

THE QUICK BROWN FOX JUMPS OVER THE LAZY DOG," Maeve whispered to herself, deliberately striking each key on the typewriter as she said it. Why had she thought working in Mr. Malloy's private investigator's office would be exciting? The first thing he and his partner, Gino Donatelli, had wanted her to do was learn to use the typewriter. She would never get the hang of this. She should have been content just being a nanny to the Malloy children. Taking little Catherine to and from school and getting her and her brother, Brian, ready for bed was so much easier than this. At least being a nanny didn't require using machinery.

She looked up when the main office door opened, grateful for the interruption.

To her surprise, a lovely young woman came in. She looked nothing like their usual clients. She was obviously

Italian, and she wore what must be her Sunday best, including an interesting little hat. She twisted her gloved hands nervously in front of her.

"May I help you?" Maeve asked brightly.

"Is this Mr. Malloy's office?" she asked without a trace of an accent. She glanced around uncertainly at the utilitarian office space with its plain wooden desk and chairs and a pair of windows that provided a stunning view of a brick wall. She'd probably been expecting something grander.

"Yes, it is."

"And Gi—I mean, Mr. Donatelli, too?"

Maeve somehow managed not to wince. This beautiful young Italian woman was looking for Gino Donatelli, and Maeve didn't even want to know why. She also shouldn't care, so why did she?

Should she lie? Did she dare send the woman away? But that was foolish. She'd only come back. Besides, the door to Gino's office was open, and he'd apparently overheard the woman's question, because he'd already come out.

"Teo?" he asked, surprised but also much too pleased to see her. Of course he was. Any man would be happy if a woman this lovely had sought him out.

"Oh, Gino!" she cried, hurrying to him and giving him both her hands, which he took with a familiarity that made Maeve furious.

"What's wrong?" Gino asked. "Is it—?"

"No, no, nothing with the family, but Gino, it's something terrible," she said, bursting into tears.

"There now, don't cry," Gino said, which is what men always said, but only because it made them feel helpless to see a woman cry. He slipped his arm around her shoulders without the slightest hesitation—they knew each other very well!—and led her into his office. "Maeve," he called back over his shoulder, "would you get Teo a glass of water?"

How dare he ask her to wait on his paramour! But the washroom was just next door to their offices, so Maeve was back in no time. By then Mr. Malloy had come out of his office to see what all the commotion was about.

"What—?" he began, but Maeve cut him off.

"Gino has a lady visitor." Did she sound disgruntled? Mr. Malloy's eyebrows rose, so she must have. Oh dear, that would never do.

Gino hadn't closed the door, though, so Maeve went right in. Teo—what kind of a name was that?—had produced a handkerchief to dry her tears, and she gratefully accepted the glass of water Maeve handed her. Her face, Maeve was annoyed to see, did not blotch up when she cried, and when her tears had dried, she looked as lovely as ever.

"Can I get you anything else, Miss . . . ?" She glanced expectantly at Gino, waiting for an introduction.

"It's missus," Gino said with a sly grin. "Mrs. Donatelli."

Maeve usually prided herself in her ability to conceal her emotions, but this time, she couldn't stop her jaw from dropping or her eyes from widening in shock. *Mrs. Donatelli*, and she certainly wasn't his mother! Was it possible? Anything was possible with these Italians. She couldn't imagine Gino had gotten married without telling them, but hadn't he mentioned that his parents had found a bride for his brother? If they arranged marriages for their children . . .

"Mrs. Donatelli?" Mr. Malloy echoed, having followed her into Gino's office. "How do you do? I'm Frank Malloy."

Mrs. Donatelli gave him an uncertain smile.

"And this is Miss Smith," Gino said, still smiling slyly. "She's learning to typewrite."

Maeve glared at him, but his grin never wavered.

"And which brother are you married to, Mrs. Donatelli?" Mr. Malloy asked.

"Rinaldo," she said proudly. "He is the oldest."

Rinaldo? Of course. She was married to one of Gino's *brothers*—he had about twenty-seven of them, if she remembered correctly—so of course she would be *Mrs. Donatelli*. What had she been thinking? "So nice to meet you, Mrs. Donatelli," she said with complete sincerity.

"Teodora was just going to tell me why she's here," Gino said. "Something terrible, you said, but not something with our family."

"No, not with our family, but terrible, yes." Her uncertain smile vanished. "Miss Harding has been kidnapped."

Maeve and Mr. Malloy looked to Gino for an explanation, but he was apparently just as puzzled as they were.

"Who is Miss Harding?" Gino asked.

"She is a worker at the settlement house. You know what that is?" she added to all of them.

They all nodded. Mr. Malloy's wife, Sarah, had been involved with The Daughters of Hope Mission, which was where Maeve had found shelter when her grandfather's death had left her alone in the world. Maeve had first met Mrs. Malloy there, and that had eventually led her here. Do-gooders of all types were opening settlement houses all over the city, so called because volunteers from more prosperous neighborhoods would "settle" there, living among the poor so they could more accurately discern their needs and therefore meet them. And of course Mrs. Malloy had recently opened a maternity clinic on the Lower East Side.

"What do you mean, she was kidnapped?" Maeve asked. "Has there been a ransom note or something?"

Teo shook her head. "Not that I heard, at least not yet, but she disappeared yesterday. She did not return to the house after she went to visit some neighbors, and she was gone all night. She would never be gone all night unless something happened to her. Some children said a man stopped her in the street, but after that, no one saw her again."

"That does sound serious, but maybe there's a simple explanation," Mr. Malloy said. "She might've just gotten tired of the work and decided to go home."

"She left all of her things behind, though," Teo said, "and there is more."

"What?" Gino asked.

"It is the Black Hand." She crossed herself against mention of this evil secret organization.

"The Black Hand?" Gino echoed in alarm. "Surely not . . ."

"They kidnapped Mrs. Cassidi. They held her for a month, until Mr. Cassidi could pay them."

"A month!" Maeve cried. "How horrible for her!"

"Isn't Mr. Cassidi the man Rinaldo works for?" Gino asked in amazement.

"Yes, he is. I do not think Mrs. Cassidi will ever be herself again. She refuses to even see visitors who come to comfort her, and she won't leave her house, not even to go to church. And there were others, too. Usually children of the Italian businessmen who have done well and have money, like Mr. Cassidi. I don't want this to happen to Jane—Miss Harding—so I told Mr. McWilliam—he is the head resident at the settlement—that I would ask Gino and Mr. Malloy to help."

"Why didn't you ask the police to help?" Mr. Malloy asked.

She gave him a pitying look. "The police do not care about the Italians, Mr. Malloy."

"But Miss Harding isn't Italian, is she?" Maeve asked.

"No, but the police do not challenge the Black Hand, because they do not concern themselves with the Italians."

"But what about Detective Sergeant Petrosino?" Gino asked.

"Yes," Mr. Malloy said. "Back when he was police commissioner, Governor Roosevelt promoted Petrosino specifically to handle crime in the Italian neighborhoods." Because the Italians were so suspicious of outsiders, Roosevelt had discovered he needed Italians on the police force to deal with crime in their neighborhoods. Gino had been one of them until he came to work for Mr. Malloy.

"Mr. Petrosino cannot be everywhere, Mr. Malloy," Teo said. "He is only one man, and besides, if you go to the police, the Black Hand will kill your loved ones."

"Have they actually killed anyone?" Gino asked, outraged.

"Not yet. The men pay the ransom and everything is fine."

"Then why not just pay the ransom for Miss Harding?" Maeve asked.

"We do not know how long it will take for them to ask, and Miss Harding, she is an unmarried American lady. She cannot . . . We must find her," Teo concluded with an uneasy frown.

"But—" Gino tried.

Maeve cut him off. "She means Miss Harding's reputation will be ruined if word gets out she was the captive of a gang of Italian criminals."

Teo nodded gratefully. "She is a good lady. She came to live at the settlement because she truly wanted to help people. We cannot let her life be destroyed because she was kind."

"Because even if nothing really happens to her, people will always assume the worst," Maeve said.

Mr. Malloy was nodding his understanding. "But Gino and I can be discreet, and if we rescue Miss Harding quickly, maybe no one will even find out this happened."

"I see," Gino said. "What about her family? Could the kidnappers be thinking they'll pay the ransom?"

"They aren't rich," Teo said, "or at least Miss Harding said they weren't, but neither are the Italians who are paying ransoms for their wives and children. I suppose the Black Hand would think Miss Harding's family could pay, though."

"Or maybe they think the settlement house will pay," Gino said.

"Those places don't have any money," Maeve scoffed. "Everyone who works there is a volunteer."

"I don't know if they think the settlement house can pay or not," Teo said, tearing up again, "but we must find Miss Harding quickly. Gino, will you help?"

"Of course."

"I will, too," Mr. Malloy said.

"No one can pay you," Teo warned them.

"We'll do it as a favor to Gino's family," Mr. Malloy said, earning a grateful smile from Teo.

Maeve wanted to volunteer as well, but she knew Mr. Malloy would remind her that her job was to be in the office in case a potential client came in. And to practice her typing. Why did men get to have all the fun?

WHERE IS THE SETTLEMENT HOUSE?" FRANK ASKED AS he and Gino escorted Teodora down the stairs and out of their office building.

"It is on East One Hundred and Fifteenth Street."

"A Hundred and Fifteenth Street?" Frank echoed in amazement. "I thought it was in Little Italy."

Gino grinned. "It is. East Harlem is the other Little Italy."

"And it is bigger and much nicer, too," Teo said.

"Oh yes, Italian Harlem. I should have remembered, but it's pretty far uptown, so I don't ever see it."

"But don't try to tell my mother how nice it is," Gino said. "She thinks Rinaldo and Teo moved into the wilderness when they settled up there."

"But Rinaldo needed work, and that is where it is."

"My brother is a carpenter," Gino said.

"He does beautiful work, Mr. Malloy," Teo assured him.

"I'm sure he does. I guess the best way to get there is to walk over to the Third Avenue El." The elevated train would carry them eighty or so blocks north far more quickly than they could travel on the streets.

Conversation was difficult as they made their way along the crowded sidewalks and crossed the busy streets. The train arrived just as they'd finished climbing up the stairs to the tracks that ran one story above.

"Does Rinaldo know you're doing this?" Gino asked when they had taken their seats in the car.

"It was his idea to ask for your help. He could not come himself because he has to work."

Gino glanced at Frank, his expression telling him this was serious indeed. Italian women didn't usually go gallivanting all over the city on their own. "One reason Mama doesn't like Italian Harlem is because she says there are too many Sicilians living there."

"That is silly," Teo said. "Besides, the Sicilians keep to themselves. They have their own neighborhoods and we have ours."

"Do you think the Sicilians could be the ones doing the kidnapping?" Frank asked.

Teo looked around in alarm, but no one was near enough to hear them. "They do not do the kidnapping," she said in a near whisper. "They steal things and make the bad money."

"Counterfeit money?" Frank asked.

"Yes. The *other ones*," she continued, probably not wanting to say the group's name in public, "they make people pay them not to blow up their stores or their homes, and they kidnap women and children."

Which was worse? Both groups were a blight on the Italian immigrants, like Gino's family, who could expect little help from the police and had no reason to trust them in any case.

"How did you get involved with the settlement house, Teo?" Gino asked.

"I go there to help mostly. They have all kinds of classes. They teach people how to speak English and all the things they need to know to become citizens. They teach adults how to read. They teach sewing and cooking and—"

"You don't need to learn how to cook," Gino teased.

She blushed and gave him a swat. "I said I *help*. And people need to learn how to cook American food. They have a nursery and a kindergarten for children so their mothers can go to work. They even have a playground. They bought five houses in a row and combined all the backyards."

A playground in the city was a rarity and would attract the children who would, in turn, bring their parents. Someone knew what they were doing.

"You said the people who work there are volunteers," Frank said. "Where do they come from?"

"From all over. They went to college first, even the women," she added in wonder. "Miss Harding just came a few weeks ago, after she graduated."

"Is she from the city?" Frank asked.

"A town up north somewhere," Teo said. "I forget the name."

Up north could mean anywhere, but certainly not a place like New York City. A naïve young woman would have been easy prey for anyone in East Harlem. Didn't the settlement give their workers instruction in how to stay safe? Frank should give this head resident—whatever that meant—a piece of his mind.

For the rest of the trip, Teo told them all about the settlement and the work they did. By the time they'd reached the place itself, which was just a short walk from the El stop on 116th Street, he saw it was just as Teo had said, a group of five row houses that looked pretty much like all the others on that street except for a large sign that read HARLEM SET-TLEMENT HALL and additional lines of what looked like gibberish to Frank but which was most likely the same thing in various languages. As Teo had explained, the settlement served everyone in the neighborhood, which included Germans, the Irish, and Jews from Eastern Europe, in addition to the Italians, who were relatively new to the area.

No one paid them any more attention than two strangers in the neighborhood would normally draw, but Frank figured if Miss Harding really had been kidnapped, someone would be watching the settlement house to see if the police had been notified. People had always recognized Frank as a cop, even though he'd worn regular street clothes when he was a detective sergeant with the police force, and they still often assumed he was one. Hopefully, someone would know he wasn't, especially if that might put Miss Harding in even greater danger.

Teo led them into what appeared to be the main door. She didn't stop to speak to anyone but took them down the hall and upstairs, past several rooms where classes seemed to be going on. Instead of children, though, the students were adults of various ages, some quite elderly. Upstairs, what had once been bedrooms had been transformed into offices. Teo stopped outside one of the doors that stood open and rapped on the door frame. "Mr. McWilliam?"

"Mrs. Donatelli, you're back," a voice said, and a man appeared in the doorway. Christopher McWilliam looked to be around thirty, an ordinary enough fellow in a suit and boiled shirt that seemed a bit limp for so early in the day. His otherwise pleasant face was drawn and his eyes were bloodshot, as if he hadn't slept.

Teo introduced the men. "Have you heard anything?" she added.

"Nothing. Please come in, Mr. Malloy and Mr. Donatelli. Thank you for coming so quickly. I'm sure Mrs. Donatelli explained the urgency."

"I will be downstairs if you need me," Teo said, closing the door behind her.

Frank blinked in surprise. Sarah and Maeve would have assumed they were welcome at a meeting like this. He'd have to let Sarah know that Teo Donatelli needed to be a little more modern.

Mr. McWilliam directed Frank and Gino to the somewhat worn sofa that sat against one of the walls. McWilliam's desk took up another, facing the windows that overlooked the street. A bookcase stood against the third wall, filled with books and papers stuck in haphazardly. Mc-William turned his desk chair around to face them. "I'm sure Mrs. Donatelli has told you everything we know."

"Why don't you tell us again yourself," Frank suggested. "Tell us everything you know about Miss Harding, too."

McWilliam took a deep breath, as if he had to fortify himself for this, and he probably did. To have a young woman under his protection disappear would reflect badly on him and his whole organization, not to mention the horror that Miss Harding would suffer. "Miss Harding is missing. From what we have pieced together, she went to call on some new arrivals over on Pleasant Avenue, to invite them to some activities here. She left them—they verified this—around three o'clock. Some children saw her speaking to a man who stopped her on the sidewalk. No one knows who the man was, or if they do, they're afraid to say. At any rate, no one has seen her since."

"How well do you know Miss Harding?"

McWilliam shifted uneasily in his chair and glanced at the door, as if checking to make sure it was closed and they couldn't be overheard. "I know her very well. I've known her since she was a little girl."

"Your families were friends, then?" Gino guessed.

"Yes. We lived in the same town. Saratoga Springs. Jane, I mean Miss Harding, was about eight years younger than I, so I never paid her much attention until she came home from her first year of college. She had grown into a . . . a remarkable young woman," he said, although Frank thought he meant she had gotten a lot prettier. "I was home for a visit, you see. I had already begun my work here. We opened the settlement house about five years ago. I wasn't here in the very beginning, but some of my friends from college had gotten involved with the settlement movement, and I thought I'd join them."

"And now you're in charge?" Frank asked.

"I'm the head resident, yes, for about two years now. I know that's an odd term," he added at their puzzled frowns. "We call the volunteers who come to live here residents, and I supervise all of them, so I'm the head resident."

"And you recruited Miss Harding?" Gino asked.

"I . . ." He glanced at the door again. "This isn't generally known, but . . . I told you I began to notice Miss Harding while she was attending college, and I started to court her. With her family's blessing of course. We . . . I had proposed to her, but I have decided to make the settlement house my life's work, and she thought she should experience it herself before giving me her answer."

Gino nodded wisely. "In case she didn't like it."

"That's not how she phrased it, but yes. And I had to agree. I wouldn't want her to be miserable, since my work will necessitate my living here in the city among the people I serve."

"And she probably wouldn't want you to give up your calling just to please her," Frank speculated, mostly to get a feeling for Miss Harding.

"She did say that, almost exactly," McWilliam admitted with obvious pride. "She really is a remarkable young woman."

He'd described her that way twice. Was he just smitten or was Miss Harding really something special? Frank's wife was certainly remarkable, and he knew many women really were, but was Miss Harding one of them? "Is it possible," Frank said, trying to sound apologetic, "that Miss Harding decided she really cannot accept this way of life and simply left the city and went home?"

"Without even speaking to me?" McWilliam asked, appalled at the very suggestion.

"She might have wanted to avoid a very painful conversation."

"No, absolutely not. She isn't like that. She isn't a . . . a coward. She would have told me if she couldn't . . . No, she wouldn't have just gone off like that. If nothing else, she wouldn't want to worry people. Besides, I'm told she didn't take any of her things with her."

"Have you spoken to her parents to be sure?"

"I . . . I didn't want to alarm them."

"I can understand that, but we do need to make sure she isn't safely at home. Maybe you can telephone them about something else. Maybe a surprise you're planning and you need their advice or something. If she's there, they'll be upset with you and let you know it. If she's not there and they haven't heard from her, they'll behave normally."

"I see, yes. We should make sure, I suppose," McWilliam said with obvious reluctance. He certainly wouldn't want to frighten them unnecessarily.

"And meanwhile, Gino and I will begin our investigation. I know you're concerned for Miss Harding's reputation, so we'll be as discreet as possible. First of all, I'd like to speak to the lady who was kidnapped, the one Mrs. Donatelli told us about."

"Mrs. Cassidi," McWilliam said with a weary sigh. "She won't speak to you. She won't even see you or any other man. She even turned away her priest. I think she finally allowed one or two of her closest female friends in, but she's still very upset by what happened to her. Terrified of everything, or so I'm told."

"That's understandable," Frank said, his mind racing.

This Mrs. Cassidi was the only person who might give them some insight into how to find Miss Harding. And if she wouldn't see a man . . . "Do you have a telephone here, Mr. McWilliam?"

"Yes, we do. You're not thinking you'll telephone Miss Harding's parents, are you?"

"No. I need to telephone my wife."

SARAH MALLOY FOUND THE HARLEM SETTLEMENT house easily enough. Malloy's instructions had been very clear. What was not clear was why he had summoned her. He couldn't discuss it on the telephone, he'd said. No one discussed sensitive information on the telephone since you never knew when the operator might be listening, and newspapers were always willing to pay for bits of gossip that might make good news stories.

She wasn't sure exactly what to do now that she was at the settlement house, though. At The Daughters of Hope Mission, where she volunteered, and the maternity clinic that she had founded, visitors had to knock in order to be admitted, for security. Here, however, she noticed as she approached the entrance, people came and went freely. In any case, she didn't have to decide anything at all because a lovely young Italian woman came out to greet her when she started up the front steps.

"You must be Mrs. Malloy," she said. "I'm Teodora Donatelli."

"So nice to meet you, Mrs. Donatelli. I assume you're married to one of Gino's brothers."

"That's right. Rinaldo. Mr. Malloy and Gino are waiting for you inside. I will show you."

She took Sarah in and down the hall to what appeared to be a classroom, empty now. Malloy and Gino were waiting for her there. They had been discussing something in whispers but they jumped to their feet when she and Teo appeared.

"You made good time," Malloy observed, coming to greet her. "And you brought your medical bag. Good."

"I must admit you have me intrigued. Is someone giving birth?" Sarah asked with a teasing smile.

"Not exactly, but we need your help."

"I will be outside if you need me," Teo said, turning for the door.

"Would you stay, Mrs. Donatelli?" Malloy asked. "I'm sure Mrs. Malloy will have questions only you can answer."

Mrs. Donatelli was surprised but apparently pleased to be included. She closed the classroom door and took one of the chairs Gino had pulled into a small circle so they could talk easily and keep their voices low. They told Sarah what they had learned about Jane Harding and her abduction.

"So Miss Harding and Mr. McWilliam are engaged?" Sarah asked.

"Not yet," Gino said. "We gather she came to the settlement house because she wanted to see what she'd be getting into before giving him her answer."

Sarah turned to Mrs. Donatelli. "Mr. McWilliam said their relationship was a secret, but did you know about it?"

Teo wrinkled her nose. "Everyone knew. They didn't speak of it of course, but you could tell how Mr. McWilliam feels about her."

"Ah yes, love and a cough cannot be hid, as they say," Sarah said, although she noticed Teo had not mentioned the way Miss Harding felt about Mr. McWilliam. She might have managed to hide her feelings better or perhaps her feelings had cooled when she realized the kind of life she would have as his wife. "So exactly what is it you need for me to do?" she asked Malloy.

"McWilliam is naturally afraid of what the Black Hand will do to Miss Harding, and she must be absolutely terrified, so we want her returned as quickly as possible. We'll have a difficult time getting people in the neighborhood to talk to us, though."

"No one will speak of those people," Teo confirmed solemnly.

"So we thought if we could question Mrs. Cassidi about where she was held for so long, we might be able to figure out where it was and find Miss Harding."

"That's assuming they were kidnapped by the same people and taken to the same place," Sarah said.

"The Black Hand is very organized," Gino said. "They kidnap people regularly, so they must have a place they can keep them without worrying they'll be found."

"But Mrs. Cassidi will not talk to anyone," Teo said.

"Not to any men, at least," Malloy said. "I'm hoping we can convince her husband to allow a woman to see her."

"But if she doesn't want to see anyone at all . . ." Sarah protested.

"If her husband tells her she must, she will do it," Gino said with a confidence that annoyed Sarah. Poor Mrs. Cassidi.

"But who will convince the husband?" Sarah asked.

"I think he will help us if we tell him what we're trying to do," Malloy said. "If we succeed, we might even be able to break up the Black Hand and stop the kidnappings."

A worthy endeavor, Sarah had to agree, but . . . "Why do

you think Mrs. Cassidi will talk to me even if her husband forces her to see me?" she asked Teo.

"If you tell her you are trying to stop the Black Hand, she probably will not. She will be too frightened. But Mr. Malloy said you are a nurse."

"I am, and a midwife."

"Maybe Mr. Cassidi thinks his wife is not well after her ordeal," Teo said. "Maybe he thinks she needs to see a nurse to make sure she is all right, but someone who is not from the neighborhood who won't spread gossip."

"That's a really good idea, Teo," Gino said, although he sounded a little too surprised for Sarah's taste. He should expect Teo to have good ideas.

"It *is* a good idea," Sarah said. "That's how you should advise Mr. Cassidi to present it to her, Malloy."

Before Malloy could agree, someone knocked on the door and a man came in without waiting for a response. Malloy introduced Sarah to Mr. McWilliam, who looked as worried as she would expect a man whose beloved had gone missing to look. He wasn't, Sarah noted, particularly handsome or even impressive, the way some men are. He looked like the kind of man Sarah's mother would have called a sensible choice for a husband—steady and kind—but was he a man who a young girl would give up everything for and live in a place like this for the rest of her life? Perhaps she had misjudged him.

"I telephoned Miss Harding's parents," he said, running an unsteady hand over his face. "I made up some story about wanting to surprise Jane with a visit home and asked when would be a convenient time. They were happy to hear from me and gave no indication that they'd heard from or seen Jane."

"I know that was difficult for you," Malloy said, "but we had to be sure. Now we can proceed with our investigation."

"What can I do to help?" McWilliam asked.

"Just try to appear as normal as possible. People will probably notice Miss Harding isn't around, but don't act like you are alarmed."

"I could say she went home for a few days," McWilliam said.

"Yes, that would work," Malloy said. "If we hope to protect her good name, we don't want people to start talking about her disappearing and wondering where she is."

Quickly, Malloy explained to McWilliam what their next step was going to be.

"And what if Mrs. Cassidi can't tell you anything that helps, or what if she won't speak to Mrs. Malloy at all?" McWilliam asked.

"Then we'll think of something else," Malloy said.

"You must not lose hope, Mr. McWilliam," Teo said. "I know Gino and Mr. Malloy will do everything they can to find Miss Harding."

McWilliam nodded almost absently, as if he had no confidence at all. "Who is going to speak to Mr. Cassidi?"

Sarah expected Malloy to say he would, but he turned to Gino instead. "Do you think he would take my advice?"

Gino shook his head. "He'd be too suspicious of you. He'd see you as a policeman. Besides, I don't know how well he speaks English."

"That's what I was thinking, too. You're the only one who can do this, Gino. Do you think you should take Mrs. Donatelli with you?"

"Me?" Teo asked in surprise.

"Yes," Sarah said. "You can speak for Mrs. Cassidi. Tell

him she may be injured or sick and not want to tell him for fear of worrying him."

"I suppose I can do that," Teo said uncertainly.

"Of course you can. If he cares for his wife at all, he must be at his wits' end to know how to help her. We'll offer him a solution."

"Should we go to see him now?" Gino asked. "He'll probably be at his office."

"The sooner we see him, the sooner we can see Mrs. Cassidi and the sooner we can find Miss Harding," Malloy said. "Do you know him, Mr. McWilliam?"

McWilliam started at the sudden attention. "I . . . yes, he has been a big supporter of the settlement. In fact, Mrs. Cassidi has been taking classes here. Or rather she had been before . . . Well, anyway, he also encourages his workers to study English here."

"Then you should go with Gino and Mrs. Donatelli, to introduce Gino. And you will have to tell him one of your volunteers has been kidnapped, too. Then Gino will explain that Mrs. Malloy will see his wife to be sure she isn't ill and also to ask what she remembers that might help us find the missing woman."

"And if he refuses to help?" McWilliam said.

Malloy smiled apologetically at Teo. "Then Mrs. Donatelli will start weeping and beg him."

She couldn't help smiling at that. "I will try, Mr. Malloy."

"Nobody could refuse you," Gino assured her.

"Let's go, then," McWilliam said. "Maybe we can find Jane before she has to spend another night in captivity."

II

Mr. McWilliam asked one of the other residents, a young woman named Kate Westrop, to give Frank and Sarah a tour of the facilities while he escorted Gino and Teo to Mr. Cassidi's office. Kate was a young woman, probably in her early twenties, who would never be called a beauty, but her fresh face and enthusiasm more than compensated. She wore a plain white shirtwaist and brown skirt and had styled her hair in a neat bun, probably to demonstrate the correct level of modesty and a lack of any ostentation that might put off her poorer neighbors.

Sarah would have liked to question her about Jane Harding, but she couldn't, since they were still pretending Jane wasn't missing. Still, she had a lot of questions for Kate, both about herself and about the workings of the settlement, and Kate answered them patiently and thoroughly.

"What made you volunteer for this work?" Malloy asked

after Kate had told them she'd graduated from college a year earlier and come straight here.

"I wanted to help people, and the settlement houses seemed to be the most effective at doing that."

"Why do you think that is?" Sarah asked.

"Because we live right here with the people we serve," Kate said, warming to her topic. "Most charities are run by rich people who make all the decisions about what poor people need, but they hardly ever ask the poor people themselves what they really need."

Had Sarah done that with the maternity clinic? she wondered with a pang. But she'd gotten the idea from the needs she saw every day as a midwife, so perhaps she'd done it correctly, even without realizing it.

"So you think it's good that you and the other volunteers live here?" Malloy asked.

"Oh yes. We started out . . . Well, not me. I wasn't here in the beginning, but the founders, I mean. They rented a house on this street and opened it as a place for people to gather. I think they'd serve tea and coffee to draw people in and have music and singing. They asked the visitors what services would help them most. Then they figured out how to do those things and started classes. A lot of the people in this neighborhood are immigrants who don't speak English, so we started teaching that first thing. The children seem to pick up English at school or in the streets, but the adults need more formal training."

"I guess the children learn because their lessons in school are all in English," Sarah said.

"And because children just learn everything faster," Kate said. "We have classes in the daytime for the mothers and older people and in the evening for people who work."

"Mrs. Donatelli said you have a kindergarten," Malloy said.

"Yes, and a nursery, too. A lot of the women have to work, but they didn't have anyone to take care of their children, so that was another need we were able to fill."

Kate took them through all the buildings. Someone had cut doors between the row houses so residents and visitors could move between them without going outside. One of the houses had a dormitory for the female residents and another one had one for the male residents, far enough apart to satisfy even the strictest of standards. In between were rooms dedicated to child care and learning for people of all ages.

They had just completed their tour and Kate had asked if they would like some refreshment when Gino, Teo, and Mr. McWilliam returned. Gino and Teo were smiling and Mr. McWilliam looked relieved.

"Mr. Cassidi has agreed to let Mrs. Malloy visit his wife," Mr. McWilliam said.

"I didn't have to cry or beg either," Teo reported with satisfaction. "After Gino explained what we wanted to do, Mr. Cassidi told us his wife has been refusing to see people because she thinks they just want to find out what happened to her so they can gossip about her. She doesn't even trust her friends."

"But I won't gossip," Sarah said. "I hope you made that clear."

"Of course we did," Gino said. "That's why Mr. Cassidi agreed. He wants to help find Miss Harding, too, if we can."

"Although we didn't tell him who had been kidnapped," Mr. McWilliam added quickly. "Please don't mention her name."

"We won't," Sarah promised. "Does Mrs. Cassidi speak English?"

"She has been taking lessons here and she speaks very well, but I told Mr. Cassidi I would go along in case you needed help. I don't think she'll want me there, but . . ." Teo shrugged. "Mr. Cassidi said he would meet us at his house."

NO WONDER THE BLACK HAND HAD CHOSEN MRS. CAS-sidi as a potential kidnap victim, Sarah thought. The Cassidis lived in a comfortable house a few blocks from the settlement, rather than in one of the many new tenements that had sprung up in East Harlem to house the seemingly endless waves of immigrants settling in the city. A wrought iron fence surrounded the tiny front yard, and flowers grew in beds on either side of the front stoop. They looked a bit neglected now, with weeds sprung up here and there, and no wonder, if Mrs. Cassidi had been gone for a month and now refused to leave her house.

A middle-aged Italian man opened the door at their knock. He wore a tailor-made suit and a worried frown. His thick black hair and heavy mustache were shot with gray. Teo introduced Sarah.

"My wife, she is very upset since she is come home," he told Sarah apologetically.

"I'm sure she is. Most people would be after an ordeal like that. Does she know I'm coming?"

"I tell her and . . ." He shook his head.

"If she doesn't want to see me—"

"No, it is not . . . I am . . . I do not understand. For days she will see nobody. Then I tell her a stranger is coming, and she is happy."

This was good news, at least. "Mrs. Donatelli came with me in case there is something she needs to translate, but I'd like to see Mrs. Cassidi alone, at least at first, if that is all right."

"*Sì, sì*, I think this is what she would like best. Please come in."

Teo waited in the parlor, and Mr. Cassidi took Sarah upstairs. The house, she noticed, had been carefully furnished with quality pieces that all looked quite new. Sarah had been in enough homes all over the city to recognize that the Cassidis were financially well-off but they weren't ostentatious about it. Their neighbors would envy them but not hate them for flaunting their success. Unfortunately, this also enabled the kidnappers to identify them as people with the resources to pay a ransom.

Mr. Cassidi stopped outside a closed door and knocked. Then he said something in Italian that included Sarah's name. He must have heard something in response because he opened the door and motioned Sarah inside. The bedroom furniture was heavy and dark, but the bedspread and curtains were bright yellow, giving the room a welcoming glow. The bedroom was almost painfully neat, and Mrs. Cassidi rose from where she had been sitting in a rocking chair by the window. She was a small woman in her forties. She wore a simple house dress, and her dark hair hung down her back in a braid. Her eyes were red-rimmed and haunted, and Sarah guessed she had not been sleeping well since her return. She probably hadn't slept or eaten well during her captivity either.

Mr. Cassidi introduced her to his wife, whose first name was Violetta.

She didn't offer her hand, so Sarah simply smiled. "I'm

very pleased to meet you, Mrs. Cassidi. What a lovely name you have. Violets are such a pretty flower."

Mrs. Cassidi smiled weakly and said something to her husband in Italian that sounded like a rebuke. He scurried away and returned immediately with another chair, which he placed facing the rocking chair where his wife had been sitting. Then he hurried out, closing the door behind him.

"Teo Donatelli came with me, if we have any trouble understanding each other," Sarah said.

"I have been studying English at the settlement," she said. "This will be practice for me. Please, sit."

Sarah set her medical bag down and took the offered seat. "I was so sorry to hear what happened to you, Mrs. Cassidi. Your husband has been very worried about you, so Mr. McWilliam asked me if I would come to see you. I'm a nurse, and I thought perhaps you might be sick or injured in some way and not want to worry your husband by telling him."

Mrs. Cassidi stared back at Sarah for a long moment, her troubled gaze searching Sarah's for something. Sarah hoped her genuine concern was plain enough to see. Then Mrs. Cassidi's dark eyes filled with tears and in the next moment she was quaking with great, soul-wrenching sobs.

No stranger to pain, Sarah sank to her knees in front of the woman, wrapped her arms around her, and let her weep. Sarah wondered if Mrs. Cassidi had allowed herself to really grieve what had happened to her until this moment and realized she probably had not. She had been putting up a brave front for everyone, even her husband, which explained why she had refused visitors and not left her house. Being brave for others was simply too difficult.

Sarah's knees were numb when Mrs. Cassidi finally fell silent and pulled away, muttering apologies in two languages.

Sarah waved away her concerns and handed her a handkerchief. "Would you like some water?" she asked, spotting a carafe on the nightstand.

Mrs. Cassidi nodded, too spent to reply. Sarah gave her a glass and waited while she drank and finished composing herself.

"I am sorry—"

"Don't be sorry," Sarah chastened her. "You have every right to grieve for what was done to you. They took your freedom and put you in fear for your life for weeks! I don't know how you stood it. I think I would have gone mad, but you're not mad. You're just sad and angry, which is perfectly normal."

"Yes, I am very angry. I do not know how to hold all the anger I feel for what they did to me."

"Mrs. Cassidi, I really did come as a nurse, to make sure you are all right. Did they hurt you at all? Hit you or beat you or . . ." Sarah stopped when she saw the look of horror that twisted Mrs. Cassidi's face.

"They hurt me."

"In what way?" Sarah asked as gently as she could, because she was starting to suspect what Mrs. Cassidi was going to say.

"One of them. He . . . he forced me."

Sarah winced in physical pain at the thought of what this poor lady had endured. "I'm so sorry. Are you—?"

"Look at me," she demanded angrily. "I am not young. I am not pretty. He did it only to shame me."

Which was always why men raped women, but Sarah didn't say that. Mrs. Cassidi wasn't interested in learning more about rapists. "Are you injured? Was there blood?"

"A little but it is gone now. I am . . . not hurting anymore. Except in here." She laid a hand over her heart.

"I wish I could tell you that pain will go away, but you *can* learn to live with it."

Mrs. Cassidi shuddered. "I have told no one. Only you."

"I'm glad I came, then. You needed to tell someone. Now it will be easier to tell other people."

"I cannot tell other people," she said, suddenly angry again. "How can I tell my husband another man has taken me? He will never be able to look at me again."

Sarah wanted to reassure her, but she really had no idea how Mr. Cassidi would react. "He may guess even if you don't tell him."

She shrugged. "I will deny it. And I cannot tell other women. They are . . . What do you call the birds who eat the dead?"

"Vultures?"

"Yes, vultures. They come to find out my shame so they can feast on it. I will never speak of it again."

That was her right of course, although Sarah would have advised against it. Perhaps she really had no one whom she could trust, though. The only thing worse than being violated by a stranger was having your friends gossip over it afterward.

Sarah reached into her medical bag and pulled out one of her cards. "Here. If you need anything or you just want someone to talk to, please send for me."

After a moment's hesitation, she took the offered card. "I cannot think about this, so how can I talk about it?"

Sarah had no answer for her. "You might help someone else, though."

"Who?" she scoffed.

"Another woman has gone missing. One of the young

ladies who works at the settlement house. They fear she has
been kidnapped by the same people who took you."

Her eyes widened in horror. "No! Why would they take
one of those girls? They have no money."

"Perhaps they think the girls' families will pay, or maybe
the people at the settlement house."

"That is foolish!"

"The young lady has not been seen since yesterday. She
took nothing with her, and she hasn't returned to her home."

Mrs. Cassidi shook her head. "This is very bad."

"Yes, it is. We were hoping . . . If the same people took
her, they are probably holding her in the same place where
you were. If we could find that place . . ."

Mrs. Cassidi's reddened eyes narrowed suspiciously. "Who
is this *we* who will find it?"

Ah yes, she'd be worried they might call in the police.
"Mrs. Donatelli's brother-in-law is a private investigator.
Mr. McWilliam has asked him to try to find the young lady
and rescue her."

"Not the police?"

"No, not the police." Sarah gave her a few moments to
consider that. "If you could remember the place where you
were kept, what it looked like and any sounds you heard,
perhaps that would help Mr. Donatelli locate it."

"I did not see the outside. I was here, at home, and someone knocked on the door. I open it and they grab me. They
put a sack over my head and carry me to a motorcar. We
drive a long time. I do not know how long. I am too afraid
to remember."

"Of course," Sarah said, nodding her encouragement.

"They carry me inside and drop me on a bed and leave

me alone in a room. I take off the sack, but I can see nothing to know where I am. There is a window, but it is nailed shut and the glass is painted black."

"So you cannot see outside and no one can see you," Sarah guessed. "Was anyone else there?"

"There are children."

"Children? In the neighborhood, you mean?" In the city, children played outside on the sidewalks and the streets, in all weather and wherever they could find an open spot.

"No, in the house. Upstairs. I could hear them."

"In the house with you?"

"Yes. I hear them play. I hear them cry."

But of course. Mr. McWilliam had explained that the Black Hand mostly kidnapped children. How horrible to think of a group of them locked away day and night for heaven knew how long. "Do you know who they were?"

"I do not see them."

If they could locate the house, they could rescue those children as well. "Did you hear anything that might tell us where the house is located?"

"It was quiet. Not like the city."

"Did you hear anything at all outside?"

"A train. It goes by sometimes, but not too close."

So someplace outside the city near a train track. Someplace that could be reached by motorcar. That really wasn't much help. "Would you recognize any of the men who took you?"

"They have masks. When they bring me food, they wear them. I never see faces. I will always remember that one's voice, though. If I hear it again, I will kill him."

Sarah believed her. She asked a few more questions, hoping to stir some memories, but the kidnappers had been very careful not to reveal anything that would have given them away.

"I did not help you," Mrs. Cassidi said at last. "I would like to help you find this lady."

"I know, and maybe we could find those children as well. But I thank you for speaking with me. If you think of anything else, please let me know."

She nodded sadly.

"Is there anything I can do for you? Anything at all?"

"You listen. That is good."

"Please remember, if you need me . . ."

Mrs. Cassidi waved away her concern. "I will do better. I will see my friends. I will tell them lies about how brave I was and how I spit on those men."

Sarah reached out and took her hand. "You are brave. You survived, didn't you? You are one of the strongest women I know."

FRANK HAD TO AGREE WITH SARAH, MRS. CASSIDI HADN'T given them much new information. The kidnappers could have taken her in any one of several directions to get to a quiet place outside the city. Not to New Jersey, which would have involved a ferry, but across the Brooklyn Bridge to the south, or north to the farms that lay not far away.

"It makes sense that they'd have a place north of the city," Gino said. They had all met back in the same classroom at the settlement house. Teo had gone home, but Mr. McWilliam had joined them, hoping Sarah had learned something that would help find Miss Harding. "If they're kidnapping people in East Harlem, that would be the closest."

"And driving through the city with a captive could be

risky," Sarah said. "If she got loose and managed to scream, someone would surely notice."

"Someone knows where this house is," Frank said.

"But they aren't going to tell us," Gino reminded him. "They're terrified of the Black Hand."

"Won't the police already be looking for those children, though?" Sarah said. "Maybe they know something we don't."

"I could find Detective Sergeant Petrosino and ask him," Gino said.

"He won't know anything about it," Mr. McWilliam said grimly. "Mr. Cassidi never went to the police, and the parents of those children probably haven't either. They're—"

"—terrified of the Black Hand," Sarah finished for him. "I know. So how can you hope to find this house if no one will talk?"

"If the windows are painted black, people will have noticed it. Gino and I can come back with the motorcar tomorrow and drive north. There are only a few places to cross the Harlem River, so we can stop along the way and ask people. Once we're out of the city, they might not be as scared to talk."

But he was only putting on a confident face for Sarah's benefit. Any place the Black Hand operated, people would be frightened.

"I'll see if I can find Petrosino," Gino said. "He has a secret office somewhere in Little Italy. My mother will know where it is."

"If it's a secret, how will your mother know?" Mr. McWilliam asked.

Gino gave McWilliam a pitying look. "My mother knows everything."

"He means," Sarah added, "that his mother knows everyone else's mother. There are few secrets in Little Italy."

"Or in Italian Harlem either," Gino added. "It's just that they don't tell them to outsiders."

Mr. McWilliam nodded and ran a hand over his face again. The poor man must be going crazy with worry for Miss Harding. Frank could imagine how he'd feel if Sarah had been kidnapped.

"We'll find her, Mr. McWilliam," Sarah said, laying a hand on his arm.

He nodded, although Frank could see he only wanted to believe her.

"Let us know if you hear from the kidnappers," Frank said. "Meanwhile, Gino and I will try to find Petrosino."

GINO'S MOTHER DID INDEED KNOW WHERE THE SECRET office was located, but she insisted on feeding Frank and Gino before allowing them to escape, since it was supper time by then and they surely were hungry. Frank had to admit he was grateful. Sarah had gone home and would be sitting down to supper with Maeve and their children about now, but he had no idea when he'd make it back home this evening.

Petrosino's office was above a barber shop in the heart of Little Italy. The stairs leading up were located in the rear of the building, where casual passersby wouldn't see people coming and going. Although it was early evening by the time they arrived, they found Petrosino working at his desk.

"Donatelli," he said by way of greeting and rose to shake Gino's hand. Petrosino was a short, stocky man, probably no taller than Sarah, but he gave the impression of being much larger. His dark eyes missed little, and he had a reputation for getting justice when no one else even tried.

"You remember Frank Malloy, don't you?" Gino said.

"Of course," Petrosino said, shaking Frank's hand. "What brings you here?"

"A young woman has been kidnapped from the Harlem settlement house, and we think the Black Hand is responsible," Frank explained.

Petrosino's face tightened with quiet fury, but he just said, "Clear off a chair and have a seat so you can tell me about it." The room held several desks, all piled high with folders and other papers. WANTED posters hung haphazardly on every wall. Frank and Gino found some chairs and sat down. Frank allowed Gino to tell the story.

"This is exactly why we need men like you on the police force, Donatelli," Petrosino said when he'd finished. "You know as well as I do that the Italians won't trust anyone else. They hardly trust me. I've been begging for a squad of Italian Americans to deal with the Black Hand and the other criminals in the Italian community, but so far, my requests have been ignored. Meanwhile, there probably aren't a dozen men on the entire force who speak Italian and none who speak Sicilian."

"Mrs. Cassidi told us they were holding children in the same house where she was," Frank said.

"I'm sure there were. We questioned a boy who was released—we knew he'd been kidnapped, but we weren't able to find him. Then he just showed up one night. His uncle saw him walking down the street. His parents wouldn't admit to paying the ransom of course. We always tell them not to, because that just encourages these villains to kidnap more people, but we can't stop them, so we figured they paid, since the boy was released. Anyway, the boy told us there were other children there with him, but we hadn't been notified of any other kidnappings, so we couldn't do anything."

"Do you have any idea where this house might be?" Frank asked.

"No, and the description you got from Mrs. Cassidi is the most information I've heard about it. The boy who was released couldn't tell us anything at all except to describe the room where he and the other children were held."

"We think it must be north of Harlem," Gino said. "Mrs. Cassidi said it was very quiet, like the country."

"Which would explain why no one claims to know where it is. I wish I could help you, but you seem to know more about this place than I do."

"How long do you think the Black Hand will wait before asking for a ransom?" Frank asked.

"A few days. They want people to be frantic with worry first, but let me tell you something about the Black Hand. It doesn't really exist."

"What?" Gino and Frank cried in unison.

Frank shook his head. "But you just said—"

"I said people have been kidnapped, but they weren't kidnapped by some big, organized group that is responsible for all the crime in New York City, which is what the newspapers claim."

"Then who is responsible?" Gino asked.

"Small groups of crooks. They'll have a leader and a few men to do the work, but they aren't connected in any way with the other small groups of crooks. The kidnapping idea is something they brought over from Italy, and somebody decided to decorate the ransom letters with pictures to frighten the families. They drew a hand holding a dagger dripping with blood, and people called it *La Mano Nera*, the Black Hand. Or maybe it was the newspapers who called it that.

Whoever started it, the newspapers spread the name and also the fear."

"Of course they did," Frank said bitterly. "They love to scare people. It sells more newspapers."

"Americans always think criminals are smarter than they are, too," Petrosino said, "so they think the Black Hand is run by some really clever criminal who has hundreds of men doing his work for him all over the city."

"I see," Frank said. "But it's really just a small gang of men. Or rather several small gangs."

"That makes it harder to stop them, too, because if no one knows who you are, no one can betray you."

"Do you have any idea who might be behind the kidnappings in Italian Harlem?" Gino asked. "Is it the Sicilians?"

Petrosino shook his head. "Everybody wants to blame the newcomers, but the Sicilians are just ordinary crooks. They also do a bit of counterfeiting and run a lottery, too. It's the Calabrians who do the kidnapping and extortion," he said with an apologetic smile. Gino's family was from Calabria.

"Any Calabrian in particular?" Frank asked.

"A name I've heard a lot is Nunzio Esposito. He's been in East Harlem for almost ten years, and he's done pretty well, although he doesn't seem to do any of the work himself."

"Any idea where we could find him?"

"He owns a saloon on a Hundred and Sixteenth Street, but you can see him parading all around East Harlem, too. He likes to toss pennies to the children and give the impression that he's helping the community."

"We'll find him," Gino said.

"Yes," Frank agreed. "And we should probably find him before we go looking for that house."

"Then we should go looking for him tonight," Gino said. "He's not likely to be holding court in the morning."

"He won't be alone, no matter when you go," Petrosino warned. "If he's the one behind the kidnappings, he isn't going to appreciate you asking him about it, and his men won't either."

But in the end, it didn't matter because Nunzio Esposito was nowhere to be found in East Harlem that night, even though several people told them he would surely be at his saloon. They did get some dirty looks for asking about him, though.

"Do you suppose Esposito oversees the kidnappings himself?" Gino asked as he and Frank headed for the El station for the ride home.

"Petrosino said he doesn't get his hands dirty," Frank reminded him. "He's probably just taking a night off, or maybe he has a lady friend he's visiting."

"I hope he's not taking a personal interest in Miss Harding. I keep thinking about what Mrs. Cassidi went through." Sarah had waited until McWilliam had left them to share the news that Mrs. Cassidi had been raped, since she didn't want to terrify him even more than he already was. The news had terrified Frank and Gino almost as much, though.

"So do I, but maybe we'll be lucky and find her before she comes to any harm." But even if she wasn't raped, a young woman as innocent as Jane Harding might never recover from an experience like this.

THE NEXT MORNING, GINO CAME TO THE MALLOY HOUSE early so they could take the motorcar. Frank still preferred not to drive it himself, which was more than fine with Gino and even more fine with Frank. Sarah saw them off. She was planning to spend the day at the maternity clinic on the Lower East Side, although she made Frank promise to telephone her if he got any news about Miss Harding.

They stopped at the settlement house before setting out on their search, just in case Miss Harding had returned. They didn't hold out much hope of this, but it didn't hurt to check.

"Not a word," Mr. McWilliam told them when they found him in his office. He looked as if he hadn't slept at all, although he'd taken pains to shave and dress in fresh clothes. "I don't know how long I can just sit here and do nothing."

"You're protecting Miss Harding's reputation," Frank said. "And it's not likely you'd be able to learn anything if you did start demanding answers from people. Leave this to Gino and me."

"You're right of course, but the waiting . . ."

"We'll find her, Mr. McWilliam, and if we don't, the kidnappers will probably want to release her quickly when they realize someone is looking for her."

"How are we going to pay a ransom, though?" McWilliam asked. "The settlement doesn't have any funds for something like that. We can barely make ends meet as it is."

"Maybe her parents could pay it," Gino said.

"I can't imagine they have the money for something like that, and we can't even ask them," McWilliam said, nearly panicked at the thought. "If they find out she's been kidnapped, they'll make her come home, and they'll never allow her to marry me, not if it means she'll be living here."

Of course they wouldn't. Frank knew he'd never let his own daughter marry a man whose work put her in constant danger. He didn't bother pointing out that Miss Harding herself was probably not going to want to stay at the settlement after this experience either. No sense upsetting McWilliam any more than he was already.

"Gino and I are going to see if we can locate the house Mrs. Cassidi described. We'll telephone around noon to let you know how we're doing and to see if you've had any news about Miss Harding."

"Is there anything I can do in the meantime?" McWilliam asked.

"I'm afraid not," Frank told him.

Leaving a discouraged McWilliam in their wake, Frank and Gino went back downstairs, where they found a rather shady-looking character lurking on the sidewalk near the settlement's front door.

"You Malloy?" he asked as Frank and Gino came down the front stoop. His pockmarked face wore a forbidding scowl, as if he'd practiced it in front of a mirror. He wore a cheap checked suit with a gaudy gold chain across his vest, from which a number of fobs dangled. He apparently had a nervous habit of fingering them, which made a slight jingling sound that was oddly festive.

"That's right," Frank said, unimpressed. "What's it to you?"

"Mr. Esposito is looking for you."

"That's good. We were looking for him last night."

"He knows. You shouldn't go around asking about him."

"Why not?" Frank asked with all the innocence he could muster, which probably wasn't much.

This seemed to stump the man, who just stared back with unabashed irritation. "You need to come with me."

"Why?" Gino asked, not to be outdone by Frank's brazen lack of respect.

"Because Mr. Esposito wants to see you."

"Where would he like to meet?" Frank asked, as if Esposito were inviting him for a social event.

"At his saloon. Come with me."

"We'll take our motorcar, if you don't mind. We'll meet you there," Frank said, nodding to Gino, who had to bite back a smile.

Frank climbed into the motor, which they'd parked in front of the settlement house, while Gino cranked the engine to life.

"Wait a minute," the man protested. "You was to come with me."

"There's no need to escort us," Frank assured him pleasantly. "We know where it is."

Gino hopped into the motor and eased it into gear while the thug stood there sputtering helplessly.

"That was rude," Gino informed Frank as they drove away. "He'll be looking for revenge."

"I hope so," Frank said. He'd felt like hitting something ever since Teo Donatelli had told him about the kidnapping.

The saloon was closed, so Frank let Gino pound on the front door until someone came to answer it.

Another thug, this one more puzzled than threatening, finally answered their summons. "What do you want?"

"We're here to see Esposito," Frank informed him, pushing his way inside before the thug could stop him. Gino followed, still trying not to smirk. "He's expecting us."

The thug suddenly seemed to understand, and he stuck his head out the door and looked up and down the street. "Where's Balducci?"

"Is he the gentleman who was sent to fetch us?" Frank

asked. "He'll be along in a few minutes, I'm sure. Now, where is Esposito? We haven't got all day."

This lack of respect obviously shocked the thug, who scurried away wearing a horrified expression.

"Are you sure you want to antagonize this fellow?" Gino asked.

"We aren't policemen, so they'll know we don't have any real power. I like to give the impression that I do anyway."

Gino nodded his understanding.

After only a few minutes, the thug returned and said, "Mr. Esposito said he'll see you."

Frank thought this very generous of him since he'd ordered them to come, but he didn't bother to say so. They followed the thug to the back of the saloon and down a dark hallway to an office. It was furnished well, with an impressive oak desk and several wingback chairs for visitors. A sofa along one wall looked as if it might serve as overnight accommodations in a pinch.

Nunzio Esposito was a remarkably handsome man of about forty. He wore a neatly trimmed mustache and his hair was thick and dark and just curly enough to be attractive. His suit was tailor-made and a diamond ring winked from his right hand. He didn't bother to rise.

"Mr. Malloy," he said with what sounded like mild surprise. "I understand you have been looking for me."

Frank sized up the seating situation and took one of the wingback chairs, motioning for Gino to do the same. He didn't want to be left standing like a supplicant to this man who was probably used to people showing him a lot more respect than Frank was prepared to do.

"Yes, we have," Frank said when they were seated. "We were told you might be able to help us."

"Help you with what?" Esposito was no longer pretending to be surprised or even unconcerned. Now he just looked annoyed.

"A young lady is missing from the Harlem settlement house. We were told you might be able to help us locate her."

Esposito narrowed his eyes and studied Frank for a long moment. "*Missing*, you say?"

"Yes. We believe she may have been kidnapped for ransom, and the people at the settlement house are very concerned because they don't have any way of paying a ransom."

"Of course they do not. Everyone knows this."

This wasn't exactly the response Frank had expected. "Then why would someone have kidnapped her?"

Esposito sat back in his chair and considered both of them for a time. "I fear you have wasted your time, Mr. Malloy. No one from the settlement house has been kidnapped."

III

Frank exchanged a glance with Gino, who looked as confused as Frank felt. "How can you be so sure no one has been kidnapped?"

This of course was a trick question. If Esposito knew who had been kidnapped and who had not, that would mean he was behind the crimes.

But Esposito didn't seem to mind the tricky question or its implications. "I did not say no one has been kidnapped. I said no one from the settlement has been." He gave them both a small, smug smile.

Frank considered this information for a long moment, trying to figure out what hidden meanings it might hold. "Can you speak for all the other Black Hand groups, too?"

"I do not know who this Black Hand is, but I do know what goes on in my neighborhood. No one has taken anyone from the settlement house. I would not permit this, you see. The settlement does many good things for our people."

"And yet a young woman is missing," Frank said, refusing to be sidetracked.

"Perhaps she is, but she has not been kidnapped."

"And you can be sure of this?"

"On my mother's grave, Mr. Malloy. The young lady you are concerned about is perfectly safe."

"How can you know this?" Gino asked, obviously forgetting that he was supposed to let Frank do the talking.

Esposito gave him a pitying look. "I told you, I know everything that happens in my neighborhood. You can stop searching for this young lady and go back to doing whatever you usually do in some other part of the city."

Gino would have argued, but Frank stopped him with a gesture. "I'm sure your word is good, Mr. Esposito," Frank lied, "but I'm also sure you'll understand that her friends and family would feel much better if they could see her for themselves."

"They will probably see her soon, Mr. Malloy. In the meantime, you can reassure them that she will come to no harm at all."

Before Frank could reply, they were all distracted by a disturbance in the hallway. Esposito called out something in Italian, and the disturbance ceased immediately. The door opened slowly, and the man who had accosted Frank and Gino outside the settlement house tentatively stuck his head in. The look he gave Frank and Gino should have curdled their blood, but they just stared back impassively.

"They rode off in their motorcar and left me behind, boss," he told Esposito.

"We'll talk about this later, Balducci. Mr. Malloy and Mr. Donatelli are leaving. Please escort them out."

Frank wasn't quite ready to leave, but the chances that they'd learn anything more from Esposito were pretty small, so he rose from his chair. "If you're wrong about this young lady, we'll be back," he told Esposito.

"I am not wrong," he said confidently.

Balducci looked as if he wanted to strangle both of them, but he contented himself with muttering imprecations as he escorted them back through the empty saloon to the front door. He slammed the door a little too hard behind them, making the glass rattle ominously. When Gino had started the motor and they were safely away from the saloon, he turned to Frank.

"Do you believe him?"

Frank frowned. "I think he believes himself."

"What does that mean?"

"It means I think he was very sure that he was telling us the truth, but it doesn't make any sense. How could a respectable young woman be safe if she disappeared from her home—and the settlement house is her home at the moment—without a word to anyone?"

"She couldn't," Gino said. "It's impossible."

"And yet Esposito seems certain that she's fine."

Gino did something with the gears, and they turned a corner, somehow managing not to collide with a wagon going the opposite direction. Frank only managed to stay in the motorcar by clinging frantically to the side. "Do you think he knows what happened to her?"

Frank straightened in his seat and tried to look calm. "I think he must. Otherwise, he would've claimed he didn't know anything about it at all. And he wasn't at all surprised that a young lady is missing. I got the feeling he even knew her name, which makes me really nervous."

"So should we keep looking for the house Mrs. Cassidi described?" Gino asked, nearly running down a peddler who didn't seem to realize just how fast the motorcar was going.

Luckily, Frank's gasp was drowned out by the roar of the motor. "I'd like to go back to the settlement house and ask Mr. McWilliam a few more questions before we do anything else."

"What kind of questions?"

"Oh, like how Esposito could know so much about what goes on at the settlement, for example."

"He probably has a lot of spies. Hundreds of people go in and out of there. Some of them would be happy to tell him anything he wants to know."

"Yes, and I suspect somebody at the settlement knows more about Miss Harding than Mr. McWilliam has told us, too."

"Like what?"

"I don't know, but McWilliam—who claims to be practically engaged to Miss Harding—has no idea where she is, but a gangster who shouldn't know her at all seems very sure she's perfectly safe."

"That does seem strange, but if he kidnapped her, he'd know that, wouldn't he?"

Frank considered this theory. "I guess he would, and he might consider her 'safe' because she's in his hands."

Gino cast him a worried frown before maneuvering the motorcar into a spot along the curb in front of the settlement house. "Should we tell Mr. McWilliam what Esposito said about her?"

"It might make him feel better, but it also might scare him to death. I think I just want to find out what he knows about Esposito and his connection to the settlement house."

They'd just entered the main door when Christopher Mc-William came bustling down the hallway. "Mr. Malloy, Gino," he called, hurrying toward them. "I have wonderful news!" He caught himself then and glanced around, aware of the curious looks from the people coming and going to the various classes. "Please, come up to my office and I'll tell you."

Gino and Frank exchanged a bewildered glance and followed McWilliam up the stairs. As soon as he had closed the door behind them, he said, "Miss Harding is back. She arrived a few minutes ago, safe and sound."

This was good news indeed, but it raised a whole host of new questions. "Where was she?"

McWilliam's smile faded. "She, uh, she wouldn't say."

"What *did* she say?"

"I, uh, I don't know. That is, I haven't seen her myself. She came into the building and went straight to her room. Mrs. Donatelli saw her, though, and told me immediately."

"Didn't you try to speak to her?" Frank asked.

McWilliam frowned in obvious frustration. "I wanted to of course, but men aren't allowed in the ladies' dormitory. I did ask Mrs. Donatelli to see if she needed anything, but she wouldn't open the door and just told Mrs. Donatelli she was fine."

And he couldn't send anyone else because nobody else knew Miss Harding had been missing. But Miss Harding wouldn't know they'd tried to keep her absence a secret either. She'd think people must have noticed, and she probably wouldn't want to face anyone just yet. Like Mrs. Cassidi. But Frank wouldn't jump to conclusions. "I see."

"Do you suppose they let her go because they heard you were investigating?" McWilliam asked.

"It's possible," Frank allowed, glancing at Gino, who obviously shared Frank's doubts. But maybe this was why Esposito had said Miss Harding was safe. Did he somehow know she was free? Had she escaped or been released? So many questions and so little chance of asking them. But maybe someone else could.

"Mr. McWilliam, may I use your telephone?"

SARAH HAD JUST FINISHED VISITING WITH ALL THE CUR-rent residents of the maternity clinic and determining that no one was in imminent need of her midwife services when she received the telephone call from Malloy. This time she didn't have to wonder why he needed her at the settlement house. When Malloy had cryptically said their lost sheep had returned and could she come to tend it, she'd understood immediately: Miss Harding was back at the settlement house—either rescued, freed, or escaped—and Malloy wanted Sarah to minister to her.

Wishing for a motorcar of her own—even though she knew the train would probably be faster—Sarah caught an elevated train to East Harlem. Teo Donatelli greeted her when she reached the settlement house.

"Gino and Mr. Malloy have gone," Teo explained in a whisper. "They did not want people wondering why they were here. I am to take you to Miss Harding."

Sarah nodded her understanding and followed Teo through a maze of rooms and hallways to the farthest row house in the group. This had been reserved for the women's residence. It was quiet now, since the other female residents would be out working at this hour of the day. Teo took Sarah upstairs and rapped on one of the doors.

"Miss Harding?" she called. "Mr. McWilliam has sent a lady to see you. She is a nurse."

"I'm not sick," a voice called from inside. "I don't need a nurse."

"Mrs. Donatelli," Sarah said loudly enough for Miss Harding to hear. "Would you leave me alone with Miss Harding?"

"Yes," Teo said in surprise, then nodded her understanding and said, "Yes," again more loudly. "I'm leaving now, Miss Harding. Mrs. Malloy will take care of you."

Teo made as much noise as she could, clattering down the stairs.

When she was gone, Sarah called through the door, "Miss Harding, I know what happened to you. Mr. McWilliam sent me."

Sarah had half expected another dismissal. Instead, after a long moment, the door opened wide enough for her to see the woman peering out at her. Plainly, she had been weeping, but now she merely looked alarmed.

"What do you mean, you know what happened to me?"

"We know you were kidnapped by, well, probably by the Black Hand or someone like them. As soon as Mr. McWilliam realized you were missing, he sent for . . ." Sarah glanced around, painfully aware of how easily they could be overheard if anyone chanced to enter this part of the house. "Perhaps we should discuss this more privately."

Miss Harding frowned, but she stepped back, opening the door wide enough for Sarah to enter, then closing it behind her. She was a striking young woman with hair like spun gold—a bit mussed now but still nicely arranged— and cornflower blue eyes. Her flawless complexion was blotched from weeping, but the redness was fading quickly since Sarah had distracted her. "Who are you?"

"I'm sorry. I should have introduced myself. I'm Sarah Malloy. I'm a . . . a nurse." No sense in calling herself a midwife. Miss Harding would hardly be comforted by that knowledge. "My husband is a private investigator, and when Mr. McWilliam realized you were missing, he sent for my husband and his partner, Gino Donatelli."

"Who must be some relation to Teo Donatelli," she said grimly.

"Rinaldo's brother," Sarah said.

"Why did Christopher send for a private investigator?"

"When he realized you had been kidnapped, he wanted to protect you as much as he could. He knew the police had not been very successful at dealing with the Black Hand, and calling them in would make your abduction public."

"And ruin my reputation," she added sharply. "Christopher would be very aware of that."

"As I said, he wanted to protect you. Perhaps you'd like to sit down, Miss Harding. I know you've been through an ordeal."

The room was spartan, furnished only with a narrow bed, a washstand, a dresser, and one wooden chair. Miss Harding had added a few feminine touches—a bouquet of flowers in a glass vase, drooping now after her absence, a framed photograph of an older couple who were probably her parents, and a bright blue bedspread—but nothing she could do would make the place appealing. She gestured less than enthusiastically toward the lone chair, realizing belatedly that she'd thrown her jacket on it. She picked it up and hastily hung it on one of the wall pegs that held her other clothing.

The baby blue of the fabric stood out from the rest of the garments, which were all sensible black or brown. Only then did Sarah notice Miss Harding's skirt matched the jacket, and if Sarah wasn't mistaken, it was made of silk. What an unusually fine outfit to be wearing while working at the settlement house.

Miss Harding seated herself on the bed. Sarah saw that she was clutching a soggy handkerchief. She touched it lightly to her eyes as Sarah sat down on the chair.

"Miss Harding, I'm terribly sorry for what you went through, but if you can tell us anything at all about your captors or where you were held, that might enable the authorities to track down the men who are doing this and also free the others they are holding."

Miss Harding frowned. "Others?"

"Yes. I spoke to Mrs. Cassidi. She was kidnapped as well, but you probably know that. She said she could hear children who were being held in the same house. Just imagine how terrified they must be, and their poor parents, too. If we could find that house, we could free them."

Miss Harding went very still, and she seemed to be studying Sarah carefully. "You think I was kidnapped by the Black Hand?"

"According to what we have learned, they are the ones behind the kidnappings, yes. Mrs. Cassidi was taken in a motorcar out to a house in the country somewhere. Is that where you were held, too?"

Miss Harding's startling blue eyes closed for a long moment, as if she was trying to shut out a terrible vision. "No," she said at last. "That is not where I was."

Could the Black Hand have more than one place where they kept captives? Of course they could, especially in a city like New York. Maybe this wasn't even the same group that had taken Mrs. Cassidi. "Do you know where they took you?"

Some emotion flickered across her beautiful face that Sarah could not identify. "Not far. Some place in the city."

"Then not in the country, like Mrs. Cassidi."

"No, not in the country."

"And you managed to get away."

"Yes." Her expression hardened, and Sarah hated herself for making her remember.

"I'm sorry. I know this must be very difficult for you. Was anyone else being held where you were?"

"I . . . No, not that I know of."

"You were very brave to escape, since you didn't even know where you were. Do you . . . Do you mind telling me how you managed that?"

Miss Harding lifted the handkerchief to her face again, pressing it tightly to her lips as if to hold back another spate of weeping. Sarah swallowed down the lump of guilt rising in her throat. But if anything Miss Harding remembered could help them find the kidnappers . . .

"I . . . It was a flat in some tenement building. They locked me in a room, but this morning, when I woke up, the door wasn't locked anymore and the guard was gone, so I left. I ran out of the building, and then I just ran and ran."

"Where was it? This building, I mean."

"I don't know. I didn't pay any attention. I just ran away as far and as fast as I could. I ran until I couldn't run anymore. That's when I looked up at a street sign. It's so easy to find your way in New York, isn't it? Not like other towns with streets like Main Street and Church Street that don't help you find your way at all. Here, almost all the streets have numbers. It's so sensible. When I saw the sign, I realized I was only a few blocks from here, and I came back. I . . . I didn't know what else to do."

"Naturally, you would have been concerned, since you would assume everyone knew what had happened."

"That I'd been kidnapped," she said flatly. "Did Christopher tell my parents?"

"Mr. McWilliam thought it best not to alarm them," Sarah said as diplomatically as she could.

"What about Lisa?"

"Lisa?"

"My cousin, Lisa Prince. She lives here in the city."

"Mr. McWilliam didn't mention her."

"He doesn't know her. She's . . . too good for the likes of us."

Sarah decided she didn't need to ask any more about Cousin Lisa. "Mr. McWilliam wanted me to see you, as a nurse, to make sure you weren't injured in any way from your experience. Since I'm a stranger, he thought you'd feel more comfortable confiding in me."

"Because someone from the neighborhood would most likely tell everyone what happened to me," Miss Harding guessed.

"People can be thoughtless," Sarah agreed.

"And cruel. You have no idea. But I'm not hurt. I was not . . . *mistreated*, merely inconvenienced."

What an odd way to phrase it. Sarah studied her for a moment, looking for any traces of trauma, but thankfully, she saw none. Perhaps she really did consider being kidnapped a mere inconvenience. "I'm glad to hear that. You're very brave. I'm sure you must have been terrified as well."

She blinked. "Of course, although no one actually threatened me."

"Did they give you any indication who they thought would pay your ransom?"

She considered this question carefully. "They did not, and I could have told them that my parents are not in a position to do so." Was that bitterness in her tone? Surely not. She was simply angry at those who had done this to her.

"Do you feel safe here?"

"What?" she asked in surprise.

"Someone who has been through what you've been through is often frightened of it happening again. You'll need to feel safe while you recover from your ordeal."

"But I told you, I wasn't hurt."

"Perhaps not physically, but I think you'll find it takes some time before you'll feel truly yourself again."

"I see. I hadn't thought of that."

"You may want to go home for a while."

"To Saratoga Springs?" she scoffed. "No amount of safety would be worth that."

"Of course, if you're comfortable here, I'm sure—"

"I could go to Lisa's house."

"You mean your cousin?"

"Yes. She married well. Her husband's family is rich. Joseph Prince. He's not really a prince, but he might as well be."

What a strange thing to say, but Sarah couldn't expect Miss Harding to be completely tactful after what she had been through for the past two days. "Would you like someone to contact them for you?"

"No. I'll . . . I'll write Lisa a note."

"What will you tell her?"

"Not that I was kidnapped," Miss Harding snapped. "She'd tell my parents, and they'd make me go right back to Saratoga Springs."

Most young women in her situation would probably have found that prospect very appealing, but Sarah had no idea what Miss Harding's life had been like before she came to New York. Perhaps she had a good reason for not wanting to return home, even to recover from a bad experience.

"If I can do anything for you—"

"I'm fine, really," Miss Harding assured her. "I'll send Lisa a note, and I'm sure she'll come for me. Women like her understand family obligations."

What did she mean by that? Most women understood family obligations. And wasn't it just a few minutes ago she had said something almost insulting about her cousin? Or was it her cousin's husband? Well, it wasn't Sarah's job to figure all of this out. She pulled out one of her cards and offered it to Miss Harding. "If you change your mind, I can come at any time."

"You're a midwife," Miss Harding said in surprise after looking at the card. "Why did they think I'd need a midwife?"

"I'm also a nurse, as I told you."

"I don't need a nurse either, as *I* told *you*," she added sarcastically.

"I'm very glad to hear it."

Sarah got up to leave, but Miss Harding stopped her. "Wait, could you . . . ? I need to write a note to Lisa. Could you mail it for me? I don't . . .." She gestured helplessly.

She wouldn't want to show herself in public just yet, in case people were talking about her. Sarah could understand that. "Of course I can. Shall I wait downstairs?"

"The writing desk is down there, in the parlor. We all share it. If you don't mind, we can go down together."

Miss Harding led the way. They found the room deserted, as Sarah had expected. A worn sofa and several chairs filled most of the space. A small desk and some bookshelves occupied the rest.

Sarah sat down in one of the chairs while Miss Harding composed her note. It was the work of only a few minutes. The less said, the better, Sarah supposed.

"Here," Miss Harding said, handing the envelope to Sarah. "I'm afraid I don't have a stamp, but Christopher will. Mr. McWilliam. He'll probably want to speak to you anyway, to find out how I am."

"And what should I tell him?"

"That I'm fine, but I'm . . . *exhausted*," she said, as if she'd just decided that was the perfect word to use. "I'll speak to him, uh, later, after I've rested. Meanwhile, I'd like to be left alone—by everyone."

Sarah would have expected Miss Harding to want to see her fiancé immediately, but she reminded herself that Miss Harding and Mr. McWilliam were not really engaged. Perhaps Miss Harding had decided not to marry him—no one could blame her for not wanting to settle here after what had just happened—and was simply delaying the moment when she would have to tell him. Whatever her reasons, Sarah would certainly honor her wishes and convey her message to Mr. McWilliam.

Sarah took her leave, reminding Miss Harding once again that she was available to help if needed. Miss Harding headed back upstairs to her room and Sarah found her way to the door that connected the women's area with the next row house. Teo Donatelli was waiting just outside of it.

"How is she?" she whispered.

"She says she's fine, although she wants to rest before seeing anyone."

"She seemed very upset when she arrived back here," Teo said. "Did she tell you how she got away?"

"It sounds as if they simply let her go. She was being held somewhere in the neighborhood, so she just walked back here."

Teo frowned. "Why would they just let her go?"

"Maybe they got frightened when they heard Gino was looking for her," Sarah said with a small smile.

Teo smiled back at the ridiculous thought. "Did you see the suit she was wearing?"

"Who? Miss Harding?"

"Yes. So beautiful. I never saw anything like it before."

"Yes, it's lovely." Although not very practical for working in East Harlem. Sarah remembered the way Kate Westrop had been dressed. But then, maybe Miss Harding had been wearing the suit for a special reason and just happened to be kidnapped while wearing it. "I need to speak to Mr. McWilliam. He'll be worried."

"Yes, come. I'll show you the way."

Teo left Sarah when they reached the main entrance, giving her instructions to Mr. McWilliam's office on the second floor before going off to help with one of the classes. Sarah found Mr. McWilliam working at his desk, but he jumped up the instant he saw her. She couldn't help noticing his eyes were red-rimmed and troubled. "Mrs. Malloy, Teo told me you had gone to speak to Miss Harding. How is she?"

"She said to tell you that she is fine but very tired. She's gone to her room and would like some privacy while she rests. She said she will speak with you later."

"Later? But . . ." He reached out a hand, as if hoping Sarah would help him understand.

"I'm sorry, but she said she was exhausted. Perhaps she doesn't feel up to talking about what happened just yet."

"Did she tell you anything at all?"

"Only that her captors didn't harm her in any way and she was held at a place not far from here. It sounds as if she was allowed to escape." Sarah almost added that Miss Harding was going to ask her cousin Lisa to take her in for a few days, but then thought better of it. Telling him something like that was Miss Harding's place. "I gave her my card and offered to help in any way I can, but she just wanted to be left alone."

"I suppose I can understand that, but I hope you assured her that no one here knows what happened to her."

"I did, but I'm sure it's still difficult to believe people wouldn't be staring at her. You know how quickly news like this can spread, no matter how much you try to keep it a secret."

Mr. McWilliam needed a bit more reassurance, which Sarah provided, and then she was finally able to take her leave. She was already out the front door when she realized she hadn't asked Mr. McWilliam for a stamp. She pulled out the envelope Miss Harding had given her and checked the address. It was on her way home, just a few blocks from an El stop and in a very nice neighborhood. She could deliver it personally, and Lisa Prince would be able to fetch Miss Harding that much more quickly, maybe as soon as this evening.

THE PRINCE HOUSE WASN'T REALLY A MANSION, BUT most people on the Lower East Side would have thought it was. The marble-fronted town house rose four stories above

Park Avenue, no finer than its neighbors, but they were fine enough to impress all but the most jaded city residents.

Sarah judged the hour to still be a fitting one for a social call, although she had no idea if this was one of Mrs. Prince's days "at home," which meant a day she was receiving visitors.

The maid seemed a little surprised to see someone she didn't know on the doorstep, especially someone dressed as simply as Sarah had dressed this morning for a visit to the maternity clinic. Sarah explained she was a friend of Mrs. Prince's cousin, Jane Harding, and had a message from her. Then Sarah presented one of her calling cards, not the ones that said she was a midwife but the ones engraved on thick vellum paper with just her name and address that identified her as a lady of means who made social calls on other ladies of means. Since merely having one's maid deliver one's calling card to another lady's house constituted "meeting" her, Sarah felt confident Mrs. Prince would feel comfortable receiving her. If nothing else, she'd be dying of curiosity to know what message her cousin Jane was sending her.

After checking with her mistress, the maid returned to escort Sarah upstairs to the formal parlor, where Mrs. Prince received her with a puzzled but polite smile. Lisa Prince was an attractive young woman in her mid-twenties. She wore a pale yellow gown of a light, gauzy material that was perfect for the warm summer weather. She wore her dark hair in an elaborate style that Sarah envied but would never even try to emulate.

"Mrs. Malloy?" Mrs. Prince said a little uncertainly as she rose to welcome Sarah. Very few society matrons had Irish surnames.

"Thank you for seeing me, Mrs. Prince. I have a message

for you that your cousin Jane Harding asked me to deliver, so I thought I shouldn't stand on ceremony."

"Of course," Mrs. Prince said, still obviously confused but determined to be polite. "Please sit down. I've asked my maid to bring us some lemonade, which I thought you'd appreciate more than tea on a day like this."

"That's very thoughtful of you," Sarah said, taking the offered chair. The room was furnished in exquisite taste with furniture that was obviously of fine quality and probably imported from Europe. Mrs. Prince had decorated in pastels instead of the darker colors of previous generations, and the room was bright and welcoming.

"I must say I'm surprised to hear from Jane," Mrs. Prince said carefully, and suddenly Sarah realized exactly why Mrs. Prince seemed so puzzled.

"I gather you and your cousin aren't close," Sarah guessed, remembering how Jane had spoken of Mr. and Mrs. Prince.

Mrs. Prince smiled a little apologetically. "I don't know how well you know Jane . . ."

"Not well at all," Sarah said, deciding a bit of explanation would help the situation, even if she varnished the truth a bit. "I've been visiting the Harlem settlement house. You see, I've started a maternity clinic on the Lower East Side, and I'm interested in learning what others are doing to meet the needs of those less privileged in our city."

Mrs. Prince didn't bother to hide her surprise. "You *started* it? Do you mean you manage it or . . . ?"

"My husband and I sponsored it," Sarah explained, clarifying that she had the financial means to do so, since Mrs. Prince couldn't very well ask outright if Sarah was rich. People with Irish surnames were also seldom rich. "My parents always encouraged me to be philanthropic," she added to further establish her credentials. "Perhaps you know them, Felix and Elizabeth Decker?"

Mrs. Prince did know them or at least knew of them, as Sarah could see from her expression. "Oh yes, of course." Mrs. Prince now knew she was dealing with a woman who was her social equal, in spite of Sarah's appearance. "And you met Jane at the settlement house."

"Yes, and she asked me to give you this note." Sarah handed Mrs. Prince the envelope.

Surprisingly, she seemed a bit reluctant to accept it, and she made no move at all to open it. "I can't imagine why she would be sending me a message."

"You were saying that the two of you aren't close," Sarah reminded her.

"Oh, we were very close when we were children. Our mothers are sisters, and they wanted us to be great friends."

"You lived in Saratoga Springs, I gather."

"Yes." She smiled sadly. "I'm surprised Jane mentioned that. She hated it there."

Actually, Jane *had* mentioned how much she hated it there, but Sarah simply said, "I suppose that's why she wanted to come to New York."

"I assume so. We really don't . . . I haven't spoken to her since . . . well, since my wedding, I guess it was, three years ago."

"Then I can understand why you're surprised to hear from her now. Perhaps her note will explain."

Mrs. Prince looked down at the unopened envelope she held but still made no move to open it. "Do you know what she wants?"

How much should Sarah explain? She knew Jane didn't want anyone to know about the kidnapping, so what else could she say? "Do you know why Miss Harding came to the settlement house?"

Mrs. Prince smiled at that. "Yes. My mother told me. It seems Christopher McWilliam wants to marry Jane, but he has committed himself to serving the poor and won't be swayed. Before giving him her answer, Jane wanted to know what her life would be like if she married him. I could have told her she would hate it and she shouldn't even consider marrying Christopher, but she didn't ask me."

"You seem rather sure of Jane's preferences."

"You mean I seem rather sure of someone to whom I haven't spoken in three years. I must also sound heartless, but I know Jane far better than you do, Mrs. Malloy. You haven't asked why Jane and I are no longer close or why I haven't spoken to her since my wedding."

"It's none of my business," Sarah said.

"No, it isn't, but I don't want you to think ill of me. My estrangement from Jane is not my doing. I told you, we were close as children but . . ." She looked away for a moment, as if trying to find the right words. "I told you our mothers were sisters. My father was an industrious man who worked very hard and did very well. Jane's father was . . . well, he was not industrious. People charitably called him a ne'er-do-well. They were never truly poor, but . . . You probably know that Saratoga Springs is a resort of sorts for people from the city."

"Yes. A lot of them go there to escape the heat during the summer months."

"That's right. At first they just stayed at the hotels, but then they started building cottages and eventually some of them built mansions. The contrast between these people and those of us who lived in Saratoga Springs all year round was . . . well, let me just say that seeing this was difficult for Jane. She couldn't have all the nice things she saw these other girls have. She couldn't even have all the nice things she saw *me* have. Her jealousy was . . . unpleasant. I'm two years older, and my mother would give her my clothes when I grew out of them, but Jane wasn't grateful. In fact, she hated me for it."

"Mrs. Prince, you don't have to tell me—"

"I know, and I'm sorry to burden you with this, but you need to understand. I don't want Jane to take advantage of you." She held up the unopened envelope. "You see, she has already begun."

"Not really."

Mrs. Prince smiled again. "I hope not. Jane was extremely jealous when I married Joe. His family is . . . Well, I met him in Saratoga Springs when I was invited to a party at one of the mansions. The daughter of that family had met me and, I guess, took pity on me. A girl from the town wasn't usually invited for fear one of the boys from an elite family would fall in love with her."

"And that's exactly what happened," Sarah said, understanding completely what Mrs. Prince was talking about.

"Yes. His family objected of course, but Joe finally convinced them he'd only marry me, and they've accepted me. As you can imagine, I was rather insecure at first, and at our wedding, Jane made several unkind remarks about my *Prince* Charming that made me weep. On my wedding day, Mrs. Malloy."

"I'm sorry."

"So am I, and I haven't spoken to her since. When I heard Christopher wanted to marry her and bring her to New York to work with the poor, I actually laughed. I never imagined she'd actually come, and when she did . . . Mrs. Malloy, I know Jane has no intention of marrying poor Christopher or remaining at the settlement house. I think she just used that as an excuse to escape from her parents and Saratoga Springs and come to New York."

IV

FRANK AND GINO COULD HEAR THE CLICKETY-CLACK OF the typewriter all the way down the hall as they approached their office.

"It sounds like she's getting faster," Gino said.

"Maybe a little," Frank said. He had a feeling Maeve had more potential as an investigator than as a typist.

She stopped typing the instant they came into the office. "Did you find her?" Frank knew Sarah had updated her all about the case last night, after they'd put the children to bed.

"No," Frank said with complete honesty.

"But she came back to the settlement house this morning on her own," Gino added.

"What do you mean, *on her own*?" Maeve asked with a frown.

"We aren't sure what happened, but she just walked into

the settlement this morning and told Teo she was going to her room and didn't want to see anybody," Gino explained.

"Teo's very helpful, isn't she?" Maeve said a little sarcastically.

"Teo is a saint," Gino confirmed with more than a hint of glee. "A beautiful saint."

"Who is married to your brother," Maeve reminded him.

Gino grinned. "You weren't too sure about that at first, were you?"

"I don't know what you're talking about," Maeve lied.

Frank could listen to them tease each other all day, but that hardly seemed like a productive way to spend their time. "I don't suppose any new clients have stopped by."

"None at all, but I've been typing furiously to make people think we're very busy," Maeve said.

"Maybe you're scaring them off because they think we're too busy," Gino said.

Maeve ignored him. "Did you at least look for the house where that other woman was held?"

"No," Frank said before Gino could say something smart. "We did get to meet Nunzio Esposito, though."

Maeve perked right up at that. "You did? What's he like?"

"Dark and dangerous," Gino offered a little too melodramatically.

Frank ignored him this time. "He acted very strange, though. He insisted nobody had been kidnapped from the settlement house."

"Maybe he just didn't know about it," Maeve said.

"He knew all right," Gino said. "He knew and he said that she hadn't been kidnapped and she was perfectly safe."

Maeve frowned. "That *is* strange. What do you suppose he meant by that?"

"We think he must have known she'd been released," Frank said.

"But why would they release her? Did someone pay a ransom?" Maeve asked.

"Not that we know of," Frank said.

Gino grinned. "I think he was just terrified when he found out we were investigating and let her go."

Maeve gave him a dark look. "It couldn't have been that."

"Whatever his reason, at least she's safe," Frank said.

"Was she able to tell you anything?" Maeve asked.

"She didn't want to see anybody," Gino said.

"Not even Saint Teo?" Maeve taunted.

"Not even Saint Teo," Gino confirmed sadly.

"But I telephoned Sarah and asked her to go see Miss Harding, so hopefully she'll have better luck."

"If she knows anything at all, Mrs. Malloy will find out," Maeve said.

"Let's hope she does. Petrosino could use all the help he can get with these kidnappings."

THE MAID ARRIVED WITH LEMONADE JUST AS MRS. Prince made her startling prediction about Jane Harding, so Sarah had some time to consider it before responding. When the maid had gone, she said, "I should warn you that the note Miss Harding sent you is a request to come stay with you."

"Stay with us? Why on earth would she want to stay with us?"

"I can't speak for her of course, but you may be right that she doesn't enjoy her volunteer work at the settlement house." Good, that explained Jane's desire to leave without mentioning the kidnapping. "Moving into your home is a respectable way for her to leave there without returning home to Saratoga Springs, which you indicated is probably the last thing she'd want to do."

Mrs. Prince obviously saw the logic of this, and she didn't like it one bit. Before she could reply, however, the parlor door opened and a man stepped in. He was tall and attractive and probably not yet thirty, although he carried himself with a confidence that belied his youth.

"I'm sorry to interrupt, darling, but I was told someone had brought a message about Jane." He gave Sarah a polite and very formal smile. "Not bad news, I hope."

"That depends on what you consider bad news," Lisa Prince replied with more than a hint of sarcasm. Mr. Prince's eyebrows rose, but a man of his breeding would never betray family secrets in front of a stranger, so he merely waited for some more information. "Mrs. Malloy, this is my husband, Joseph Prince. Mrs. Malloy has brought me a note from Jane." She held it up as proof.

"You haven't opened it," he said, making it sound like a question.

"Not yet, but Mrs. Malloy has warned me that Jane would like to come and stay with us for a time."

"Would she?" he asked, still trying not to give anything away, but he couldn't conceal all of his true feelings. Plainly, he was not happy at this prospect.

Sarah could certainly understand their reluctance, but she also knew that whatever Jane Harding may have done in the past, she really had endured a horrific ordeal and needed a sanctuary of some kind. "I'm afraid Miss Harding has found life at the settlement house more difficult than she anticipated," Sarah said, hoping she could convince them without giving away too much. "She desperately needs some time away, and you would be doing her a great kindness to let her visit you."

Sarah could see her plea had touched their sense of duty if not their sense of pity, but they still weren't quite convinced.

"What does she say in the note?" Prince asked, coming over to where his wife sat on the sofa and taking a seat beside her.

With a sigh, Mrs. Prince tore open the envelope and read the brief missive. "She says the work at the settlement house has disturbed her far more than she could have imagined and she begs me to let her come and stay with us for a week or two until she decides what course she should take."

"The course she should take is back to Saratoga Springs," Prince said, no longer bothering to hide his anger.

"Of course it is," his wife said. "But once her parents get her home, she'll never be allowed to come to the city again."

"So she wants to come here and plant herself so she can enjoy the delights of New York without censure and at no cost to her or her parents."

"You may be judging her too harshly," Sarah felt compelled to say. "As Mrs. Prince pointed out to me, you know her far better than I, but I saw her today, and I know how distressed she is. I think she would be very grateful for your assistance, and you are under no obligation to keep her more than a few days. You can always ask her parents to come and take her home if she proves troublesome."

Mrs. Prince sighed again. "I would never forgive myself if Jane really needed help and I refused to give it."

"And I will never forgive you if you allow her to abuse you in your own house," Prince said with a loving smile to soften his words. "So it's settled. We'll take her but only on sufferance."

"We have an engagement tonight, though," Mrs. Prince recalled with dismay.

"She isn't expecting a response until tomorrow at the earliest," Sarah said. "She actually asked me to mail the note, but I was passing here on my way home so I thought I'd make sure you received it promptly."

This was obviously a relief to Mrs. Prince. "We'll send the carriage for her tomorrow, then, and I suppose I should go myself to fetch her."

"I know Miss Harding will appreciate your generosity," Sarah said, thinking she was probably telling the truth. Miss Harding might be jealous of her cousin's lot in life, but she would also be grateful to escape her current situation for one not only more secure but also much more luxurious.

"I'm sorry you became involved in our little family dramas, Mrs. Malloy," Mrs. Prince said. "And I appreciate your kindness to Jane."

"I have a family of my own, so I know how difficult things can be." And they could be much more difficult than this, as Sarah knew only too well. At least no one in this family had died. Jane Harding would probably recover from her ordeal, and one hoped she would show the proper amount of gratitude to her cousin.

Sarah didn't have to worry about any of that, though. Her part in this family drama was now over.

Gino left the motorcar at the curb outside the settlement house and went in, looking for Mrs. Malloy. Late-afternoon classes were letting out, so he had to step aside in the foyer to make way for those exiting the building. He found Teo tidying up one of the classrooms.

"You're back," she said.

"Yeah, Mr. Malloy suggested I drive up here to see if Mrs. Malloy is ready to go home yet."

"She already left, I'm afraid, but if you don't have anything else to do, why don't you stay and have supper with me and Rinaldo tonight. Unless you need to get the motorcar back or something."

"No, I don't. Mr. Malloy doesn't even know how to drive it, and I'd love to see Rinaldo."

When Teo had finished her duties, Gino drove her the six blocks to the tenement where she and Rinaldo lived. Gino drove slowly and carefully, since it was Teo's first time in a motor and he didn't want her to be frightened. Also because she wanted to be sure all of her neighbors had a chance to see her in it.

Rinaldo came home a little later. Everyone said all the Donatelli boys looked alike, but Gino had always thought Rinaldo was the handsomest of the six. He was also the smartest. He'd married Teo, hadn't he? He and Gino sat on the front stoop drinking wine and telling each other lies in between showing neighbors the motorcar until Teo called them in for supper. As Gino had said, Teo didn't need anyone to teach her how to cook. The meal was delicious, and afterward they all went outside again to catch what breeze they could as the sun sank and the city cooled down a bit. Teo joined a group of women gathered on a neighboring stoop while more men joined Rinaldo and Gino on theirs. Gino kept them entertained with tales of the crimes he and

Mr. Malloy had investigated, until the sky had darkened completely and people started heading inside for bed.

"I guess I should be going," Gino said, rising from his place on the stoop. Teo had just left the group of ladies, who all appeared to be going inside as well.

"Gino, wait," she called. By the time she reached him and Rinaldo, the other men had gone. "I heard something you should know."

"Gossip," Rinaldo teased, giving Gino a wink. "The women know everything."

"Mama usually does," Gino reminded his brother.

"And so do I," Teo said unrepentantly. She glanced around to make sure no one else was near and lowered her voice. "It seems Nunzio Esposito has a new flat in the tenement they just built on Pleasant Avenue."

"But he already has a house," Rinaldo said.

Teo nodded sagely. "Where his *wife* lives. They say the new flat is to keep his other woman."

A dozen possibilities flashed through Gino's mind, but one seemed more likely than all the others. "Was this woman there of her own free will?"

"No one knows, but someone did see a woman there. She had yellow hair."

"Which would make her unusual in this neighborhood," Rinaldo said.

"And Jane Harding has yellow hair. Where exactly is this flat?" Gino asked.

So Miss Harding will be taken care of," Sarah concluded after telling Frank how she had spent her afternoon.

Frank wasn't so sure, but maybe Miss Harding didn't need as much care as they had originally assumed. When he'd come home from his office and found Sarah in the parlor, he'd been surprised to learn she had missed Gino and had created an errand for herself on her way home. "You didn't need to personally deliver that note, you know."

"Of course I didn't, but you can't think I'd pass up an opportunity to help out if I could, can you?"

"Or to get a look at the Princes," he added with a grin. "I'm sure they were grateful for your interference."

"I doubt it, but at least I was able to convince them to give Miss Harding a place to stay. I had the impression that Jane had hurt Mrs. Prince very much, so Miss Harding may not have been at all welcome there if I hadn't gone in person to convince them. So what are you going to do now?"

"We'll have to tell Gino what you learned from Miss Harding, but I'm thinking there isn't much more we can do if she doesn't have any idea who kidnapped her or exactly where she was held. I'll tell Petrosino what she said, just in case it helps him with any of his cases, but with Miss Harding home safe, I think our work is done."

After supper, Sarah helped Maeve tuck Brian and Catherine into bed and then the two women joined Frank and his mother in the parlor. Mother Malloy had her own quarters in the large house, but she preferred to join them in the evening. Sarah filled Maeve in on what she'd learned from Miss Harding and what she'd learned about her from Lisa Prince.

"That sounds odd," Maeve said when Sarah had finished.

"Which part?" Sarah asked with a smile.

"Well, all of it," Maeve said. "But if she's so upset that she has to leave the settlement house, why doesn't she just go home?"

"And why would she go someplace she isn't welcome?" Frank's mother remarked, not even looking up from her knitting. Sarah held that it was too hot to knit in the summer, but that never seemed to bother his mother.

"I wondered that myself, Mother Malloy," Sarah said. "We think—that is, Mrs. Prince and I think—that Miss Harding wants to stay in the city, even though she's not eager to work at the settlement house."

"I can't blame her for that," Maeve said.

Frank couldn't either, but . . . "Even after she was kidnapped?"

"Doesn't sound like she suffered too much," his mother said. "A respectable girl would be scared out of her wits."

"Was Miss Harding scared out of her wits?" Frank asked his wife.

"She had been crying, but . . ."

"But what?" Maeve asked too eagerly.

"But she didn't seem as upset as I expected, and she didn't want anyone to comfort her either."

"Not that it matters," his mother reminded them. "You're done with her now, aren't you?"

They were of course, and Sarah deftly changed the subject to more pleasant topics for the rest of the evening. Maeve and his mother had already gone up to bed when the doorbell rang.

"Who could that be at this hour?" Sarah wondered.

Frank got up to answer it. "I'd guess it's Gino returning the motor. He was probably giving everybody in East Harlem a ride around the block."

Sure enough, Gino was on the front steps. "I'm sorry it's so late, but they told me at the settlement house that Mrs.

Malloy had already gone home, so Teo invited me to supper and . . ."

"And naturally, you stayed. You want to come in?"

"No, it's late. I just wanted you to know I brought the motor back. I also thought you'd like to know that the women in East Harlem are gossiping about Nunzio Esposito."

"And what are they saying about him?"

"That he's set up an apartment on Pleasant Avenue for some woman who isn't his wife."

"Who is the woman?"

"Nobody knows, but they say she has yellow hair."

Frank's mind was racing, but Sarah had overheard them and come to the door, too.

"Do you suppose he intended to kidnap Jane and keep her there as his mistress?" she asked.

"I wouldn't put it past him," Gino said. "A man like that . . ."

"But then, why did he let her go?" Frank asked.

"Because you were looking for her," Sarah suggested. "He didn't want a scandal."

"Do you think a man like that would be worried about a scandal?" Frank asked.

"And would he really think he could keep it a secret, in any case?" Gino asked. "In that neighborhood?"

"Who knows what he thought," Frank said, "but that at least explains why he knew Miss Harding was safe. He'd released her himself."

"Anyway, I thought you'd want to know."

They thanked Gino and bade him good night.

"Good heavens, what a horrible man," Sarah said.

"If it's true. Maybe the Black Hand just decided they

needed a closer place to keep their kidnap victims. You know how gossip can get things twisted."

"I hope that's all it is. We'll probably never know."

THIS WAS FOOLISH. AND RECKLESS. MR. MALLOY WOULD tell him that and talk him out of doing it, but then Nunzio Esposito would get away again, just like he'd been getting away with everything all of his life. Gino couldn't let that happen, not if he could stop it. Not if he could do something to keep women and children from being kidnapped—Italian women and children mostly. Instead of Mrs. Cassidi, it might've been Gino's own mother. Or Teo. He'd joined the police force because he wanted to help the Italians, who were his people, because nobody else seemed to care about them. When he'd realized the police weren't going to be the solution, he'd partnered with Mr. Malloy so they could get justice when no one else could. Or would.

He'd lain awake most of the night thinking about all this, which was why he was in East Harlem this morning. He'd taken the elevated train up from the other Little Italy, crammed in with all those going to their jobs, because he wanted to get an early start. Not that he expected Esposito to be up and around at this hour, but Mr. Malloy had taught him that catching a man when he wasn't quite awake gave you an advantage.

Too bad he didn't know where Esposito lived. He could probably find out, though. He banged on the door of Esposito's saloon until somebody finally came to answer. The man had obviously been awakened by Gino's insistent pounding. He wore an undershirt and was still adjusting his suspenders, probably because he'd just pulled on his pants.

His unshaven face scowled at Gino through the glass, which rattled when he yanked the door open.

"What do you want?" At least it wasn't Balducci, who was already pretty angry at Gino and Mr. Malloy for leaving him standing on the sidewalk when they drove away to see Esposito.

"I need to see Esposito."

"You won't see him here, not until tonight."

"It's an emergency," Gino tried. He glanced around as if checking for eavesdroppers, then leaned in and lowered his voice. "It's about the woman."

"What woman?" the man asked, but Gino could see he was bluffing. His eyes had widened just a bit and suddenly his manner wasn't quite so confident.

"You know what woman. I need to find Esposito."

"Did you try his house?" the man asked. This time he was the one who glanced around nervously.

Gino scowled the way he'd seen Mr. Malloy do it when he doubted someone's honesty. "Do you think he's at his house?"

The man chewed his lip for a long moment while Gino waited patiently for him to fill the silence. "Try the flat."

"Where is it? I know it's on Pleasant Avenue, but . . ." He gestured helplessly. Teo hadn't known the exact address.

The man needed a little more convincing, but he finally gave Gino the address and the apartment number. "But don't tell him I told you."

"I'm not going to tell him anything except what I know about the woman." Gino strode away with an air of confidence he didn't feel. The man wouldn't know that, so maybe he wouldn't tell anyone that Gino had been looking for Esposito. Not that it would matter. Gino would be in as much trouble as he could be in when he found the Black Hand leader.

As Teo had said, the tenement was new, although it seemed to be already full. At the rate people were coming to the city, he supposed they could fill as many tenements as they could build. The streets were full of men going off to work and women visiting the many pushcarts in search of the food they'd feed their families that day. No one paid him any mind as he made his way along the sidewalk and into the building. The hallway was dark, since no natural light penetrated the stairwell except through a skylight six stories up. He gave his eyes a few minutes to adjust and then started up the stairs. According to the number, the flat Esposito had rented was on the second floor, in the front. This was a prime location, since it was above the dirt and noise of the street but with only one flight of stairs to climb. The people on the sixth floor had a quieter life but much farther to go.

The place smelled of garlic and onions and people, but not yet of filth and decay, like the older tenements in the city. He paused at the top of the stairs and took a deep breath to still his jangling nerves. He wasn't sure exactly what he was going to say to Esposito, but he knew he had to say something. Even a man like him would have a heart, wouldn't he? How could he take children from their parents and lock them up for weeks? How could he betray his own people?

Drawing another breath, he forced himself to walk down the hall to the correct door, lift his hand, and knock. To his horror, the door moved at his first touch, opening a few inches, and he realized it hadn't been latched. That seemed careless in the extreme. Even the leader of the Black Hand must be concerned that someone could break into his apartment. Gino stepped back, not wanting to be accused of forcing his way inside.

But no one came in response to his knock. He tried again, this time rapping on the door jamb since knocking on the door would only make it open farther. Still no one came, and Gino listened, stepping closer to the door and putting his ear to the opening. No sound at all. If Esposito was keeping a woman here, neither of them appeared to be home at the moment.

He started to step back again, and that was when he saw it, through the small opening, illuminated by a shaft of sunlight coming through the front window: a man's foot. Or rather a shoe, just visible, but it was pointing up so it had to be on someone's foot. Someone who was lying on the floor. Was he imagining it? He checked the hallway to see if anyone was watching. He saw no one, so he pushed the door open a little farther.

It was a man's shoe and a man's pant leg. The man attached to them wasn't visible, but he was apparently lying on the floor of the front room, near the doorway into the kitchen, which was the room the front door opened into.

"Hello? Anybody home?" Gino called.

The shoe and the leg attached to it didn't move. Emboldened, Gino pushed the door all the way open and stepped inside. The room was indeed the kitchen, although it seemed strangely empty of any signs it had yet been used for cooking or eating. Everything in it—furniture, dishes, pots, and pans—was brand-new and seemed oddly neat and orderly.

"Hello?" he called again, then walked over to the doorway that led to the front room. The man lying there did not move because, as Gino could now clearly see, he was dead. The handle of a large knife protruded from his stomach, and his dark suit and white shirtfront were saturated with blood.

The man was Nunzio Esposito.

Before Gino could even begin to make sense of this, he was distracted by the sound of men's footsteps hurrying up the stairs in the hallway.

Someone said, "In there," and before he could understand what was happening, a policeman came barging into the apartment. Gino could hear whoever else had been with him retreating back down the stairs. The policeman stopped for a moment, just inside the door, taking in the scene with one swift glance, and then he smiled an evil smile. "Caught you in the act, didn't I, *boyo*?"

BY THE TIME MAEVE ARRIVED AT THE OFFICE—SHE'D had to walk Catherine to school in the morning before she could begin her duties—Frank had been pacing the floor for at least half an hour.

"Did Gino tell you where he was going this morning?" he asked her.

Maeve frowned and shook her head. "But Mrs. Malloy said he was out pretty late last night. Maybe he just slept in."

"Maybe," Frank said, although that wasn't like Gino. Usually, he told Frank if he was going to be late. Gino's parents weren't on the telephone, though, so Gino would have no way of letting Frank know if he'd decided that after leaving the Malloy house last night. Frank chided himself for worrying over nothing, although somehow it didn't feel like nothing.

Maeve settled in with her typing practice—maybe she *was* getting faster—and Frank went back to reading the morning newspapers. Since the settlement house case hadn't really been a case someone had hired them to do, he didn't have to write up a report.

The rest of the morning passed slowly and still no sign of Gino. Maeve had just asked Frank if he was ready for lunch when they heard someone running down the hallway outside. The office door flew open and Teo Donatelli burst in. She was gasping for breath, having obviously run much farther than just down the corridor, and was holding her side.

Maeve hurried to her and helped her into one of the wooden chairs they kept for clients. "What's wrong? Are you all right?"

Teo nodded, still not able to speak, and Maeve went to fetch her a glass of water. By the time she returned, Teo had almost caught her breath, and she gulped down the water eagerly. When she was done, she looked up at them anxiously. "It's Gino. He's been arrested."

"Arrested?" Frank and Maeve echoed in unison, exchanging a shocked glance.

"Why was he arrested?" Frank asked.

"For murder, we think. Nobody knows for sure, because the police wouldn't say anything, but they took him away in a paddy wagon."

"Why do you think they arrested him for *murder*?" Maeve asked, obviously horrified.

"Because Nunzio Esposito is dead."

Frank just stared at her for a long moment, hardly able to comprehend what she was saying. "How did he die?"

Teo didn't even blink. "I told you, they didn't tell us anything, so all we have is rumors, but people are saying he was murdered. And Gino was there when the police came and—"

"Gino was *where* when the police came?" Frank interrupted her.

"At the flat I told him about, the one everyone says Esposito got for his lady friend."

"What flat is that?" Maeve asked. No one had bothered to tell her what Gino had reported last night, since the case was closed.

"It's in one of the new tenements on Pleasant Avenue," Teo said. "He already has a house where his wife lives, so he didn't need another place. Everyone said—"

"But nobody knows for sure," Frank said quickly. "It's all rumors."

"But that's where he was killed. Mr. Esposito, I mean. In that flat. They carried him out. Everybody saw that. He had blood all over him, and he was dead."

Frank was sure there must be some mistake. "And you think Gino was in there with him?"

"He was. Everybody saw them bring him out, too, but he wasn't hurt. He had those things on his wrists . . ." Teo wrapped the fingers of one hand around her other wrist to illustrate, but Frank already knew.

"Handcuffs." So they really had arrested him. This was not good.

"Yes, the handcuffs."

"Why would Gino have been in Esposito's flat?" Frank asked.

No one had an answer for that, which made Frank want to swear, but with two ladies present, he had to restrain himself.

"Where would they have taken him?" Maeve asked.

"To their station, probably, but eventually to the Tombs. How long ago did this happen, Mrs. Donatelli?"

"I don't know for sure. A few hours, at least. I didn't hear at first. I was at the settlement, and people started coming to tell me. I went to the building on Pleasant Avenue to find out more. The police were gone by then, but the people there, they told me what happened. Then I came straight here."

"You did the right thing. We'll take care of this."

"How can you take care of it if they arrested Gino for murder?" Teo asked in apparent despair.

"Don't worry. We've handled this kind of thing before." And not so very long ago either. "Maeve—"

"I know. I'll go find Attorney Nicholson," she said, naming the well-known defense attorney who had assisted them the last time. "What are you going to do?"

"Go up to Italian Harlem. I'll see Mrs. Donatelli home and try to find out as much as I can from the neighbors and then try to get the police there to talk to me."

"Where shall we meet up?"

"If you can get Gino out of jail—"

Teo gave a startled yelp.

Frank smiled apologetically and continued. "If you can get Gino out of jail, take him to our house."

She nodded, but Teo said, "I should go to Little Italy and tell the Donatellis what happened."

"And get them all upset for nothing?" Frank scoffed. He hoped he sounded believable because he wasn't at all sure it was nothing. "Better to wait until we've got him out on bail."

"Can you do that?" Teo asked tremulously.

"A good lawyer can do anything," Maeve promised rashly. "And Mr. Nicholson is a good lawyer."

Or a bad one, depending on your point of view, considering how many criminals he got freed, but Frank didn't point that out. He'd been one of the criminals who'd gotten freed, after all.

Maeve was already gathering her things and covering her typewriter. "I better telephone Mrs. Malloy and tell her what's happening so she can get Catherine at school if I'm not back in time."

"Do that, and tell her you'll bring Gino back there." Frank turned to Teo. "Mrs. Donatelli, if you're ready, we'll head back uptown."

"Yes. I can take you to the building. The people there, not many speak English. I can help you."

As much as he hated involving her, she was right. He'd need help, and with Gino in jail, his options were limited.

"Before we go, can I use the, uh . . ." She gestured to the hallway where the washroom was located.

"Of course." In fact, he was glad for the chance to speak to Maeve alone for a minute.

As soon as Teo was gone, he went to Maeve's desk and stopped her from picking up the telephone. He pretended not to notice her hand was shaking. "Do you think Gino could have done this?"

Maeve's face paled visibly. "What do you mean?"

"Just what I said. Could he have killed Esposito?"

"I . . . I don't know," she admitted.

Frank didn't know either. Obviously, Gino had gone to confront Esposito. He'd also been furious about what the Black Hand was doing to the Italian community. Anything could have happened if Gino got angry enough. "If he did or even if Esposito's men just think he did, his life is in danger. That's why I said to take him to our house. We'll need to keep him hidden until we can figure this out."

Maeve nodded, and Frank realized he'd truly frightened her. He didn't think he'd ever seen Maeve actually frightened. But it wasn't surprising. Frank was frightened, too.

V

MAEVE COULDN'T BELIEVE THIS WAS HAPPENING. HOW could Gino have gotten himself into a fix like this? And what on earth was he doing in East Harlem in the first place? The case was over. Or at least Miss Harding was safe, which was all they'd been asked to accomplish. Did Gino think he could scare Nunzio Esposito into . . . into what? Becoming an honest man?

The very thought made her want to laugh out loud, but the other people on the El would think she was crazy if she started laughing for no apparent reason. Besides, none of this was funny. Gino was in jail and probably charged with murder, which made her stomach roil in terror, because Gino was in far more trouble than the average murderer in New York City.

In New York City, they could simply figure out whom to bribe and get the charges dropped or simply lost, which was often done, even in cases of murder. But not in *this* case of murder. In this case, the real problem was convincing Esposito's men not to kill Gino in revenge.

She hadn't even thought of that until Mr. Malloy mentioned it, although it probably would have occurred to her eventually. The Italians were famous for their vendettas. Everybody knew that. Gino wouldn't even be safe in jail. They needed to get him bailed out today and then taken someplace safe, or at least someplace safer.

And what if he actually had killed Esposito? There would be no place safe for him then.

Henry Nicholson's office was across the street from the Tombs, which was what everyone called the New York City Halls of Justice and House of Detention because it had supposedly been built to resemble an Egyptian tomb. It had been built on the old Collect Pond, the original source of water for New York City, which had become too polluted to use anymore. The water had been drained, but the ground had remained swampy, so the building had begun to sink almost immediately, and the whole place reeked of the damp and rot that had been seeping into it for over sixty years.

She just hoped Nicholson was in his office.

Maeve had known Mr. Nicholson for years. As the last surviving member of a family of grifters, she had encountered the attorney professionally many times when he had assisted her various relations. Fortunately, she'd never needed his services herself, and now that she'd started a new life, she was fairly certain she never would.

Of course, she'd never expected Gino would need them either.

She got off the El at Canal Street and walked over to Nicholson's office. The clerks knew her and greeted her warmly. She'd been here only a few months ago when Mr. Malloy was arrested and charged with a murder he hadn't committed. She wasn't sure what to tell Nicholson, since she had no idea if Gino was guilty or not, but luckily, defense attorneys didn't worry about things like that. They simply considered all their clients to be innocent.

She explained what she wanted to one of the clerks, who informed her that Mr. Nicholson was in court but that he would probably return shortly. In the meantime, he would take down all of the information and try to find out where Gino was being held and when he would be arraigned. This took well over an hour and several telephone calls, but Nicholson's people did this every day, so they were much more efficient and successful than she and Mr. Malloy would have been on their own.

Gino, it seemed, had been transferred to the Tombs, as they had expected, and Maeve was relieved to learn he was being arraigned that day. At least they would be able to get him out of the Tombs quickly, hopefully before the Black Hand was able to find him and take revenge.

As she waited, Maeve had time to think things through, and she realized that the Black Hand might want to kill Gino even if they already knew he was innocent, because one of them might be the real killer. With Gino dead, the police could pin Esposito's murder on him and close the investigation.

By the time Henry Nicholson returned to his office, Maeve was a wreck.

FRANK AND TEO TOOK THE THIRD AVENUE EL UP TO East Harlem, getting off at 116th Street. They spoke little during the trip. Teo was probably too frightened to even think straight, and Frank was too busy trying to figure out what he could do about all this.

Getting Gino out of jail and to a safe place was important, and he knew Maeve could take care of that. Sarah would see to securing the bail money and delivering it as soon as she'd gotten Catherine home from school. But even more important was figuring out who had really killed Esposito so Gino would be safe again.

That is, unless Gino had killed him. But Frank wouldn't think about that. Surely, Gino had more sense, even though he'd somehow decided that confronting Esposito alone was a good idea. Frank would certainly have a talk with Gino about going off alone on crazy errands.

Meanwhile, he'd find out what he could about Esposito's murder. Teo took him to the tenement building where Esposito had been killed. The building was new enough that it still looked clean, and the curtains in the windows told him that people were living there. He shouldn't have been surprised that it had filled up quickly.

A group of people—women and a few old men—were gathered on the sidewalk out front. Teo went right up to them and started conversing in Italian with much animation and hand gestures. Frank stood back, giving her a chance to find out what she could and thinking he'd been right to accept her offer of help. Even if he'd found people who spoke English well enough to converse with him, they would never have trusted a stranger enough to confide in him.

A few of the people glanced over at him occasionally, their suspicion obvious, but presumably, Teo had vouched for him because no one made any moves to send him on his way. Finally, after a long discussion, Teo returned to him.

"Let's go inside. I'll show you which flat it is and tell you what they said."

Frank nodded, tipped his hat to the group, who just stared back at him in silence, and followed Teo into the building. They made their way up to the second floor. Frank had grown up in a tenement, but this place didn't yet have the same odor of neglect. If anything, it was almost elegant in its newness. No wonder Esposito had claimed one of the flats for himself. Or for his woman, if that's truly what it was for.

"This is it," Teo said, stopping outside one of the doors.

Frank didn't hesitate. He reached for the doorknob, expecting it to be locked, but the knob turned easily under his hand. Teo gasped in surprise.

"After you," Frank said with a wave of his arm.

But Teo hesitated, her dark eyes wide with alarm. "Should we go in?"

"Why not? Esposito isn't going to complain."

Her eyes widened even more but she smiled wanly. "I don't suppose he will."

She stepped inside, walking carefully as if afraid of disturbing someone, and Frank followed. The kitchen looked entirely too neat. His mother had kept a clean kitchen and so had Sarah, back before they were married. Now they had a cook, and Velvet kept their kitchen immaculate, too, but none of those kitchens looked like this.

"No one cooks in this kitchen," Teo said.

That was it: not a trace of food anywhere. "I wonder why not?"

"Because no one lives here yet," Teo said. "The people downstairs, they tell me Mr. Esposito rented this place and had all the furniture delivered, but no one moved in." She stepped to the doorway that led to the front room but stopped short when she saw the dried pool of blood on the floor. "Oh."

"I guess that's where he was killed." Frank stepped around her and went in, carefully skirting the bloodstain. He studied the room, walking around the perimeter and examining every piece of furniture. A brand-new sofa and two matching chairs flanked the fireplace. A large cabinet with glass doors stood against one wall and a buffet against another. Frank opened doors and drawers and found all of the storage areas empty. Heavy drapes had been hung at the windows, but they were open to let in the sunlight. Missing were the knickknacks and pictures that people used to make their living space feel like home. Even the poorest immigrants had a photograph or two of loved ones left behind or a treasured memento to set on the mantel. Here only a light film of dust adorned the flat surfaces.

Teo still hadn't entered the front room. She stood in the kitchen, probably intimidated by the blood. She did look a bit pale. Frank walked past her and across the kitchen to the back room. The window in this room opened into a tiny courtyard where little sunlight penetrated, so the dim light made it difficult to see. Still, the room was clearly furnished as a bedroom.

A brass bedstead nearly filled the small space, but they'd also managed to squeeze in a clothes cupboard and a dressing table. While the other two rooms had looked bare and unlived-in, this room had certainly been used. The bed was unmade, the sheets tangled and the coverlet lying half on the floor. A silver-backed dresser set lay haphazardly on the dresser, the comb and brush obviously lying where they'd been set down after their last use, the mirror with its reflective surface turned down. The silver was bright and newly polished. Frank could easily see the few hairs tangled in the brush's bristles were blond.

He pulled open the top drawer of the dresser and to his surprise, he found it full of silky, lacy undergarments. They might once have been carefully folded, but now they looked as if they'd been rummaged through. He knew enough about ladies' clothes since marrying Sarah that he recognized these as expensive. More expensive than any women in this neighborhood could afford.

"Teo, will you look at these things and tell me what you think?" he asked, stepping back to give her room.

Teo came into the bedroom with obvious reluctance, but that faded when she saw the silver items on the dresser and the silk tumbled in the drawer. "Where did this come from?" she asked, although he didn't think she expected him to answer. She quickly checked the items in the drawer, then closed it and opened the next one. There she found a few shirtwaists, still neatly folded, and several pairs of gloves.

Without being asked, she went to the cupboard and pulled open the door. Inside hung some ladies' garments on pegs. As Teo pulled each one out and held it up, Malloy could see they were skirts and jackets, but in colors and fabrics too bright and fine for this neighborhood. Finally, she pulled out a dark brown skirt of obviously inferior quality.

"That's strange," Teo muttered.

"What's strange?"

"Everything here is brand new except for a few things, and they're old and worn."

"What's old and worn?"

"Some . . . undergarments," she said, not meeting his eye.

"One of the shirtwaists in that drawer." She indicated the dresser with a jutting of her chin. "And this skirt."

"What do you make of that?"

"I don't know, but . . ." Teo said, frowning as she considered the possibilities. "The neighbors, they said they saw a woman here."

"A woman with yellow hair."

Teo nodded. "There's yellow hair in the brush."

"I noticed."

"They said she was here for a few days."

"Was she a prisoner?"

"I don't know. She was by herself for some of the time, and nobody saw a guard or anybody who looked like they were guarding her, but she might've been locked in or tied up or something."

"What do you make of the clothes?"

Teo shook her head, then hung the skirt back in the cupboard. "Maybe she came here wearing the old clothes, and then she put on some of the new things."

"Most women would, especially if these things were for her," Frank said.

"Yes, you are right. Who wouldn't? And when she leaves, she is wearing the new clothes."

"Do you think she intended to come back?"

Teo gave this some thought. "If not, why would she leave all these nice things behind?"

"Maybe she doesn't have anything to carry them in," Frank guessed.

"Oh, that is true, too. She cannot walk down the street carrying a pile of clothing."

"No, people would think she stole it and maybe call a policeman," Frank said.

"Probably not a policeman," Teo said with a small smile. "They do not trust the police here, but everyone would know where she went, in case she did steal it, so the owner could go after her." Teo looked around again. "Except . . ." She pointed to the floor just to the right of the bedroom door.

Frank looked down and saw a medium-sized alligator Gladstone bag sitting next to the dresser. He squatted down and opened it to find it completely empty. "So she did have a way to carry things away with her." But for some reason she hadn't used it. Maybe she hadn't wanted anything to slow her down. Or maybe she was planning to return. Anything was possible. "So she didn't carry away anything except what she was wearing, and she left her old clothes here. Did anybody see her leave?"

"Yes. She left yesterday, in the morning."

"Alone?"

"Yes. They said Esposito was here all night and the night before, too, but he had already gone that morning. Then she left, too."

"Did they know who she was?" Teo shook her head, but her gaze shifted and she no longer would meet his eye. "What is it?"

"They said the woman they saw was wearing a blue dress."

"Does that mean something?"

"When Jane Harding returned to the settlement, she was wearing a blue dress I never saw before."

SARAH WAS GETTING WAY TOO MUCH EXPERIENCE AT posting bail. Mr. Nicholson's assistant was very helpful, as he had been the last time they'd been here, and took care of the paperwork. She and Maeve didn't even have to go across the street to the Tombs. Gino met up with them at Nicholson's office after his release, coming in to find her and Maeve waiting for him. They both jumped to their feet to greet him.

He looked a bit worse for wear. Was that a bruise on his chin? His usually immaculate clothes were dirty and his hair was mussed. The worst part was his eyes, though. They were haunted, and it nearly broke her heart to see it.

"It's going to be all right," Sarah said, laying a hand on his arm.

"Is it?" he asked with a bitterness she'd never heard from him before.

"Of course it is," Mr. Nicholson said cheerfully. He was a large man with a loud voice and was partial to equally loud suits. If Maeve hadn't vouched for him before their first meeting, Sarah would never have believed him to be even competent, much less an expert at his chosen profession. "Don't worry about a thing. Mrs. Malloy has posted your bail, young man. I know I don't have to explain how things like this are usually handled, so I'll wait until I hear from you before I take any action."

"I didn't kill Esposito," he said.

"Of course you didn't," Nicholson agreed, still smiling.

"No, I really didn't." He turned to Sarah. "I'm not an idiot."

"Of course you aren't," Sarah said.

"Although we are all wondering why you went up to East Harlem to find him in the first place," Maeve said. She was furious about all this, for some reason, and Sarah was pretty sure she knew what that reason was.

"I'm wondering that myself now," Gino said.

Oh dear. He never usually let her get away with her snide remarks.

"We'd best get you home," Sarah said. The sooner they could discuss all this in private, the better.

"My parents will be pretty upset. Do they know yet?"

Sarah exchanged a glance with Maeve. "No. We haven't told anyone. Teo knows of course. She's the one who told us you'd been arrested."

"Teo? How did she find out?"

"I'm sure half the people in East Harlem went to tell her as soon as it happened," Maeve said. "Then she came to the office to tell Mr. Malloy."

Gino glanced around in surprise. "Where is he?"

"He's in East Harlem, looking for the real killer," Maeve said.

Only then did Gino appear to notice how angry Maeve was. "What are you so mad about?"

"About you! What were you thinking, going up to Italian Harlem to see Nunzio Esposito all by yourself? Without even telling anybody where you were going?"

Gino blinked in surprise at her vehemence, and Sarah had to admit she was a little shocked herself.

"We can discuss this when we get home," Sarah said. "Thank you so much for your help, Mr. Nicholson. We'll be in touch."

She herded the baffled Gino and the furious Maeve out of the office. When they reached the lobby of the building, Sarah stopped them.

"We aren't taking you home to your family, Gino."

"Why not?"

"What's wrong with you?" Maeve demanded. "Because we are afraid you won't be safe there, that's why. The Black Hand thinks you killed Esposito. Do you think they're going to wait for a trial?"

"Oh," Gino said, visibly shocked. "I didn't think of that."

"Well, think of it," Maeve advised.

"Maeve, we don't need to argue about this now. The important thing is to get Gino someplace out of sight. Malloy said to take you to our house, Gino, and he'll meet us there when he's finished in East Harlem."

"I've got to let my parents know I'm fine and out of jail," Gino argued.

"They don't even know you were *in* jail," Maeve said impatiently.

Sarah gave Maeve what she hoped was a quelling look and said, "And certainly you can send word to them as soon as we get to our house, but we don't think it's a good idea for you to stay with them. That's the first place the Black Hand would look for you."

"I guess you're right."

"And you don't want to put your family in danger, do you?" Sarah added. "Now let's find a cab and get home."

They flagged down a pair of Hansom cabs, which were a tight squeeze for two people, much less three, so Sarah convinced Maeve to go alone while she went with Gino.

"You could have gone with Maeve," Gino said when they were on their way. He'd tried to scoot over as far as he could but they were still touching from hip to knee.

One did indeed need to be on close terms with someone before agreeing to share a Hansom cab with them. "Malloy said not to leave you alone."

"Why not?"

She gave him a pitying look. Gino really wasn't thinking clearly today. "Because he's afraid you'll go off and do something foolish."

"But—"

"Which you already did once today and look where it got you," she reminded him. "And I didn't think you'd want to listen to Maeve yelling at you the whole way home, so I appointed myself your guardian."

"What's wrong with Maeve anyway? What's she so mad about?"

"About you getting arrested, I suppose. That's the only important thing that happened today."

"Why would she . . . ? She wasn't mad when Mr. Malloy got arrested. It's the same thing."

Was it? Not to Maeve, apparently. "I'm sure she's just worried about you. Malloy wasn't ever in any real danger, but you are."

"We don't know that."

Sarah glared at him until he relented.

"All right, I guess the Black Hand might be looking for revenge if they think I killed Esposito, but I didn't."

"It may not matter. If one of *them* killed Esposito, they'd love to pin it on you and then kill you to make it stick."

Gino, to give him credit, looked suitably appalled at the very thought.

"And that is why Maeve is angry, so stop pretending you're not scared and start acting sensibly."

"Yes, ma'am," he said meekly. She thought he really meant it.

FRANK SHOULD HAVE GONE DOWNTOWN HIMSELF TO bail Gino out of jail. Then he wouldn't be stuck at home waiting and imagining Sarah and Maeve had run into all sorts of problems. Or worse, that someone had already managed to get revenge on Gino and he was in a hospital or a funeral home somewhere. He'd never been so happy to finally hear the front door opening.

Maeve came in alone.

"Where's Sarah and Gino?" he demanded.

"They're right behind me. We took separate cabs."

"So you got him bailed out all right?"

"Of course. He wanted to go right home, but Mrs. Malloy convinced him that wasn't a good idea. Where are the children?"

"In with my mother. They already had their dinner."

"I'll get them ready for bed, then." She sounded tired, which never happened even when she really was tired.

He wanted to stop her and ask her what was wrong, but he had no idea how to do that. "Don't you want to get something to eat first?"

"I'm not hungry."

Maybe Sarah could figure out what was wrong with her.

By the time Sarah and Gino arrived, Maeve had taken Brian and Catherine upstairs to get bathed and changed into their nightclothes. Their cook, Velvet, had kept dinner warm, so the three of them sat down to eat. While they ate, Gino told Frank how he had come to be arrested.

"What made you think you needed to see Esposito alone?" Frank asked, unable to hide his anger.

"I knew you'd be mad about that, but I thought . . . He's an Italian. I mean he *was*. I thought maybe I could remind him how much damage he's doing to his own people."

"And convince him to do it to other people instead?" Frank asked sarcastically.

"I know, you're right, but I had to try. I couldn't sleep a wink last night for thinking about it. By morning, it just seemed like the right thing to do."

"I think we can all agree it wasn't the most sensible course of action," Sarah said, quite reasonably. "And since we can't change what happened, we need to put our efforts into making sure nothing even worse comes of it. I for one am extremely curious to know why a policeman showed up to arrest you at the exact moment you went into the flat."

"And why the door was so conveniently open for you," Frank added, "although maybe the killer was in too much of a hurry to think about locking the door behind him."

"I did wonder about both of those things," Gino said.

"Did you figure anything out?" Sarah asked.

"Not really."

"Who knew you were going there?" Frank asked.

"Nobody. I mean, I didn't tell anybody what I was going to do."

"Who saw you going into the building this morning?" Sarah asked.

Gino considered for a moment. "Anybody who was on the street, but maybe somebody was watching it."

"Wait," Sarah said. "How did you know where Esposito would be?"

"I went to his saloon first. I didn't think he'd be there, but I thought they might tell me where to find him."

"Why would they do that?" Frank asked, genuinely baffled at his logic.

Gino shrugged sheepishly. "I figured I could trick them. I told the fellow who came to the door that it was an emergency and I needed to see Esposito and that it was about the woman. I figured if Esposito really was involved with some woman, they might believe me and tell me where he was."

"And it worked?" Frank asked in amazement.

"It did. The man who answered the door at the saloon told

me where the flat was. Teo had told me what street it was on, but she didn't know the address or which apartment."

"So this fellow sent you right to where Esposito's body was and then a copper shows up a minute later and arrests you for his murder."

Gino had the grace to wince. "I guess that's exactly what happened."

"Oh, Gino, they tricked you," Sarah said. "You said someone brought the policeman up to the flat. Did you see who it was?"

"No. I just heard him say something to the cop, but I didn't recognize his voice. It could've been anybody."

"But it was probably somebody from the Black Hand."

"At least it was somebody who knew Esposito was dead, maybe because he was the killer," Sarah said. "We don't know for sure it was the Black Hand."

"It was probably that fellow we insulted yesterday who brought the cop," Gino said.

"You insulted somebody in the Black Hand?" Sarah marveled.

"Not exactly," Frank said, realizing they'd needlessly made an enemy. "Esposito sent one of his men to fetch us and instead of letting him escort us back, we drove off in the motor and left him standing."

"It felt like the right thing to do at the time," Gino said, "but he hates us now."

"Ah yes. Men are so sensitive," Sarah said with a small grin.

"Some men are," Frank agreed. "We probably should have been a little more considerate."

Sarah sighed loudly but didn't confirm his theory. "So did you discover anything in East Harlem today?"

"I tried to talk to the cop who arrested Gino, but I just

got a runaround and was never able to find him. Teo took me to the apartment where Esposito was killed, though, and we were able to search it."

"You were?" Gino asked in surprise. "How did you get in?"

"We opened the door. It wasn't locked this time either, which made me wonder why, but there was nobody around to ask, so Teo and I just went on in."

"And what did you find?" Sarah asked.

"A very nicely furnished place where nobody really lives, according to the neighbors. All the furniture was brand new, but Teo doesn't think anyone has ever cooked in the kitchen. It looked very clean. Somebody used the bedroom, though."

Sarah frowned. "How do you know?"

"The bed had been slept in and not made up, and there were clothes in the cupboard and the dresser."

"Whose clothes?" she asked.

"Women's clothes. *Only* women's clothes. Expensive ones, according to Teo. Silk underwear. A silver comb and brush set, too."

"Silver?" Gino echoed in amazement.

"Oh dear," Sarah said. "This sounds like just what people thought it was, a place for Esposito to meet his mistress."

"That's what I thought, too," Frank said. "The neighbors said Esposito spent several nights there, probably when the woman was there, too."

"I don't suppose you saw any sign of her," Sarah said.

"None at all, and if she heard about the murder, she'll be long gone."

Sarah nodded her agreement. "It's not hard to believe a man like that had a mistress. He might even have had more than one, especially if he treated them this well."

"It's possible, I guess, but whoever stayed there had left behind her old clothes, and we assume she wore some of the new clothes back to wherever she went when she left."

Sarah frowned. "What did the old clothes look like?"

"A brown skirt, a shirtwaist, and undergarments, according to Teo. Nothing particularly distinctive. Teo talked to the neighbors, too. They saw the woman leaving yesterday morning."

"Did they know her?" Sarah asked, still frowning.

"No, or at least no one admitted to it, but she had yellow hair, and she was wearing a blue dress. Teo said Jane Harding was wearing a blue dress yesterday when she returned to the settlement house, a dress she'd never seen before."

"Oh dear, that's true. It was really a skirt and jacket, but it was beautiful. I thought it was awfully fine for working at a settlement house, too. But Jane Harding couldn't possibly be the woman in that apartment, could she?"

"She has yellow hair and a blue dress, and the hair in the brush was blond."

"But Jane was *kidnapped*," Gino said. "She couldn't have been that woman."

"Jane did get back to the settlement house the same morning the neighbors saw a blond woman leaving the flat," Frank said.

"Yes, but that doesn't make any sense," Gino said. "A woman who was kidnapped doesn't just walk away."

"Jane did claim that when she woke up that morning, her guard was gone and the door was unlocked," Sarah said. "So in effect, she did just walk away."

"You're right, Gino. None of this makes any sense," Frank said.

"Is it possible Esposito kidnapped her because he thought

he could win her affections with some pretty things?" Gino asked. "Would that work on a woman, do you think, Mrs. Malloy?"

Sarah's eyes grew wide as she considered Gino's question.

"What is it?" Frank asked.

"Jane's cousin, Lisa Prince, told me Jane was always jealous of her because her family was wealthy and Lisa had much nicer clothes than Jane did."

"But how would Esposito know that?" Frank asked.

"He wouldn't," Sarah said. "And how would he even meet Jane or know who she was? Teo said she'd only been here a few weeks."

"A woman like Jane would stand out in that neighborhood," Gino said. "And lots of people would've seen her at the settlement house, so they'd be talking about her, too."

"So maybe Esposito saw her, but what would make him think she'd even be interested in him?" Sarah asked.

"Nothing," Frank said, "so we're probably wasting time trying to figure this out. Besides, we know she didn't kill Esposito, so what does any of this matter?"

"How do we know that?" Gino asked.

"Because she was at the settlement house last night," Sarah said. "She locked herself in her bedroom and wouldn't come out, not even to see Christopher McWilliam."

"All right. Then the only reason we'd need to know who this mistress was is if she killed him," Gino said.

"And maybe she did," Sarah said, "but Jane Harding didn't."

"If Jane really was the woman being kept in that flat, though, she might know something that would help us find the killer," Gino said.

"We can keep that in mind," Sarah said, "but we can't go

asking her about that. If Esposito really did keep her in that flat for two days, heaven only knows what he may have done to her. She made it clear she didn't want to talk about what had happened to her, and we aren't going to force her to talk about it."

"Of course not," Frank said quickly, in case Gino wanted to argue. "The question is, who else might have wanted Esposito dead?"

"Any number of people," Sarah said, "if he's been kidnapping people's wives and children and extorting money from local businessmen."

"So the first thing we need to do is start asking around Italian Harlem," Gino said.

"Except you aren't going anywhere near Italian Harlem," Frank said.

"Why not?"

"Because you might get killed, that's why not. You're going to stay right here for the time being."

"Here? In your house?"

"I can't think of any place safer. Can you?"

Gino gaped at him for a long moment, clearly unable to.

"We'll have to send word to your family of course," Sarah said. "They'll be worried if you don't come home."

"I'll go out as soon as I've finished eating and send them a telegram," Frank said. "Then one of us will go visit your family tomorrow and explain what's going on."

"You can't go," Sarah said.

"Why not?"

"Because I'm sure everyone knows Gino works for you, so if anyone is watching their house, looking for Gino, they'll figure out why you're there."

Frank frowned. "That seems convoluted to me."

"She's right, though," Gino said. "You and I went to see Petrosino, too. Everyone in Little Italy will know that."

"So I should go," Sarah said.

"People in Little Italy know you, too," Maeve said, finally coming into the dining room. Plainly she'd heard at least part of the conversation.

"Then Maeve should go," Gino said.

"Me? Why me?" she asked, genuinely startled.

"Because nobody in Little Italy will know who you are," Gino said. "And besides, it's time you met the rest of my family."

VI

The next morning, Gino needed a minute to remember where he was when he awoke in one of the Malloys' spare bedrooms. Then he allowed himself a few minutes to be annoyed that Mr. Malloy thought he needed to hide out here for heaven knew how long, quaking in fear of the Black Hand.

He supposed he *should* fear the Black Hand. They were pretty ruthless, after all, but he certainly wasn't going to hide here for the next few days or even weeks—because it could take that long—until they found out who had really killed Nunzio Esposito. Especially because Mr. Malloy would need his help, if he hoped to have any success at all in Italian Harlem.

Luckily, he'd hit upon the perfect solution while lying in bed last night, too restless and angry at his predicament to fall sleep. He waited until Mr. Malloy had headed back up to East Harlem, where he was going to make a second attempt to question the cop who had arrested Gino. It would probably be a fruitless effort to find out who had told the cop to go find Gino in the flat with Esposito's dead body. Then he waited until Mr. Malloy's mother had taken Brian to the school for the deaf, where he learned how to sign, along with all the other stuff kids learned in school. And he waited until Maeve left to take Catherine to that fancy school she went to uptown before Maeve headed back down to Little Italy and the Donatelli house. And finally, he waited until Mrs. Malloy left after a call from the maternity clinic she ran on the Lower East Side. One of the women there was in labor, and they were worried about her. Then, when no one was around to overhear him, he used the telephone to leave a message at a certain boardinghouse for Miss Verena Rose. Miss Rose was a girl he'd met a few months ago on another case, and he was pretty sure she could be of great assistance in helping him out of his current situation.

MAEVE COULDN'T BELIEVE THIS. HOW WAS SHE EVEN GOing to communicate with Gino's parents? He'd said their English wasn't very good and Maeve spoke no Italian at all. What if she couldn't make them understand? What if they didn't even believe she knew Gino? He'd explained numerous times how the Italians didn't trust anyone they didn't know, and even then, they preferred doing business with people to whom they were actually related. Maeve didn't fit either of those categories and never would.

She could feel people staring at her as she walked down the street. They were probably staring at her red hair. Not many people in Little Italy had red hair. Gino had suggested she go at noon time, since his father would be home for lunch then and she could explain the situation to both his parents at once. He'd neglected to mention it would also be the time of day when lots of people would be on the streets. If the Black Hand didn't get him, she just might stick a stiletto between Gino's ribs for getting her into this.

At least a dozen children—those too young for school— were racing around in the street in front of the house Gino's family shared with his aunt and uncle and their family, engaged in some game only they understood. Maeve wondered idly how many of them belonged to the Donatellis. Gino's mother and her best friend had married brothers. The brothers had done well enough to buy the house and divide it for their two families. It was probably just as crowded as most tenements but with a lot more privacy, since everyone was related.

She looked up at the ramshackle house, which had been squeezed in between two others. It was the best kept of the three, with a neat but tiny patch of lawn separating it from the sidewalk and cleanly swept front steps leading up to the porch.

Maeve took a deep breath and climbed the steps. She rapped sharply on the front door, trying to give the impression that she was confident of her welcome. After a few minutes, a young man opened the door, a puzzled smile on his face when he saw her. He looked so much like Gino—just as dark and handsome—that he must be one of the brothers.

"I'm looking for Mrs. Donatelli," she said when he didn't speak.

"Mama," he shouted, making her wince. "But if you're a social worker," he added to Maeve in a normal voice, "you're

wasting your time. She's not going to change the way she does things."

What an odd thing to say. "I'm not a social worker."

"Then who are you?"

"I'm Maeve Smith. I—"

His expression changed so quickly, Maeve blinked in surprise. His amused curiosity dissolved into a worried scowl, and he grabbed her arm. "Get inside quick."

She didn't resist because she'd *intended* to go inside, but she couldn't understand why his attitude had changed so abruptly.

"Mama!" he called again, this time more urgently, as he slammed the door behind her.

She could hear Mrs. Donatelli before she saw her. She was chastening her son in Italian, probably for yelling like that inside, as she bustled out from someplace in the back of the house, probably the kitchen since she was wiping her hands on her apron as she came. She was a small woman, her body only slightly thickened from bearing six sons. Her dark hair had just a hint of silver, and her pleasant face was remarkably unlined.

When she saw Maeve, she stopped dead, and asked the young man something in Italian.

He answered her, saying Maeve's name. This led to a rapid exchange of questions and answers, punctuated by lots of hand gestures, in which Gino and Maeve's names were mentioned.

"I just need to speak to Mrs. Donatelli," Maeve tried. "And Mr. Donatelli, if he's here."

The young man gave her a horrified glance and then apparently relayed this information to his mother. She shouted, *"Angelo!"* at the same time he shouted, *"Papa!"* In another moment, an older man emerged from the back of the house, looking annoyed and dabbing his mouth with the corner of a napkin that was tied around his neck. He frowned when he saw Maeve, and when the young man announced her by name, he also stopped dead in his tracks. Both parents looked her up and down with grim interest.

Then for some reason, Mr. Donatelli started shouting at his wife, who started shouting right back. The young man merely watched, looking troubled. "I just need to talk to them for a few minutes," Maeve told him, feeling a little desperate now. "I need to tell them something about Gino."

At the mention of Gino's name, both his parents fell instantly silent and glared at her as if she were the one who had framed Gino for Esposito's murder. Since they didn't even know about Esposito's murder yet—at least she didn't think they did—that couldn't be it. She tried a reassuring smile, but that just made Mrs. Donatelli burst into tears.

The young man muttered what was probably an Italian curse and said, "We better go in the parlor." He ushered her into the room that opened off the front hall. It was full of well-worn furniture, obviously the place the family would gather. The young man motioned her to sit down on the sofa, then went back and ushered his mother into the room. She was still weeping but trying to dry her eyes with her apron. Mr. Donatelli just looked angry, and he glared at Maeve in a way she found completely unjustified. Although maybe they did already know about the murder charge and were just taking out their fury on her.

The parents sat in armchairs facing her, and the young man moved to a spot between the chairs and remained standing. He crossed his arms, and they all three glared at her for a long moment. Before she could think of how to start her explanation, the young man said, "Gino didn't come home last night. He might have run out on you."

"Didn't you get Mr. Malloy's telegram?"

The young man relayed her question. "We got it, but now that we know . . . Well, it makes sense, doesn't it?"

Nothing made sense so far, at least to Maeve. "I have some . . . unpleasant news to tell you about Gino, but—"

"We've already figured it out, miss," he assured her. "But we can't make him marry you. In fact, considering you're Irish, I doubt my parents would even want him to. Besides . . ."

Marry? What were they talking about? "Wait a minute. First of all, I'm not Irish." Which was true. She was American.

The family conferred for a moment.

"Are you even Catholic?"

Maeve was completely lost now. "What does that matter? Don't you even want to hear what I have to tell you about Gino?"

"Look, miss, I'm sorry if Gino got you in trouble, but you'll have to settle things with him. We can't—"

"I'm not the one in trouble. Gino is!"

"But he's not the one having a baby, is he?" the young man countered a little too smugly. Mrs. Donatelli understood enough of that to make her cross herself.

Baby? What on earth was he . . . ? Maeve needed only another moment to finally figure it out. Trouble. They thought she was *in trouble.*

Pregnant.

By Gino.

Good Lord! That was funny. It was, in fact, hilarious. "No!" she cried, hoping Mr. and Mrs. Donatelli at least understood that English word. "No, no, no!" By the third no, she was laughing, because it really was hilarious. She started shaking her head, figuring they'd understand that, at least.

They were staring back at her in confusion, probably wondering if she was insane.

When she could speak again, she said, "*Gino* is the one in trouble. He was arrested for murder yesterday."

The young man's mouth dropped open. "Murder?"

"Yes, but it's all right. Mr. Malloy bailed him out of jail. He stayed at the Malloy house last night, because we thought he'd be safer there for now." Should she explain about the Black Hand and the danger? She probably should, but she'd stop here and give him time to explain to his parents.

His mother was already chastening him again for not translating fast enough, and Maeve waited patiently while he did, folding her hands in her lap and trying her best to look like the kind of girl who would never have to plead with a young man's parents for help bringing a reluctant lover to the altar.

Now the parents were upset in an entirely different way and were both asking questions a mile a minute, but of course Maeve couldn't understand them, so she just continued to look virtuous until they wound down. When the brother would have translated, she held up a hand to stop him because she figured she already knew what they'd want to know.

"The man Gino is accused of killing is Nunzio Esposito," she explained. Mr. Donatelli's eyes widened at that, so he'd probably heard of him. "He's the head of a Black Hand group in East Harlem. Gino and Mr. Malloy were investigating a kidnapping they thought Esposito's men had done, and a policeman found Gino in the apartment with

Esposito's body, so they arrested him, but Gino didn't do it of course."

"Of course," the brother said faintly.

His mother started demanding some answers, so he took some time to explain what Maeve had just told him.

When he stopped, Maeve didn't wait for another question. "They don't need to worry, though. Like I said, Mr. Malloy bailed Gino out and plans to keep him hidden away until we find out who really killed Esposito."

The brother nodded. "Away from the police."

Maeve blinked at that but realized she shouldn't be surprised. Naturally, they were suspicious of the police, who always showed a particular eagerness to arrest Italians for anything at all. "No, from the Black Hand. If they think he killed Esposito, they would want revenge."

"*Vendetta*," he murmured, making his parents frown.

"Exactly," she said. "And if one of them did it, they'd want to pin it on Gino and kill him to make people think he was guilty."

He nodded and explained this to his parents in solemn tones. His mother crossed herself again. His parents had a few more questions, which Maeve answered as well as she could, since she hardly knew much more about it than they did.

She tried to be reassuring. "Like I said, you don't need to worry because Mr. Malloy will get this all sorted out and find the real killer, and meanwhile, Gino will be safe at our house."

"Our house?" the brother asked suspiciously. "You live there, too?"

Now here he was, getting the wrong idea again. "I take care of the Malloy children."

"But you work for the agency, too. Gino told us."

"Sometimes I do." Whenever she could, as a matter of fact.

"Gino told us all about it. He talks about you all the time."

"He does?"

He smiled the same smile Gino did whenever he was up to mischief. "Yes, which is why when you came here looking for him . . . Well, I'm sorry about the . . ." He made a helpless gesture.

"Misunderstanding?" she offered.

"Yes, the misunderstanding."

She'd have a thing or two to say to Gino about that. What on earth had he been saying about her to his family? "Gino asked me to pack him a bag. We don't know how long he'll be at the Malloys' house, but he'll need some clothes and—"

"Sure," he said, and translated for his mother.

She frowned at Maeve and said something to her son before jumping up and leaving the room.

"She'll pack his things," he explained. He said something to his father, who grumbled and then got up and left, too. Plainly, they were finished with her.

When she and the brother were alone, Maeve said, "What's your name?"

"Oh, I should have introduced myself. I'm Enzo." He took the opportunity to sit down in the chair his father had vacated.

"And which one are you?"

He grinned at that. "I'm the second oldest, after Rinaldo. Gino is the third."

"Are you married, too?"

His grin widened. "No. Are you interested? Because now that I know you're not Irish . . ." He did look an awful lot like Gino.

But he wasn't Gino. "I'm not Catholic."

He shrugged, as if that were of no consequence.

"What does Gino say about me?"

"Well, he never said you have red hair."

She should have known better than to ask. "I've met Teodora."

"Did you?" He was impressed. "Did Gino introduce you?"

"No, she came to the office to tell us Gino had been arrested." No sense telling him she'd first come about Miss Harding's kidnapping, since that was still supposed to be a secret.

"Oh. For a minute, I thought he might be trying to win Teo over first, before bringing you here to meet Mama."

That would have been interesting. "Why were you so quick to think I was trying to get Gino to marry me?"

He sighed, a little chagrinned. "Well, a young woman, who looks very serious, comes to the house asking for my parents, a young woman I know my brother is, uh, friendly with, and what could she possibly want to see our parents about?"

When he put it that way, she could understand. "Let me just assure you that is not even a possibility and never will be."

"Never is a long time."

It certainly was. "What do you do for a living, Enzo?"

"I work with Pop at the shop. He wants one of us to take over the business when he's gone."

"Do you like it?"

He looked at her like she was crazy. "What does that matter?"

"Gino likes his work. A lot."

"Now that I see who he works with, I can understand that."

But she shook her head. "He liked it a long time before he met me. Besides, he mostly works with Mr. Malloy, who isn't a bit pretty."

"I know. I've met him. So why is Gino supposed to have killed this Esposito?"

"Because he has been kidnapping women and children in East Harlem. Italians mostly. His men also make the local businesses pay them money to protect them."

"Protect them from what?"

"From the Black Hand."

"But they *are* the Black Hand."

"Which is why Gino was mad. In fact he was so mad, he went to tell Esposito to his face how mad he was."

"That's stupid," Enzo said.

"Of course it is. He's lucky Esposito was already dead."

"So you're going to keep Gino locked away at Mr. Malloy's house?"

"We're going to try."

"He won't like that."

"Which is why we need to find the killer quickly."

They heard some thumping on the stairs, and Mrs. Donatelli called for Enzo, who jumped up and ran to help. A minute later, he returned carrying a rather worn-looking satchel. Mrs. Donatelli was right behind him, still looking a bit angry. Maeve hoped the woman didn't blame her for Gino's predicament.

"Will you be sure to tell your mother that Gino got himself into this mess?" she asked Enzo. "I had nothing to do with it."

"Of course. I'll be happy to get him in trouble. I've been

doing it all my life." He hefted the bag. "This is pretty heavy. How far are you going?"

"I was going to get a cab."

"You won't find one in this neighborhood. I'll walk with you over to Broadway."

Mrs. Donatelli was frowning, obviously not approving of Enzo's kindly expression.

"Are you sure that's all right with your parents?"

"They raised me to be a gentleman." He said something to his mother, and while her scowl told Maeve she still didn't approve, she made no move to stop him either.

Enzo followed her out of the house and down the front steps. "I hope you'll tell Gino how nice I was to you."

"Oh, I will," Maeve promised. "Right after I tell him you thought he'd run off rather than marry me."

FRANK HADN'T REALLY EXPECTED THE POLICE IN EAST Harlem to be helpful. Yesterday, no one had been willing to give him any information about Esposito's death at all, and they had claimed the officer who arrested Gino had gone down to the Tombs with him and wasn't available. Today he'd expected more reluctance to cooperate, but he certainly hadn't expected them to lie right to his face. First they'd told him the cop he was looking for worked in another precinct, and they had sent him on a wild-goose chase. By the time he found his way back to the original precinct, he was ready to take on the whole lot of them. They must have realized it, too, so they sent him to the right street, where he finally found Officer Ogden.

Because it was such a nice day and still early, Ogden was walking his beat, swinging his locust stick with a jaunty air instead of sitting in a saloon or dozing in a doorway. He was a big man with a bushy mustache and a bulbous nose that spoke of many evenings spent bellied up to some bar. His eyes were bloodshot and held no visible spark of intelligence.

He stopped when Frank called him by name and looked Frank up and down. "And what might you be wanting with me this fine day?"

"I'm a private detective, Frank Malloy." He handed Ogden one of his business cards. "You arrested my partner yesterday."

"You're partners with a dago?" Ogden scoffed, squinting to examine the card.

"Gino Donatelli and I were both cops."

Ogden frowned, not sure how that answered his question. "If Donatelli was a cop, he should know better than to kill somebody."

"You know as well as I do that he didn't kill Esposito. Why should he?"

"I don't know. Maybe he wanted Esposito's woman. He was keeping a woman in that flat, you know. Everybody's saying so."

"I heard. Donatelli didn't want her, though. He didn't even know who she was."

"Why was he there, then?"

"He was looking for Esposito. He wanted to ask him some questions about a case we're working on."

Ogden was not impressed. "How did he know where to find Esposito? Nobody knew about that flat."

Which was of course not true. Apparently, a lot of people knew about it. "Somebody at the saloon said he'd be there. Probably the same person who took you there to arrest Donatelli."

"Who said somebody took me there?"

"Everybody who saw you." Frank figured that would be true if he'd asked any of them.

Ogden didn't like that at all. Once he'd thought about it, he'd realize that most people would be afraid to tell Frank anything like that, but for the moment, Frank would let him think they had.

"Who sent you up there, Ogden? Was it Balducci?" Frank asked, taking a wild guess.

Something flared in Ogden's bloodshot eyes that might have been alarm, but he said, "Why would Balducci send me anywhere?"

"Because he'd just sent Donatelli to the flat, and he already knew Esposito was lying dead up there and he wanted you to accuse Donatelli." Most of that was a guess and the rest was an outright lie, but Frank wasn't too concerned.

Ogden raised his locust and started slapping it into the palm of his other hand in what he probably thought was a menacing manner. "I don't take orders from the Black Hand."

"I'm glad to hear it, but maybe he just suggested you'd get your big chance to catch Esposito's killer. Nothing wrong with that, but didn't you wonder how he already knew Esposito was dead?"

"He never said Esposito was dead."

So Balducci really was the one who had sent Ogden. "What *did* he say?"

"He said . . . Wait a minute. He didn't say anything," he quickly amended. "I just saw a suspicious character going into the tenement, so I followed him."

"So you were right behind Donatelli, then. Do you really think he had time to kill Esposito before you got up the stairs?"

"I—"

"Because it's hard to believe a man like Esposito would be taken by surprise like that by a stranger. And where did Donatelli get the knife? It was a big one, wasn't it? Surely, he wasn't carrying it. People would've noticed. And if he wasn't carrying a weapon, he probably didn't intend to kill Esposito, which means he would've needed time to argue with Esposito and get mad enough to kill him and then look around the kitchen and find the knife while Esposito just stood around waiting and not trying to fight back or get away, and—"

"*Stop!*" Ogden cried, then glanced around to see who might have witnessed his outburst. No one passing by acted as if they'd heard anything untoward, which was probably a testament to Ogden's usually brutal behavior. "I don't know nothing about what happened up there. All I know is Esposito was dead and Donatelli was there, so I arrested him. I don't decide who's guilty and who's not. I leave that to the lawyers."

"So you might be wrong about Donatelli killing Esposito?"

Ogden glanced around again. "It's none of my business, Malloy, and you'd be smart to start minding your own, too."

"Except my partner is charged with murder."

"You can get him out of that quick enough."

"Maybe with the law, but not with the Black Hand."

"What do you mean?"

"I mean if they decide he did it, they'll take their revenge. They might even take their revenge if they know he didn't do it."

Plainly, this confused Ogden. "Sounds like your argument is with Balducci. He's the only one who can help you with that."

"Are you saying he's already taken Esposito's place?"

Once again alarm flared in Ogden's bloodshot eyes. "I didn't say that. It's just . . ." He glanced around as if looking for someone to get him out of this conversation.

Frank was more than happy to oblige. "Thanks, Ogden. You've been a big help."

"I have?" He obviously had not intended to be.

Frank left him scratching his head. He really should question Balducci, who seemed like the most logical person to know who killed Esposito, if he really was the one who had sent Ogden to arrest Gino and had already assumed Esposito's duties as head of his Black Hand gang. But somehow confronting Balducci alone seemed like a bad idea. A man ruthless enough to be a member of the Black Hand and who might very well have killed his own boss wouldn't hesitate to kill a bothersome private detective, given the chance. Besides, Frank wouldn't be much help to Gino if he was dead, never mind the inconvenience to himself. Sarah would be pretty mad about it, too.

Knowing he wouldn't have much luck trying to get information from anyone else in the neighborhood, he headed for the settlement house, where at least he could reassure Teo that Gino was safe for the time being. And maybe she'd even heard some gossip that could prove useful.

Frank half expected Teo to be waiting for him in the front hall of the settlement, but he saw no sign of her among the people milling about. The "residents" were easy to spot, though, the do-gooders who, like Jane Harding, had taken up residence here to help the poor. They had an air of confidence that the people from the neighborhood lacked. The kind of confidence that came from never having to worry about where your next meal was coming from or where you were going to sleep that night.

The young female resident he spoke to didn't know where Teo was, but she suggested he could find Christopher McWilliam in his office, so he did.

"Mr. Malloy," McWilliam said by way of greeting. He didn't seem overly pleased to see Frank, but he didn't groan out loud either. He got up and came forward to shake Frank's hand. "I was sorry to hear about Mr. Donatelli's arrest."

"Mrs. Donatelli told you, I guess."

He nodded. "Everyone's talking about it. Nobody believes he's really guilty of course. Everyone here understands how the police work, and I'm sure they'll figure out that he's innocent and let him go. Please sit down."

Frank took a seat on the sofa where he'd sat before, and McWilliam pulled his desk chair over. "I was wondering how Miss Harding is today."

"I . . ." McWilliam sighed and looked away, obviously trying to get control of his emotions, although Frank wasn't sure what emotions he was feeling. After a moment, he lifted his chin with what looked like determination and with what actually was a very sad smile, and he said, "She left yesterday."

Frank nodded, remembering what Sarah had told him about her intent to go visit with Lisa Prince. "My wife said she was going to stay with her cousin for a while."

"With Mrs. Prince, yes. Mrs. Prince came yesterday afternoon in her carriage. It caused quite a stir in the neighborhood, I can tell you."

Frank imagined it would have. "I can understand that Miss Harding wants to get away for a while."

"Yes but . . ." Were those tears in his eyes? "Mr. Malloy, she told me she wasn't coming back."

Frank knew what that meant. Jane Harding had supposedly

come to the settlement house to see if she could adapt herself to living there for the rest of her life as McWilliam's wife. If she wasn't coming back, that meant she had rejected more than life at the settlement. She was rejecting him, too. "I'm sorry, Mr. McWillam."

"Yes, well, I suppose it's better to know this now rather than later." Which sounded like something a man said to convince himself rather than something he really believed.

"I know how important your work here is to you," Frank said, not really knowing anything of the kind, but McWilliam's feelings were obvious.

"I don't know if I could give it up for her, but she didn't even ask. She simply said she was leaving because how could she remain in a place where she would never feel safe?"

What would Sarah say to comfort him? She always knew the right thing. Did they teach that in those fancy schools rich girls attended? Is that what Catherine was learning at Miss Spence's School? "Maybe she'll feel differently after she's been with her cousin for a while."

"Do you think so? I guess it's possible. I should go to see her, I suppose. Make sure she's all right."

Frank doubted that was a good idea. "Maybe you should give her a few days. She's probably still pretty upset over what happened."

"Yes, well, if the way she carried on when Lisa showed up is any indication, I suppose you're right."

"What do you mean?"

"I shouldn't say anything, but . . . It was awful. So embarrassing for everyone. Jane apparently hadn't expected Lisa to come for her so soon, so she wasn't packed and this upset her. Lisa went up to help, but that only made it worse.

Jane can be . . . *emotional* when things don't go her way. She was nearly hysterical when she finally left."

"Then that's another good reason to give her some time, Mr. McWillam, but I'm glad you warned me. I was hoping to ask Miss Harding some questions, but now I realize this isn't a good time."

"Questions about what?"

"About where she was held when she was kidnapped."

"What does that matter now? You'll never be able to catch whoever took her."

"I'm not so sure about that, and you're wrong. It does matter, if she was held at the flat where Esposito was killed."

"What makes you think she was?"

"Because people saw a woman with blond hair leaving the flat around the same time Miss Harding escaped."

"That's . . . No, you're wrong. Everyone is saying Esposito was keeping his mistress there, so it couldn't have been Jane."

"Maybe people just assumed she was his mistress and was there of her own free will. But this is all just guesswork. I won't know anything for sure until I talk to Miss Harding. It's possible it was a completely different woman."

"Of course it was. There are thousands of women with blond hair in New York."

"I know. I'm married to one," Frank said with a reassuring smile. "But I'm sure you can understand that with my partner accused of his murder, I'm anxious to get as much information about Esposito's death as possible."

"Of course. I'm sorry, Mr. Malloy. I'm being selfish to just be thinking about Jane."

"Not at all. It does you credit. I assume from what you said that you were able to see her before she left."

"Just for a few minutes. Men aren't permitted in the women's residence, but the other women were finally able to coax Jane out of her room later in the evening the day she got back. I met her in the hallway, just outside the door that leads to the residence, which wasn't the best place to have a conversation, as you can imagine."

"No, I don't suppose it was."

"That's when she told me she was leaving the settlement. She said she'd asked Lisa to come for her, although she expected it would be at least another day or two before she did. Meanwhile, she would remain in her room because she couldn't bear to talk about what had happened to her." Like Mrs. Cassidi. Frank hoped it wasn't for the same reason. "But even if Jane was held at that flat, she wouldn't know anything about Esposito's murder yesterday," McWilliam said.

"You're probably right, but it seemed like a good place to start. You said everyone's talking about it. Have you heard any theories about who might have killed Esposito?"

"I'm happy to say not many people think Gino Donatelli did it," McWilliam said, quite seriously. "I think they might be afraid to talk about the Black Hand, even to conjecture about this, but you have to consider the possibility that one of his own men did it."

"I'm looking very closely at Balducci."

McWilliam glanced toward the door, then leaned forward and lowered his voice. "They're saying he'll take over now that Esposito is dead."

News certainly traveled fast in this neighborhood if McWilliam had already heard it. "That seemed like a good possibility to me, too. But if Balducci or one of his men killed Esposito, they'll be anxious to pin it on Gino, won't they?"

Plainly, McWilliam hadn't considered this possibility. "That's terrible."

"They're terrible people, Mr. McWilliam."

McWilliam could only agree. Frank took his leave, not sure he'd learned anything of importance. He was relieved to find Teo waiting for him in the front hallway when he went back downstairs. She escorted him into an empty classroom where they could have a bit of privacy.

"Do you know what happened to Gino?" she asked him, her dark eyes reflecting the anxiety they all felt for the boy.

"He's fine. We bailed him out of jail, and I made him stay at my house last night because I was afraid the Black Hand might be watching his parents' house."

Teo murmured something that might have been a prayer and crossed herself. "Rinaldo wanted to go tell his parents what happened last night, but I convinced him to wait. They'll be wondering why he didn't come home, though."

"I sent them a telegram last night so they wouldn't worry, and this morning I sent Maeve to tell his parents and collect his things. He'll be staying with us for the time being."

"Maeve?" Teo echoed with a curious smile.

"Yes. Why, is something wrong?"

"No, no," she said, although she plainly found this highly amusing. Frank would have to find out why, but obviously from someone else.

"I just met with McWilliam. He said that people are saying Balducci has taken over the Black Hand."

"That's what people expect, I think, so they're saying it's true."

"I see. Have you heard anything else? We need to figure out who else might have killed Esposito. The only way to really protect Gino is to find the real killer."

"I know, so I've been listening this morning to find out what people are saying." She tugged his sleeve, pulling him farther from the open door in case someone was outside in the hallway. Then she leaned in and whispered, "This sounds so strange that it must be true. People are saying Mrs. Esposito was seen on that block late Wednesday night."

VII

THE HANSOM CAB DROPPED MAEVE OFF AT THE DOOR-
step of the Malloy house. She lugged the bag of Gino's
clothing up the front steps and used her key to open the
front door. During the entire trip from Little Italy, she'd
been planning what she'd say to Gino, trying to find the
exact phrasing that would adequately convey her outrage at
having his parents think she was Gino's paramour (or whatever they actually thought she was) while also revealing how
Enzo had flirted with her. She was pretty sure she had figured out what to say.

She stepped inside and closed the door behind her.
Should she call out to make sure Gino had heard her arrive?
She really wanted to make a dramatic entrance.

No sooner had she completed the thought than a strange
man stepped out of the parlor. Obviously Italian, his raven
hair was shot with gray and he wore a full beard. His dark

eyes glared at her from beneath bushy brows, and he made an odd growling sound in his throat that was unmistakably threatening. Then he started toward her.

"*Gino!*" she shouted. "Hattie! Velvet!" she added, naming the servants who should also be here. Where were they? Had this man done something to them? "Who are you? What do you want?" she demanded, dropping the bag and reaching back for the doorknob. She could escape out into the street if she had to, although he still might catch her. "*Gino!*" she tried again.

"Ah, *signorina*, do not be afraid," he said in a thick accent.

This was, of course, exactly what someone who was intent on murdering you would say, so Maeve wasn't fooled. She frantically fumbled for the doorknob, knowing she dared not take her eyes off the stranger. Where was Gino? Why didn't he come? What on earth was going on?

"Do you not recognize me, *signorina*?" he asked, coming closer and closer, dangerously close.

Maeve opened her mouth to scream, but the sound of a woman's laughter stopped her.

"It worked!" the woman cried in obvious delight.

The man stopped and straightened ever so slightly, which miraculously changed everything about the way he looked, and when he smiled, sharing the woman's delight, Maeve instantly recognized him.

"*Gino,*" Maeve said, and this time it was an accusation.

The pretty blond woman who had laughed stepped out into the hall. "How nice to see you again, Mazie," she said.

"You know that's not my name, Miss Rose," Maeve said.

"Oh yes," Verena Rose said. "I keep forgetting."

No she didn't. She just liked to annoy Maeve. And of

course Maeve had used the name *Mazie* when she'd first met Verena during a case a few months ago. Verena had been performing in a play with an actor who had gotten himself murdered. "Did you do this?" she asked, indicating Gino's transformation with a wave of her hand.

"Yes, I did," Verena said with obvious pride. "I even showed him how to walk so he'd look older."

"It worked, too. I even fooled you," Gino added with even more pride.

"I could give you a few pointers, too," Maeve couldn't resist adding.

"But you're not a professional actress," Verena said. "I have training."

"And I knew she'd be able to help me with the hair and the beard," Gino said. "They do that stuff all the time in the theater."

Maeve could have shown him a thing or two about disguises, but she wouldn't mention it. If being an actress was only a fairly respectable profession, being a grifter wasn't respectable at all, and that was where she'd learned what skills she had at formulating a disguise. "Are you wearing greasepaint?" she asked, squinting at Gino's face.

"Just a little," Verena said. "I thought his complexion should be darker."

"From years under the Calabrian sun," Gino said, still not bothering to pretend he wasn't delighted at having fooled her, even for a moment. "Look, she even gave me some wrinkles."

Maeve didn't look. "All right, so you managed to figure out how to disguise yourself. What do you hope to accomplish by it?"

"Now I can help Mr. Malloy in East Harlem. He'll need

me because nobody there will talk to him, even if they can speak enough English for him to understand."

"And do you think they'll talk to a stranger, even one who's Italian?"

"Teo and Rinaldo will help, too."

"And what if somebody recognizes you and tells the Black Hand?"

"Nobody will recognize me," Gino assured her. "Nobody in Italian Harlem really knows me except my family there."

Maeve thought it was possible he might pull it off, but she certainly wasn't going to admit it. "Does Mr. Malloy know about this?"

Of course he didn't, as she could see from Gino's expression. "Not yet, but he'll think it's brilliant."

Brilliant was a stretch, but Mr. Malloy would probably appreciate the effort. "We'll see." She turned to Verena. "You did a good job. I really didn't recognize him at first."

Verena blinked in surprise. She hadn't expected a compliment from Maeve, which was the only reason Maeve had given her one. "Thanks."

"Don't I get a little credit for my acting?" Gino said with mock despair.

"Yes, but just a little."

"And you're going to take me out to dinner at Delmonico's to thank me," Verena said sweetly.

"I sure am, as soon as all of this is over," Gino said with much more enthusiasm than Maeve thought was necessary.

"I brought your clothes," she said to change the subject.

"Did you tell my parents I was arrested?" he asked with a frown.

"Yes. They took the news pretty well. They've probably been expecting it for quite a while now."

That made Verena laugh out loud, which made Gino frown murderously, but he needed only a moment to recover.

"How did you talk to them?"

"Enzo was there," she said.

"Enzo," he repeated, obviously not pleased, which was just what Maeve had been hoping for.

"Yes, he was very helpful. He even asked me to marry him."

Sarah had missed supper at home that night. One of the women at the maternity clinic had had a very difficult birth, and she'd stayed until the woman and her baby seemed well out of danger. The resident midwives could certainly have handled the situation without her help, but she'd felt obligated to stay in case the outcome had been bad. She didn't want the staff alone to take the blame for the first death at the clinic. Fortunately, no one had died this time. It would happen sooner or later, though. Poverty bred all sorts of dangers that took women and their babies with impunity. Rickets was a common killer, having malformed a woman's bones years earlier, when she was only a child, and making it impossible for her to give birth naturally. Often the operation to take the baby—even if performed in time—would cause a fatal infection. And that was just one of the silent killers of vulnerable mothers and their infants. Giving women a safe place to deliver wasn't even half the battle.

By the time Sarah got home, the children were in bed and even Mrs. Malloy had retired to her own rooms. Maeve and Gino were in the parlor with Malloy, probably talking about the case. They all jumped to their feet when she entered. Malloy came forward and kissed her cheek.

"Have you eaten?" Maeve asked.

"Yes, I had supper at the clinic."

"Is everything, uh, all right?" Malloy asked uneasily. He knew the dangers of childbirth all too well, having lost Brian's mother that way.

"Yes, everything went well. Mother and baby are doing fine." A slight exaggeration, but Sarah hoped it would prove true. "Did you find out anything about Esposito's murder today?"

Malloy told her about his visit with Officer Ogden and Mr. McWilliam and the information Teo had relayed.

"Mrs. Esposito was seen on Pleasant Avenue?" Sarah asked when he was finished.

"That's what people are saying."

"But would that be unusual? She probably lives in the neighborhood somewhere."

"This was very late, apparently," Malloy said. "Long after respectable women were safely in their houses."

"And I don't suppose Esposito's wife is too worried about being kidnapped," Gino said, "so she wouldn't be scared to be out that late."

"Do you suppose she went to the flat?" Sarah asked.

"If I found out my husband was keeping a mistress, I'd certainly go there to see for myself," Maeve said.

"Would an Italian woman do that, though?" Sarah asked Gino.

"A lot of them would. I wouldn't be surprised if she was the one who stabbed him, too. Italian women are pretty emotional about these things."

"Finding out my husband had set up a place for another woman right under my nose would make me mad enough to stab him," Maeve said.

"Are you sure you're not Italian?" Gino asked with a grin.

Maeve ignored him.

"So it's pretty likely Mrs. Esposito went to the flat the night Esposito was murdered, possibly to confront him or maybe just to make sure the rumors were correct," Malloy said.

"She knew he wasn't at home." Maeve continued the theorizing. "That meant he could have been at the flat and probably the woman was, too."

"Although if the woman was Jane Harding, we know she wasn't there, because she'd already escaped and returned to the settlement house by then," Sarah pointed out.

"But we don't know the woman was Jane Harding," Malloy pointed out right back. "If it wasn't her, then that woman might have gotten mad when Mrs. Esposito showed up."

"Maybe she didn't know Esposito was married," Maeve said. "That could make a woman mad enough to stab him."

"But people saw the woman leave the flat that morning," Gino said.

"She could have come back," Maeve said. "If she was there of her own free will, she probably did."

"Or she could have killed him before she left," Sarah said.

"So maybe Mrs. Esposito went there to confront her husband and killed him or maybe his mistress got mad about something and killed him," Malloy said.

"And maybe Balducci killed him for some reason or just because he wanted to take his place as boss," Gino added.

"And maybe somebody we haven't thought of yet killed him for a reason we haven't figured out yet," Sarah added.

"Like somebody the Black Hand had kidnapped," Maeve said.

"Or more likely one of their family members, since they mostly kidnapped children," Gino said.

"Except Mrs. Cassidi," Sarah said. "Although I can't see

her sneaking out late at night to confront Esposito. She was too frightened to even leave her house after her ordeal."

"Her husband might have, though," Malloy mused. "Especially if he found out what they'd done to her."

"Or any parent of a kidnapped child," Sarah said. "If someone took Brian or Catherine from me, I'd probably murder them myself."

"I'm sure you would, my dear," Malloy said, "and so would I. But think how much courage it would take to confront the leader of the Black Hand."

"Not if you could catch him alone and unprotected," Gino argued, "the way he was in that flat."

"But whoever killed him didn't go there intending to kill him," Maeve said.

They all turned to her in surprise.

"She's right," Malloy said after a moment. "Because he was stabbed with a knife that was probably already in the flat."

Maeve nodded. "So the killer didn't bring a weapon with him, which means he—or she—probably hadn't planned to kill him."

"Unless he thought he could kill Esposito with his bare hands," Gino said.

This time everyone turned to him, but with disdain.

Gino threw his hands up in surrender. "I know it sounds crazy, but it's at least possible."

"Or maybe the person was so angry, he just didn't think to take a weapon," Maeve said generously.

"So it is at least possible," Malloy said, equally generous.

"And let's not forget the mistress or whatever she is—the woman who was in the flat with Esposito," Sarah said. "She might also have a family member or husband or lover with a very good reason for hating Esposito."

"So we need to find out more about Mrs. Esposito, and who the woman was that Esposito was keeping in the flat, and which ones of the kidnapping victims' family members were brave enough that they might have confronted Esposito," Malloy summarized.

"How are you going to do all that when you can't even communicate with most of the people in Italian Harlem?" Sarah asked.

"Gino is going to help me."

Sarah frowned when she saw Gino's smirk. "I thought we were afraid the Black Hand wanted to murder Gino."

"Verena Rose came by for a visit today," Maeve reported sourly.

Sarah could understand Maeve's disgust at such an event. Gino had seen Verena a few times after they had finished the case in which she'd been involved. Sarah and Malloy had privately remarked on how jealous that had made Maeve, although Maeve would never have acknowledged such a weakness. But what did Verena's visit have to do with any of this?

"She fixed Gino up with a disguise," Malloy reported. "I didn't recognize him at all when I got home, and he even fooled Maeve."

"Only for a minute," Maeve claimed, but Gino gave a snort of derision that earned him a glare.

"I had to take off the beard so I could eat supper," Gino said, "but you can see it when I get dressed up tomorrow. You can still see the gray in my hair."

"Is that what that is?" Sarah asked, looking more closely. "I thought it was just the lighting in here."

"But he won't be able to question Mrs. Esposito," Malloy said. "A new widow isn't likely to accept a visit from two men she doesn't know, so we're going to need you to go to East Harlem tomorrow."

"What makes you think she'll accept a visit from me?" Sarah asked.

"Nothing, but we thought we'd try sending Teo with you and have you pretend you're a nurse from the settlement house, the way you did with Mrs. Cassidi," Malloy said.

"What makes anyone think she'd need a nurse?" Sarah scoffed.

"Nothing, of course," Malloy admitted. "And if she killed her husband, she's probably not exactly prostrate with grief, but we thought it was worth a try."

"Does she have children?" Sarah asked.

Gino and Malloy exchanged a questioning look.

"Not that we know of," Gino said.

"Teo will know," Maeve said.

"Of course she will," Sarah said. "Maybe she can also figure out why Mrs. Esposito would need to see me. How can we find out who the woman at Esposito's flat was?"

"Gino and I are going to question the neighbors and also talk to Mr. Cassidi."

"And if Mr. Cassidi killed Esposito, do you expect him to admit it?" Sarah asked.

Malloy grinned at that. "Not at all, but we'll see his reaction and we might be able to judge from that if it's possible. In addition, he can probably tell us about anybody else who might've been foolish enough to confront Esposito."

Sarah held out little hope Mr. Cassidi would identify the killer for them, but who knew? "Maeve, how did your visit with the Donatellis go?" she asked to change the subject.

"They took the news about Gino's arrest pretty well, although they were upset, as you can imagine."

"Aren't you going to tell her my brother proposed to you?" Gino asked with a smirk.

"*What?*" Sarah and Malloy said in unison.

"Enzo was quite charming, and I'm afraid he got the wrong idea when I asked if he was married," Maeve said primly.

"Enzo can't be trusted," Gino said grimly.

"I'm sure he can't," Maeve said. "But maybe he just felt sorry for me. You see, Gino's parents assumed I was there because I was in a family way and wanted their help in forcing Gino to marry me."

Sarah burst out laughing and Malloy joined her. Gino was not at all amused, but Sarah was glad to see Maeve was.

"How awkward for you," Sarah said when she could speak again.

"I think they were more embarrassed than I was. They actually suspected that Gino didn't come home last night because he'd run out on me."

"I'd never do that!" Gino cried, outraged.

"Of course you wouldn't," Sarah said, although Maeve just gave him a skeptical glare. "So what are you going to do next?" she asked Malloy.

"I guess I'll go back to East Harlem with Gino and see how effective his disguise is. We need to question the people in that tenement where Esposito was killed and talk to Mr. Cassidi. I'd also like to question Miss Harding, to see if she was the woman Esposito was keeping in his flat, but McWilliam said she was pretty upset when her cousin came for her yesterday morning."

"Why would she be upset?" Maeve asked. "She got just what she wanted."

"I don't know. I guess she wasn't expecting Mrs. Prince to come for her so soon, so she wasn't ready or something.

McWilliam hinted that she gets *emotional* when things don't go her way."

"Then he should be happy she decided not to marry him," Gino muttered.

"Let's not judge her too harshly," Sarah said. "She has been through a lot in the past few days."

"Maybe she needs to see a nurse," Maeve said with feigned innocence.

"That's exactly what I was thinking," Malloy said.

But Sarah was shaking her head. "I can't just barge into the Princes' house again. At best they'll decide I'm a busybody and at worst they'll refuse to see me at all. The most I can do is offer my services, which I'll do in a very nice note in which I express my hopes that Miss Harding is faring well."

"Do you think Miss Harding will want to see you again?" Maeve asked.

"Probably not, but I think I made a friend in Mrs. Prince, and if Miss Harding is still being *emotional*, Mrs. Prince might appreciate a sympathetic ear."

"But if Mrs. Prince refuses your help, won't that end your chances of visiting her again?" Malloy asked. He'd learned a lot about the way people in society behaved since they'd been married.

"Probably, but as a last resort, I can always ask my mother to go with me for an unscheduled visit. Not many New York society matrons would turn her away."

IN TRUTH, GINO HADN'T BEEN TOO SURE ABOUT HIS DISguise, but it seemed to be working. He and Mr. Malloy had taken the El up to East Harlem the next morning after deciding that having Gino drive the motorcar would only make people notice and perhaps figure out his ruse. They stopped at the settlement house first, and no one batted an eye at him when he asked for Teo, but she wasn't there. They made their way over to Teo and Rinaldo's tenement, and they found her just finishing up her housework before heading over to the settlement.

To Gino's delight, she didn't recognize him.

"I was lazy this morning," she explained to Mr. Malloy, a little chagrined at being caught making such a late start to the morning. She gave Gino a quizzical glance, obviously wondering who he was.

"This is Detective Sergeant Salvatore Pizzuto," Frank told her with a perfectly straight face. "He's going to be heading up the investigation into Esposito's death. I was hoping you'd take him over to Pleasant Avenue and introduce him."

She didn't like that idea at all. "The police? I don't know. Rinaldo thinks I should stay away from there now."

"Ah, *signora*, we would not ask you to do anything dangerous," Gino said in his fake voice. "All I need from you is to show me who to speak with."

Teo frowned. "People will wonder why I'm helping the police."

"But don't you want to save your brother-in-law?" Gino asked plaintively. "He is in danger, and he needs your help."

"He wouldn't be in danger if he hadn't put himself there," Mr. Malloy said, making Gino wince. "But I'm sure his parents would be grateful for any help you can give him."

Mention of the senior Donatellis obviously swayed her. "I can show you who you should talk to, but I will not do more than that. The Black Hand will be watching now."

Gino sighed dramatically. "Thanks, Teo. The whole family will appreciate it."

Teo stiffened and took a closer look at him. "Gino?" she asked, still not quite sure.

"What do you think? Will I fool the people on Pleasant Avenue?"

She called him a few choice names in Italian, probably not wanting Mr. Malloy to hear her acting unladylike, and when Gino laughed, she gave him a swat. "I should let the Black Hand have you for pulling a trick like this."

"Mr. Malloy isn't going to get anybody to talk to him up here, and I can't show my face in case the Black Hand is looking for me, so . . ." He shrugged.

"All right, but Rinaldo will be angry. He told me to stay away from Pleasant Avenue."

"I'll protect you, Teo," Gino promised with mock sincerity, knowing full well his brother would never harm her.

"I won't protect you, though," she replied.

SARAH SPENT A LITTLE TIME ON HER NOTE TO MRS. Prince, trying to get it just right. When she had, she put it out for the postman to collect when he delivered the morning mail. Mrs. Prince should get the note tomorrow, and Sarah had suggested she could telephone if she needed Sarah's services quickly. People didn't usually use the telephone to arrange social visits, but this was a special case. Besides, Mrs. Prince might be feeling desperate if Jane Harding was as difficult as people had indicated.

Sarah was finishing up her own correspondence when she heard the mail coming through the slot in the front door. Before she could get up, her maid, Hattie, brought it in to her. Sarah thanked her and flipped through the missives quickly, not seeing anything of importance until she found an envelope addressed to her in a feminine hand. She recognized the return address immediately and tore open the letter from Mrs. Cassidi.

Her written English was not quite as good as her spoken, but Sarah had no trouble at all understanding her request for a visit from Sarah, nor did she miss the underlying tone of desperation.

"Hattie, I'll be going up to East Harlem this morning," she called.

FRANK KNEW HIS PRESENCE ON PLEASANT AVENUE would only make people less likely to tell what they knew, so he headed over to Mr. Cassidi's office. He and Gino had decided that Frank's time could best be used approaching the businessman who was the most likely of all the people involved to answer Frank's questions.

Unless, of course, Cassidi himself was the killer.

Cassidi plainly wasn't happy to see Frank, though, especially after Frank introduced himself as Gino Donatelli's partner. In fact, he actually seemed angry. "What do you want?" he asked when Frank had been escorted into his office. "I already told Donatelli everything I know."

"I was hoping you could give me some information that would help me figure out who killed Esposito."

"And why should I even care about that? It is enough that *bastardo* is dead after what he has done." Cassidi turned back to the work he had been doing when Frank walked in, silently dismissing him.

"I know it's a lot to ask, Mr. Cassidi, but you may have

heard that my partner has been accused of the murder, and even though I can probably get him off, I can't stop the Black Hand from taking revenge if they think he did it."

Cassidi looked up impatiently. "I do feel bad for Gino. His brother is a good employee, but I do not know how I can help you, Mr. Malloy."

"I don't either, but maybe you know something that will help me figure it out, maybe something you don't even realize you know."

Mr. Cassidi's expression told him he doubted this very much, but he reluctantly gestured for Frank to take a seat.

Frank cleared his throat. "I understand that the Black Hand has kidnapped children from the neighborhood."

Cassidi's dark eyes narrowed dangerously. "Yes. This is true. Some of them are still missing."

"Has anyone . . . Or rather, have you heard anyone making threats or promising to get revenge for a kidnapping?"

Cassidi glared at Frank for a long moment, making him want to squirm in his chair. What right did he have to ask a question like that, after all? "Even if I did hear such a thing, why would I tell you? You would just try to blame that man for killing Esposito."

"But if he really did kill Esposito—"

"I do not care. Esposito was scum. He should not have been allowed to live. He stole children from their parents and violated women—" He caught himself, obviously realizing that he had said too much.

So he knew what they had done to his wife. No wonder he was angry. And now he had an even better reason to have killed Esposito himself. "You're right. I shouldn't have asked you to implicate your friends, Mr. Cassidi, but Gino is *my* friend and I don't want him to take the blame and possibly get himself killed for something he didn't do."

"Are you sure he did not do it?"

"Oh yes. Positive. The trouble is that I know a lot of people wanted Esposito dead. I just don't know who all of them are."

"You know one of them, Christopher McWilliam."

Frank blinked in surprise. "McWilliam? Why do you say that?"

Cassidi shifted uneasily. "You should ask him."

Frank didn't have to ask. Jane Harding's kidnapping would be reason enough, but how did Cassidi know it was Jane who had been taken? Or at least it appeared he did, since that's the only reason McWilliam would want Esposito dead. They had been careful not to tell either of the Cassidis who had been kidnapped in an effort to keep it secret, though. "I'd appreciate it if you'd let me know if you hear anything that could help Gino." Frank laid one of his cards on Cassidi's desk.

He made no move to pick it up. "Have you asked Balducci? He had the most to gain from Esposito's death."

Frank smiled grimly at that. "He's on my list."

"Don't go alone."

Frank had no intention of it.

SARAH TOOK THE EL UP TO EAST HARLEM AND WALKED over to the Cassidi home. Mrs. Cassidi answered her knock after peering out the front window to identify her caller. Sarah wondered if the woman would ever feel comfortable opening her front door again. It seemed unlikely.

"Thank you for coming, Mrs. Malloy," she said, ushering Sarah in quickly and closing and locking the front door carefully behind her.

"I was happy to do it. Are you all right?"

"Come inside." She led Sarah into the parlor, which was a room obviously kept just for company. "Let me get you some lemonade."

Mrs. Cassidi served the tall glasses on a silver tray, obviously anxious to impress her visitor. Sarah thanked her and waited patiently for her hostess to gather herself enough to tell her why she had been summoned.

"My husband knows what they did to me," she said at last.

"Telling him must have been very difficult."

Mrs. Cassidi shook her head. "He knew. He said it was his biggest fear the whole time I was gone. He did not think they would kill me because they wanted the money, but there was nothing to stop them from anything else. He said he knew as soon as he saw me what had happened."

So Mr. Cassidi had a good reason to go after Esposito. "I'm sorry. I hope . . . If there's anything I can do . . ."

"He is very angry."

Of course he was. "If you don't feel safe, I can arrange—"

"No, he is not angry at me."

Thank heaven for that.

"He is angry at Esposito and the men who did this. He . . . I am afraid."

"What are you afraid of?" Sarah asked as gently as she could.

Mrs. Cassidi looked away, her face twisted in pain. "He was so angry and then Esposito was dead."

Sarah's nerves prickled. "Do you think your husband had something to do with it?"

"No! He could not do that. He would never . . . My Arturo, he could not kill, no matter how angry he was, but he went out that night. He said he went to the settlement house, but . . ."

"Do you know why he went to the settlement house?"

"He wanted to warn Mr. McWilliam, to tell him they must get the young woman back at all costs and quickly, before . . ."

"Yes, of course. He was very kind to do that, and he couldn't have known she'd already returned to the settlement."

"But you see, that means he was out that night. I am afraid someone will accuse him. I know they arrested Gino Donatelli, but they say he did not kill Esposito either."

"No, he didn't. My husband and Gino are partners. They are private investigators, and my husband is investigating Esposito's murder. He's trying to find the real killer because he's afraid the Black Hand will kill Gino in revenge."

"*Sì*, that is something they would do. You must find the real killer, Mrs. Malloy, to protect Gino and my husband both."

But Sarah was shaking her head. "I'm afraid we don't even know where to start. So many people wanted Esposito dead. We even heard that his wife was seen on Pleasant Avenue the night he died."

"Olympia?"

"Is that her name?"

"Yes. She is . . . I have done what you said. I let my friends come to visit me. They were full of gossip about Esposito. They tell me he has a flat on Pleasant Avenue where he is keeping a woman, and Olympia is furious. He has had women before, you understand, but he never made a place for them like this. And he gave this woman something that belonged to Olympia, something valuable, at least to her. She . . ." Mrs. Cassidi shrugged helplessly.

"I see. Of course she would be furious. Any woman would be. I wonder if she actually went to the flat that night. She might have seen something that would help us find the killer."

Mrs. Cassidi allowed herself a rare smile. "Or she might have killed him herself."

Sarah smiled back. "I'd ask her that if I could speak to her, but I doubt she'd welcome a visit from me."

"No, she would not," Mrs. Cassidi said, "but maybe . . ."

"Maybe what?" Sarah prodded.

"She goes to Mass every morning and tomorrow is Sunday, so she will surely be there. If we met her there, you could ask her whatever you like."

VIII

THIS IS SALVATORE PIZZUTO," TEO TOLD THE NEXT PERSON they encountered in the tenement, who happened to live just down the hall from Esposito's flat. This was a sturdy young Italian woman with a baby on her hip and a worried frown on her face. "His daughter is missing, and he is trying to find out if she could be the woman that Esposito was holding in his flat here." This was the story she and Gino had concocted, figuring it would win sympathy and perhaps inspire the neighbors to tell what they knew to a stranger. They were speaking in Italian for ease of communication and because that's how most people in the neighborhood spoke to each other.

The woman shook her head at Gino, although she looked sad to do so. "That woman was not Italian. She was American. She had yellow hair."

Most of the neighbors had claimed not to have seen her, so Teo brightened at once. "Did you know her?"

"No. She was not from here."

Teo managed a worried frown and leaned close so they wouldn't be overheard. "Do you think she was here against her will?"

The young woman bounced the baby, who was making fussy noises. "How would I know that?"

"Did you hear anything?" Gino asked. "Was she crying for help?"

"No, nothing like that."

"Did they argue?" Teo tried.

"Oh no." The young woman smirked. "That man, he can be charming when he wants to be, and always to the women."

"And you didn't see anyone guarding the flat?" Gino asked.

"Esposito . . ." She took a moment to pretend to spit on the floor at the mention of his name. "He always has a man to guard him. When he is here, somebody was in the hall or outside on the stoop, but he leaves with Esposito. He is guarding him, not her."

"Are you sure about that?" Gino prodded.

She gave him a sad smile. "The woman leaves when she wants to."

"Did you see her go?" Teo asked.

"Everyone sees her go. She is wearing such a fine dress, everyone notices her. She pretends not to see us, but we see her."

"What day was this?" Gino asked.

"The day before they find Esposito dead, I think. Wednesday morning."

"And no one tried to stop her from leaving?" Gino asked.

"I am sorry, sir, but this woman is not your daughter and this woman was not a prisoner. I know they . . ." She glanced around, suddenly nervous, then lowered her voice. "I know they kidnap people, but they do not keep them here. If they took your daughter, she will be somewhere else."

Gino was about to thank her and take their leave, but Teo said, "When she left, what color was her dress?"

"Blue, like the sky on a fine day. If he buys her clothes like that, I wonder why she leaves."

SATURDAY WAS A BUSY DAY AT THE SETTLEMENT HOUSE. Children were out of school and many had come to use the playground. A lot of parents milled around, apparently gossiping and catching up with friends. The classrooms were all full, too, and few of the residents were unoccupied, so no one really noticed Frank's arrival. He found Christopher McWilliam in his office.

"Mr. Malloy, what brings you here?" he asked, jumping up to greet Frank, although his expression was more wary than welcoming. He still looked as if he wasn't sleeping well.

"I'm still trying to figure out who killed Esposito." McWilliam had no response to this. After an awkward pause, Frank said, "Have you heard anything from Miss Harding?"

McWilliam flinched slightly, so obviously this was still a painful subject. "Uh, no, and I didn't really expect to. I think Jane has left this part of her life behind." And left him behind as well, apparently. "How is Gino Donatelli doing?" he asked, returning the barb.

"I've sent him to a safe place until we can find Esposito's killer."

McWilliam frowned. "Do you think you'll be able to do that?"

"I'm pretty good at finding killers, Mr. McWilliam."

The news did not seem to please McWilliam. "I . . . Did you think I would be able to help you?"

"As a matter of fact, I did need to ask you something," Frank said. "Can we sit down for a minute?"

Plainly, McWilliam didn't want Frank there at all, but he somehow managed a falsely friendly smile and motioned to the sofa. "Of course. Please, make yourself comfortable." McWilliam moved his desk chair over as he had before and perched on the edge, as if unsure he really wanted to stay.

Frank settled in, silently telling his host that he meant business. "I went to see Mr. Cassidi today."

"Did you? Why on earth did you need to see him again?"

"Because I thought it would be a good idea to speak to the people I knew might want to see Esposito dead."

"Did you really think Cassidi might have killed him?" McWilliam asked in wonder.

"A lot of people in this community had good reason to hate Esposito, and Mr. Cassidi was only the most recent addition to that list."

"Which makes me wonder why you chose him."

"Because I knew about him. I didn't know who else might have had a family member kidnapped, because the Italians don't usually go to the police about these things."

McWilliam nodded. "We can't seem to convince them they should trust the police."

"And there's really no reason why they should. So I asked Cassidi if he could tell me who else had been victimized by the Black Hand."

McWilliam shifted uneasily in his chair, slipping even

closer to the edge as if preparing to flee. "And what did he tell you?"

"That he wouldn't give me any names because he was afraid I'd accuse them of the killing."

"As I said, we can't seem to get the Italians to trust the police."

"But he did tell me about someone else, someone who isn't Italian."

"And who is that?" he asked uneasily.

"You."

He didn't seem shocked. "I suppose he told you he came to see me the night before they found Esposito's body."

Frank's nerves tingled. This was news to him. Frank didn't have to wonder why Cassidi hadn't mentioned it either. It meant he was out the night Esposito was killed and could easily have gone to the flat, too. But why would Cassidi have gone to see McWilliam? "Yes," Frank lied, "he did tell me he saw you that night."

McWilliam reached up and rubbed his eyes. Then he slowly lowered his hands but didn't quite meet Frank's gaze. "Do you know what they did to . . . ?" He couldn't seem to force himself to finish the sentence.

So that was it. Of course. "Do I know what they did to Mrs. Cassidi?" Frank asked gently. "Yes, I do. She told my wife."

McWilliam looked up at the ceiling, anywhere but at Frank. "He didn't know exactly who was missing from the settlement. He didn't know the woman was my fiancée, but he wanted to tell me that we needed to find her at once, that we couldn't wait weeks or months because . . ." He stopped to swallow and all the color had drained from his face.

"I'm sorry, Mr. McWilliam, but we don't know what happened to Miss Harding, and she was only gone for a short time," Frank said, still being kind because McWilliam looked as if he might shatter if Frank pressured him at all. Still, he needed more information. "By any chance, did Miss Harding tell you where she was being held?"

McWilliam frowned. "No. I didn't even ask."

"But we know it was nearby. She was able to walk back here when she escaped, after all."

"I . . . I suppose so."

"Don't tell me you didn't suspect she was being held at the flat where Esposito was killed."

McWilliam shook his head. "I didn't . . . I couldn't . . ."

"Hadn't you heard the gossip?"

"I don't gossip, Mr. Malloy," McWilliam said stiffly.

"Then maybe Mr. Cassidi told you when he came to warn you."

But McWilliam was shaking his head again. "I hadn't heard about that place until I heard Esposito was dead."

"Then you didn't go there that night to confront Esposito?"

"And kill him?" McWilliam scoffed. "Hardly, and I'm highly insulted that you should accuse me of such a thing."

He looked more frightened than insulted, but Frank didn't point that out. Instead he said, "Sorry," without very much conviction.

This did make McWilliam angry. "I'm not a killer, Mr. Malloy."

"No one would blame you for killing a man like Esposito, especially if you thought he'd hurt the woman you love."

"I must ask you not to make these insinuations about Miss Harding again. Even if we aren't engaged, she deserves my protection, and I intend to offer it."

"Of course. I meant no disrespect," Frank said sincerely.

"So can I assume that you were here at the settlement house the entire night after Mr. Cassidi visited you?"

"I don't think I need to answer any more of your ridiculous questions, Mr. Malloy. You've insulted me and Miss Harding quite enough for one day. I must ask you to leave."

Frank didn't really need to ask any more questions, ridiculous or not. "Thank you for your time, Mr. McWilliam." He rose from the sofa and McWilliam jumped up from his chair in response. "I hope you'll let me know if you hear anything that would help me clear Gino Donatelli's name, however. Like Miss Harding, he is an innocent victim in all of this."

McWilliam's face contorted with whatever emotions were roiling within him, but he merely said, "Of course," and gestured toward the door.

As she made her way into the sanctuary of Our Lady of Mount Carmel in East Harlem the next morning, Sarah wondered if going to church specifically to question a possible murder suspect was some kind of sin. She'd never seen anything in the Bible about it or heard a sermon on the subject. Since she was quite possibly the first person to have done it, she supposed it was too rare an occurrence to even merit a mention.

The church itself was magnificent. The stained glass shone brightly in the morning sun, and the quiet hum of the organ and the sweet smell of incense spoke of genuine peace.

Mrs. Cassidi was already seated in the back pew when Sarah arrived. Sarah knew the Catholics had more than one Mass on Sunday morning, unlike the Protestants, who made do with one service. Mrs. Cassidi had been very certain that Mrs. Esposito would attend the earliest Mass, which meant a very early start for Sarah, but she arrived well in time. The worshippers were still filing in as Sarah slipped into the pew beside Mrs. Cassidi.

"Good morning," Sarah said, suddenly realizing that she had no idea how to participate in a Catholic worship service. Kneeling was involved, she knew, but how did one know when to do it? "I'm not Catholic. You'll have to tell me what to do."

Mrs. Cassidi nodded absently. She was scanning the people making their way down the aisle. "There she is." She nodded to the woman who had just passed them.

Mrs. Esposito was an imposing figure. Taller than most of the women in Italian Harlem, she held herself rigidly erect and moved with a stately grace. Was she always like this, or was she simply bracing herself for all the gossip she knew must be swirling around her after her husband's murder? How humiliating to have everyone saying he'd been killed while visiting his mistress. She was dressed in unrelieved black, but it was a stylish ensemble that looked brand new. She clutched what must be a prayer book in her gloved hands, and her unnecessarily tight grip on the book was the only thing that betrayed her tension. Her face was expressionless and strangely beautiful, although time had softened her features somewhat. The word *tragic* seemed to fit her, somehow.

Mrs. Esposito claimed a seat a few rows in front of them and knelt instead of sitting, bowing her head and crossing herself before she started fingering the beads of her rosary as she apparently began to pray. Sarah wondered for what she prayed, but perhaps she was just going through the motions to keep curiosity seekers at bay. She wouldn't want to acknowledge any false expressions of sympathy, after all.

Then the service started, and Sarah had to focus all her attention on standing and sitting and kneeling at all the proper times. Since everything was in Latin, she couldn't get any clues from the priest leading the service, so she had to mimic Mrs. Cassidi, who graciously prompted her with discreet hand motions. As soon as the service ended, Mrs. Cassidi and Sarah moved quickly to execute the maneuver they had decided would work best for them.

Mrs. Cassidi left their pew and moved up the side aisle while Sarah moved up the center aisle. Then they each slipped into Mrs. Esposito's pew from either end, effectively boxing her in. She had been gathering her things, preparing to leave, and she glanced up at Sarah with some annoyance before noticing that Mrs. Cassidi had moved in on her other side.

"Violetta, what are you doing?" she whispered furiously, turning to give Sarah a brief glare to include her.

"Olympia, I just wanted to tell you how sorry I am," Mrs. Cassidi said in a normal voice, in case someone was listening.

"*Grazie*," Mrs. Esposito said through gritted teeth, then she asked a question in Italian.

"English, please. My friend is American."

"Who is this woman and what does she want?" Mrs. Esposito repeated in a furious whisper.

"This is Mrs. Malloy. Her husband's partner, Gino Donatelli, has been accused of killing your husband, but we know he did not do it."

Mrs. Esposito stiffened at this, and the look she gave Sarah almost made her wince. "I know nothing of this."

"You were seen on Pleasant Avenue the night your husband was murdered, Mrs. Esposito," Sarah said. "I just want to know what you saw when you went to the apartment."

"I saw nothing. I did not go there." But she was clutching her prayer book in a death grip again.

Sarah chose to ignore her denial. "What did you plan to do that night? Were you going to confront your husband or the woman?"

"I was not going to do anything." She glanced up apprehensively as some of the exiting worshippers slowed down to eye the strange trio curiously. Mrs. Esposito quickly crossed herself and began praying again, or at least pretended to. Mrs. Cassidi was already kneeling, ostensibly praying but really just trying to more effectively block Mrs. Esposito's exit.

Sarah waited until their observers gave up and moved on. "I think you found out your husband had rented a flat and was keeping his new mistress there. I think you decided to confront him and demand that he give her up."

She laughed at this, a harsh, mirthless sound that was more like a grunt. "I do not care if he has a woman. She is *puttana*. I am his wife. Nothing can change that."

"Then why did you go there that night if you didn't care?"

She turned to Sarah, and her beautiful face was now twisted into a rictus of fury. "He took . . . something from me. Something of mine, and he gave it to her. I go to get it back."

"And did you? Get it back, I mean?"

Mrs. Esposito glared at Sarah as if she would have gladly ripped her heart out with her bare hands, but finally she simply said, "No."

"He wouldn't give it to you?"

"She took it and she was gone. She left him," she added with a bitter smile. "He was crying like a *bambino* when I find him."

"And you were so angry that you stabbed him to death," Sarah tried.

Mrs. Esposito's smile widened and grew even more bitter. "Why do I kill him? I have nothing now. I am the widow of a man they feared, and now they hate me. Let me out before I scream and tell the priest two witches are putting the evil eye on me."

Mrs. Cassidi gasped in outrage, but Sarah rose immediately and made way for Mrs. Esposito to leave. No sense causing a scene when she'd already gotten all the information she was going to get.

When Mrs. Esposito was gone, Mrs. Cassidi muttered something in Italian that sounded like something Mrs. Esposito wouldn't have wanted to hear about herself. "I am sorry, *signora*. I thought she would be ashamed when she saw me, because she knew her husband's people had kidnapped me. I thought she would answer your questions."

Sarah slid back into the pew. "She did answer them, although she probably didn't think so. We know she went to the flat and that she was angry enough to have killed her husband. Do you have any idea what her husband could have taken from her and given to the other woman?"

Mrs. Cassidi glanced around to make sure they were not being observed, and even then, she leaned in close. "We do not brag. The devil takes notice." She crossed herself. "But sometimes you cannot help yourself. Olympia would not want people to know she has something very valuable. Someone might steal it away, but she also would want people to envy her. Her husband is a brutal man, but he has power and money. He gave her something. She said it would protect her always."

"What does that mean?"

Mrs. Cassidi shrugged. "People do not ask, because she is so anxious for us to ask. She is very . . . I do not know the word." She made a prim face that almost made Sarah laugh out loud until she remembered they were still in church.

"Smug?" she guessed.

"*Sì*, smug. But when people do not ask, she gives hints. She makes us know her husband gave her a diamond."

"A diamond?" That didn't sound right. "A diamond ring perhaps?"

She shrugged again. "Something with a diamond. Or diamonds. So if she is ever in need, she can sell the diamond. If he gave this thing to this *puttana*, that would be very bad."

"And Mrs. Esposito would be very angry, especially when she found out the woman had left him and taken it with her."

"And now her husband is dead, so she needs it."

Sarah sensed someone had come close, and she looked up to find a priest frowning down at them and looking very menacing in his black robes.

He said something in Italian, probably chastening them for lingering in the sanctuary to talk. Sarah rose and smiled and nodded politely. Mrs. Cassidi murmured something back to him that sent him scurrying away.

"What did you say to him?" Sarah asked as they made their way out of the church.

"I told him we were giving Olympia Esposito the evil eye."

I'VE GOT TO FIND OUT MORE ABOUT THIS EVIL EYE," Maeve said when Sarah had told all of them about her visit to Our Lady of Mount Carmel after they'd eaten Sunday dinner and sent the children off to play.

"I'm sure my mother would be happy to explain it to you," Gino said, "but you'd need to learn Italian first."

"I'm sure Enzo would be willing to translate for me," she replied sweetly.

"You shouldn't joke about the evil eye," Mother Malloy said.

"Don't tell me the Irish believe in it, too," Maeve marveled.

"The Irish believe in every way disaster can befall you," Malloy said.

His mother gave him a look that an Italian might have thought was an evil eye. "Not that kind of superstition, but you still shouldn't make fun. The devil is always listening."

Sarah had an urge to cross herself. This was getting out of hand. "At any rate, I think we now know that Mrs. Esposito was at the flat the night her husband was murdered and that she had a very good reason for killing him."

"But she was right," Mother Malloy said. "If she kills her husband, what will become of her?"

"Maybe he left her a lot of money," Maeve said.

"Do you think men like Esposito put their money in banks and have their lawyers draw up a last will and testament to provide for their families?" Malloy scoffed.

"When you say it like that, it doesn't sound very likely," Sarah admitted. "But she probably wasn't thinking about that. Maybe she was just furious that he'd been taken in by some female who managed to get something really valuable from him—well, actually from her, if the diamond thing was supposed to be hers—and then disappeared. If she was angry enough—and that would have made her pretty angry—she might grab a knife and stab him on impulse."

"I can understand that," Maeve said. "She might be sorry later, and maybe she didn't even intend to kill him, but he's dead all the same."

"I saw things like that all the time when I was a cop," Gino said. "People get mad and lash out. They cool down later, but that doesn't change what happened."

"And she admitted she was there. That's more than Cassidi or McWilliam did," Malloy said.

"Or Balducci," Gino added with a smirk. "How are we going to find out where he was that night?"

"We could ask him," Malloy said.

"Do you have any idea how to do that?" Gino asked.

"Maybe you could corner him in church," Maeve suggested with a smirk.

"I can't believe none of you have thought of the most logical person," Mother Malloy said.

They all turned to her in surprise. "Who are you thinking of?" Sarah asked.

"The mistress. She got the diamond or whatever it is. Maybe she had to kill him to get it."

"But she'd left that morning," Malloy argued. "Everybody saw her go."

"Maybe she came back."

They took a minute to consider this. Sarah could see how it made sense. "She'd left that morning, but maybe she got to thinking that she should have taken the diamond as well and went back for it."

"I see," Maeve said, brightening. "Maybe she didn't expect Esposito to be there either."

"But he was," Gino continued, "and he wouldn't let her take it, so she had to kill him."

"Was this before or after Mrs. Esposito killed him?" Malloy asked, deadpan.

"Before," Maeve replied smugly. "But after Balducci killed him."

"We really need to talk to Balducci," Gino said. "I wish we hadn't been so rude to him."

"Maybe you could offer him a ride in your motor to make up for it," Sarah said slyly.

"Or maybe you could just offer him your motor," Maeve added.

"Why don't you just ask that Italian policeman to talk to him?" Mother Malloy said, not even looking up from her knitting, so she didn't see them all gaping at her.

FRANK AND GINO—WEARING HIS DISGUISE FOR SAFETY— left early on Monday morning, heading for Little Italy and Petrosino's not-so-secret office. He wasn't there, so they spent some time looking for him. Fortunately, the people in Little Italy were helpful and knowledgeable, and they finally tracked him down. He'd been walking the streets in search of a man suspected of breaking into a store a few days earlier. So far, he hadn't had much luck.

Frank introduced Gino by his new name, and Petrosino never blinked. "He's helping me with the Esposito case because I don't speak Italian," Frank added.

Petrosino nodded. "Do I know you, Mr. Pizzuto? You seem familiar."

"I have family in Little Italy. You may have seen me."

"Yes," Petrosino said thoughtfully. "I think their name might be Donatelli."

Gino grinned and shook his head. "I hoped to fool you."

"You are with Malloy. That helped," Petrosino demurred. "But I wouldn't hang around Little Italy too long. Other people might catch on, too."

"We just needed to speak to you about Esposito's murder," Frank said.

"I haven't heard anything new."

"I didn't expect you would, but we need your help. It seems Balducci has taken over Esposito's Black Hand group, and it's possible he's the one who killed Esposito."

"It wouldn't be the first time that happened."

"I want to question Balducci, but there's some bad blood there, so I can't just go see him."

Petrosino grinned at that. "I heard how you left him standing and drove away."

Frank winced. If the news had spread all the way down here, he'd never get near Balducci. "Yeah, well, I know now that was a mistake."

"Men have been killed for far less," Petrosino said, his grin disappearing. "I'm guessing you know that, which is why you're here."

"I don't think I'll be able to solve Esposito's murder if I'm dead," Frank said without irony. "So I was hoping you might intercede for me."

"What is it you want me to do?"

"I need to know if there's any chance Balducci or one of his men killed Esposito."

"There's always a chance," Petrosino pointed out. "But usually, when something like that happens, there are rumors, both before and after."

"What kind of rumors?"

"Of trouble. Somebody is mad or Esposito isn't treating

his men fairly or they're being told to do things they don't like."

"And you didn't hear anything like that about Esposito?"

"No. In fact, his men were very satisfied and loyal. Esposito knew how to handle them, and he never got too greedy. He also never took so much from the businessmen that they went out of business, so the community tolerated him. I know they were kidnapping women and children, but the victims were always returned, so he wasn't asking his men to kill innocent people. That would have caused hard feelings."

"I'm sure, and as much as I want Balducci or one of his men to be guilty, I'm more afraid that they'll decide Gino is and try to take revenge."

"Ah yes, vendetta. They are already angry with you, so this would be easy for them, too."

Gino sighed dramatically. "I'm right here, remember."

Petrosino spared him a sympathetic glance. "I can remind them that Donatelli had no reason to kill Esposito."

"He also didn't show up at the flat until Esposito had been dead for hours. We heard that Esposito always had a bodyguard with him. Where was he when Esposito was killed?"

"I will ask. In the meantime, you should get out of Little Italy, Gino."

SARAH HEARD MAEVE COME IN, RETURNING FROM EScorting Catherine to school. Mother Malloy and Brian had left long ago and wouldn't be back until the end of their school day. Maeve found her in the parlor.

"I need to do something," Maeve said, sitting down beside her on the sofa.

Sarah laid aside the book she had been reading. "What did you have in mind?"

"I don't know, but I'm not helping anyone just sitting around here or practicing my typing at the office."

Sarah only stared at her for a long moment, not believing for a minute that Maeve didn't have a plan.

"All right," Maeve relented. "I was thinking I could volunteer at the settlement house."

This was a surprise, and Sarah didn't bother to hide her reaction. "Are you serious?"

"I can't help thinking that we need to talk to the people there and find out what they know. So far our best information has come from gossip, and Teo can't be everywhere."

"The people in that neighborhood aren't going to confide in you."

"I know, but they might confide in the residents. That's what they're called, isn't it? The ones who volunteer to live there?"

"Yes, residents. I suppose they could have heard something, but I'm sure they have some sort of process by which they select volunteers, and I think someone said they have all graduated from college."

"I can lie and say I went to college."

Sarah wasn't sure she should encourage such a deception. "You don't look old enough."

"I'll fool them. Please, Mrs. Malloy. If I do this, you'll need to take Catherine to school and fetch her home, but it will probably only be for a few days, and even if it goes on longer, school will be out soon." The school year ended in time for the July fourth holiday.

Sarah could see Maeve's frustration, and she could also see that Maeve might be right about this being a good way to get information they couldn't get any other way. "I don't mind fetching Catherine, but you have no guarantee that Mr. Mc-William will accept you as a volunteer. Why should he?"

"Because he wants to find out who killed Esposito."

"Are you sure?"

That stopped her. She frowned. "Why wouldn't he?"

"Why *would* he? If Esposito kidnapped Jane Harding, he's probably glad the man is dead."

"Oh, I see. And if Jane killed him, he wouldn't want me to find that out."

"I don't suppose he would, but Malloy thinks McWilliam knows more about it than he's telling and there's always a chance that he himself is the killer, so that's another reason he might not want you around."

"Can't I just go to the settlement house and ask them if I can volunteer and see what happens? Teo will vouch for me."

"I don't see any harm in asking," Sarah said. "The worst that can happen is that they say no. I'll be here today if you aren't back in time to get Catherine from school."

Maeve rewarded her with a big smile, but before she could say anything else, the telephone's shrill bell cut through the peaceful morning.

Sarah jumped up to answer it.

"Mrs. Malloy, is that you?" a voice asked.

"Yes, this is Mrs. Malloy."

"This is Lisa Prince. I got your note this morning."

Sarah's nerves tingled with anticipation. "I'm glad you telephoned. Was there something I can do for you?"

"Yes, there is. I was wondering if you could call on me."

Did she sound desperate? Perhaps that was too strong a word. She certainly sounded a bit harried. Sarah glanced at Maeve, who had followed her out into the front hall. "I'll need to get my daughter from Miss Spence's School this afternoon, and that's not too far from you. Could I call on you after lunch today?"

Her sigh was audible. "That would be wonderful, Mrs. Malloy."

"Who was that?" Maeve asked when Sarah had hung up the earpiece.

"Lisa Prince, Jane Harding's cousin. She would like me to visit her this afternoon."

"How long has Jane been there now?"

"She got there on Thursday, and today is Monday, so . . ."

"So long enough to drive Mrs. Prince to ask for help," Maeve said with a grin.

IX

In the end, Frank convinced Petrosino to take
him along when he went to see Balducci, even though Petrosino was sure Frank would just be inviting Balducci to hate
him even more.

They found him in Esposito's saloon. If the dead man
really had owned the saloon, Frank couldn't help wondering
who owned it now. Mrs. Esposito, maybe. Somehow, Frank
couldn't imagine an Italian matron sitting in Esposito's office and ordering kegs of beer and kidnappings, the way her
husband certainly had. Balducci seemed more than comfortable doing so, however. He didn't even bother to stand up
when Frank and Petrosino were escorted in.

"They didn't tell me Malloy was with you," he said, giving Frank a look that could curdle milk. Frank couldn't help
thinking of the evil eye.

Petrosino said something to him in Italian that seemed

to placate him, however, and Balducci turned his attention to Petrosino.

"What do you want?"

"First of all, I want to apologize," Frank said, even though Balducci hadn't addressed him, figuring this wasn't going to cost him anything and might even win him a little grace. "Donatelli and I didn't have to be so rude to you the other day."

Balducci snorted. "You need to learn some respect."

Frank saw no reason to reply to that, so he just waited, letting Petrosino take the lead.

"I want to talk to you about Esposito's murder," Petrosino said in English, making it clear that's the language they should use.

"What about it?"

"Do you have any idea who killed him?"

Balducci gave them an evil grin. "I thought it was Donatelli. Wasn't that why the police arrested him?"

"You know he didn't do it," Frank said. "By the time he got there, Esposito was cold."

Balducci shrugged. "How would I know that?"

Ah, finally, a way to get to him. Flattery was always effective on men with little self-confidence, and Balducci must still be feeling a bit insecure in his bid to take over the Black Hand. "Because you're the boss now, and you know everything that goes on. What I can't figure out is how somebody was able to get to Esposito in the first place. Didn't he always have a bodyguard with him?"

Balducci barked something in Italian to Petrosino, who replied, "He's helping me. Answer his question."

Balducci growled but then bared his teeth in the parody of a smile. "Nunzio was a fool over that new woman of his.

He told Dante to go home that night. He didn't want Dante looking at the woman."

"He wasn't worried that somebody might try to kill him?" Frank asked, not bothering to keep the sarcasm out of his voice.

Balducci shrugged. "No one ever tried it before."

"Who knew this Dante wasn't guarding him that night?"

"Dante and Nunzio. Maybe the woman."

"But she wasn't there, was she?"

"How do I know? Nunzio expected her to be or he would not have been there himself."

That made sense. Esposito had spent the previous two nights with his mistress at the flat. He might have been surprised that she wasn't there, but he'd probably have expected her to return soon. Maybe she did or maybe she was already there. And maybe the woman didn't like knowing that a strange man was outside, hearing heaven knew what. "I see, but that doesn't explain how you knew Esposito was dead the next morning."

Color flooded Balducci's homely face. "What do you mean?"

"I mean Gino Donatelli came here that morning, looking for Esposito. Somebody—not you, but probably one of your men—told him Esposito would be at the flat on Pleasant Avenue. As soon as Gino walked into the flat and found Esposito's body, a cop shows up and arrests him. The cop didn't go there by accident. Somebody sent him so he'd find Gino with the body."

Balducci just glared, but Petrosino gave Frank an appreciative glance. "So how *did* you know Esposito was dead?" he asked Balducci.

Balducci gave a beleaguered sigh. "Dante. He went back

to the flat the next morning. Nunzio would come here to the saloon when he got up, and Dante knew he'd want to be guarded on the way. He was worried when he saw the door was open."

"Unlocked, you mean?" Frank asked.

"No. Open partway. When nobody answered, he went in and found Nunzio. He came running back here. I live upstairs."

"And you decided to pin the murder on the next person who came to the door?" Frank surmised, sarcastic again.

This time Balducci's smile held real mirth. "Not exactly, but it did work out pretty well. Donatelli came knocking a little while later, and I sent Dante to find Ogden."

"Why go to all that trouble?" Petrosino asked. "The police weren't going to be looking too hard for Esposito's killer."

"Maybe, but I could not count on that, and if they did decide to look, I'm the first one they would look at. Me and the rest of our crew. Better if some other dago got the blame."

"Or maybe you killed Esposito yourself and that's why you tried to blame it on Gino," Frank tried.

But Balducci just chuckled. "You know nothing. You think because I sit behind this desk that I am the new boss."

"Aren't you?"

Balducci leaned back in his chair and gave Petrosino an expectant look.

Petrosino sighed this time. "I think what Mr. Balducci is saying is that with Esposito dead, nothing is certain. One of the other men in their crew can challenge him for leadership. His men might leave him and join another Black Hand group if they don't want to work for him. Or another Black Hand group could take over this neighborhood and push Balducci out."

"They were afraid of Nunzio, but they are not so much afraid of me," Balducci said.

"Even if you killed Esposito?" Frank challenged.

"If I did, then I cannot be trusted," Balducci said. "You see, you know nothing."

Frank was beginning to think that was true. "Then you're not planning to take revenge on Donatelli?"

"*Vendetta?*" Balducci scoffed. "When I know he did not kill Nunzio?"

Frank shrugged. "If you killed Gino, that would make people think you were innocent and believe he was guilty."

"That is too twisted, Malloy. We are simple men."

Frank doubted that, but Balducci's arguments made a certain kind of sense. And it would be great if Gino's life wasn't in danger. He wasn't about to test that out just yet, because he certainly had no reason to trust Balducci, but at least he had a spark of hope now. "So we're back to the original question. Do you have any idea who *did* kill Esposito?"

"If I did, I would go right to the police," he said without a shred of sincerity.

"Don't you want justice for your friend?"

"There is no justice, Malloy. Even you should know that."

Frank did know it. He had long been trying to change that.

MAEVE HAD DRESSED CAREFULLY FOR HER TRIP UP-town, trying to look like a young lady who had been to college. Luckily, that didn't require much effort. Young ladies who went to college were usually not very concerned with fashion, so Maeve actually had to tone down her outfit quite a bit.

The El wasn't particularly crowded during the middle of the day and it was always much more pleasant to ride than the trolleys with their mashers always putting their hands where they shouldn't and people stepping on your feet. It was much faster, too.

She paid particular attention to the neighborhood as she walked the few blocks from the El station to the settlement house. The cacophony of languages being spoken by pedestrians and shouted by street vendors gave testimony to how many ethnic groups lived in East Harlem. A lot more than just the Italians that had given it the nickname of Italian Harlem, to be sure. How ambitious to think one set of idealistic volunteers could serve such a disparate group of people in any meaningful way. Still, the number of people frequenting the settlement house showed that they must be doing something to benefit someone. Maeve supposed she could understand why an idealistic young person would want to be part of that.

She found the settlement house easily enough. The sign was helpful, but the number of people going in and out of the row houses was a good indicator that she had reached her destination. She and Mrs. Malloy had decided she should ask for Teo first, tell her their plan, and then ask her for help.

Teo was in a cooking class, helping the students—all middle-aged women of various ethnicities—master the proper way to make fried chicken. In preparation for the Fourth of July holiday, the staff had apparently thought the women should learn how to make a proper American picnic. The smell sent Maeve's stomach growling, and she happily accepted Teo's invitation to join them in sampling the final results.

Only when the students were gone did Teo finally turn

to Maeve and say, "Why are you here? Is everything all right?"

"Yes, everything is fine. Gino is fine. I'm just tired of sitting in the office doing nothing. I thought I could volunteer here for a while and maybe pick up some useful gossip."

Teo frowned and took Maeve to the corner of the room farthest from the door, where they would be least likely to be overheard. "Mr. McWilliam must approve all the volunteers. He would want you to apply and give him references and it would take weeks. I think it is better if you just pretend you live in the neighborhood and go to some classes."

"Would anybody believe I live in this neighborhood?" Maeve asked with a grin.

Teo frowned. "Maybe not."

They stood there thinking for a long moment. "I know," Maeve said at last. "How about if I say I'm *interested* in volunteering, but I'm not sure. I'd like to find out more about the work you do and observe some classes and—"

"Oh, that is a good idea!" Teo cried. "We would not even have to tell Mr. McWilliam, because he would certainly ask you a lot of questions that you maybe could not answer, and he might decide you would not suit and send you away. I can get one of the residents to show you around. I could even let her think Mr. McWilliam has assigned her this duty."

"Teo, you are a very clever woman," Maeve said with approval.

Teo grinned. "I am a woman. We are all very clever or we do not survive."

Which was so true. "Who is the resident you want to introduce me to?"

"Kate Westrop. She showed Mr. and Mrs. Malloy around

when they were here. She is the one Mr. McWilliam always chooses for that because she is so friendly, but . . ." She glanced around, making sure they were still alone. ". . . she is *too* friendly, I think. She sometimes says things she should not."

"And if I was very interested, she might say even more?" Maeve asked.

"I think so. Come, we will find her."

Kate Westrop was outside, watching the children on the playground. Teo introduced Maeve and told Kate the story they had settled on.

"Mr. McWilliam, well, you know how careful he is," Teo concluded. "Miss Smith needs to know what we do here and if she thinks she will fit in before she applies to become a resident, and we thought you were the best one to show her."

Maeve could not have done it better herself. Now Kate Westrop thought McWilliam had assigned her this task.

"How did you hear about the settlement, Miss Smith?" Miss Westrop asked.

"I had a friend in school, and she was coming to volunteer at the settlement after graduation. I thought it would be fun to volunteer at the same place, but Mrs. Donatelli tells me she's not here at the moment."

"Who is your friend?" Kate asked with a worried frown. She was one step ahead of Maeve already.

"Jane Harding. She made the settlement house sound so wonderful that I just had to come and see for myself."

Kate exchanged a glance with Teo, who just stared innocently back. Did Kate have any suspicions about why Jane had left? Maeve would know what they were before the day was out.

* * *

THIS TIME THE MAID ADMITTED SARAH TO THE PRINCE house immediately and took her right up to the parlor, where Mrs. Prince was waiting.

"Mrs. Malloy, how kind of you to come," she said, jumping up and coming to meet Sarah.

"I'm glad I was able to," Sarah said, accepting Mrs. Prince's invitation to sit on the sofa with her. They exchanged a few pleasantries about the weather and Sarah answered some questions about Catherine and her school, and then the maid brought in some delicious iced fruit drinks and little tea cakes.

Up until that moment, Mrs. Prince had been cordial and very proper, but Sarah had still felt the tension in her. She was like a violin string pulled too tightly and almost ready to break. As soon as the maid left, she gave a shuddering sigh.

"Are you all right?" Sarah asked, setting down her glass.

Mrs. Prince hadn't even picked hers up yet. "I don't know what to do with Jane. She's behaving so strangely."

"What do you mean?"

"I mean she's been polite and considerate, just as a houseguest should be, but there's something wrong with her. She sits for hours in her room, just staring out her window. I tried taking her shopping, but she was too distracted, hardly even noticing anything in the shops. I . . . I know this sounds foolish and even selfish, but at least if she was disagreeable, I would have a reason to send her home to her parents. Having her here is very uncomfortable for Joe and me, but I can't think of a single reason to ask her to leave. I also have the feeling that if I did, she would be devastated. I'm at my wits' end."

Oh dear, it was as bad as Sarah had feared, and plainly Jane had not told her cousin about her ordeal. "I believe I told you that Jane's experience at the settlement house was somewhat unpleasant."

"Yes, you did, and I asked her about it, but she refused to discuss it. Mrs. Malloy, if something happened that affected her so badly, I feel I need to know what it was. Someone does, at least, so we can help her."

Sarah picked up her glass and took a sip to moisten her suddenly dry mouth. She couldn't possibly betray Jane, but Mrs. Prince was right, she really did need to know what had happened. Their past relationship may have given Mrs. Prince no reason to feel kindly toward Jane, but now Jane needed kindness. How could Lisa Prince help Jane or even feel the proper amount of sympathy, if she had no idea of the situation?

"Mrs. Prince, I can't betray Jane's confidence, but perhaps if I could see her, I could convince her to tell you about her experiences. I think you'd feel much differently if you understood what she's been through."

"Good heavens, you make it sound like . . . Well, I suppose it must have been awful, whatever it was. She's in her room, as she usually is. Shall I ask her to come down? Do you think I should tell her that you're here?"

"Perhaps not by name. Just say a friend has come to see her."

"I'll send the maid, so she won't be able to ask her any questions about who the friend is."

"Good idea."

Mrs. Prince rang for the maid and gave her instructions.

Then they waited in awkward silence for the message to be delivered. After what seemed an eternity, the parlor door opened and Jane Harding came in. She wore a plain brown skirt and a shirtwaist. Her hair was in a haphazard bun, and her expression was blank, at least until she saw Sarah.

"Oh, it's you," she said, more puzzled than anything.

"Mrs. Malloy was in the neighborhood and decided to check on you, Jane," Mrs. Prince said with forced cheerfulness. "Wasn't that kind of her?"

Jane plainly didn't think so, but years of deportment lessons overruled whatever her true emotions were. "Yes. How nice to see you, Mrs. Malloy."

"Come and join us, Jane," Mrs. Prince urged a bit too enthusiastically. She asked the maid to bring another glass.

Jane took a chair opposite them, her reluctance obvious. Sarah thought she looked a bit pale, but that was probably to be expected.

"Your cousin is very concerned about you, Miss Harding," Sarah began, not sure exactly how far she should go.

Jane's gaze flitted to Lisa and back to Sarah. "She needn't be."

"When I delivered your note to her, I told her that your experience at the settlement house had been unpleasant. I didn't feel I could tell her more than that, but she's having a difficult time understanding why you seem so withdrawn."

Finally, Jane showed a reaction. The color bloomed in her cheeks and her eyes flashed with sudden anger. "And you think I should tell her something?"

"That's your decision of course, but I've found that sharing our troubles with people who care about us can often help us deal with them."

"What do you think I have to deal with, Mrs. Malloy?" Jane asked sharply.

Sarah glanced meaningfully at Lisa Prince. "I don't want to betray your confidence . . ."

"Don't worry about that. Tell Lisa about my unpleasant experience. Go ahead."

Sarah could believe that Jane was angry but not that she wanted Sarah to be the one telling her story. "Are you sure?"

"Yes. Tell her." Jane folded her hands and lifted her chin in silent defiance of Sarah's hesitation.

Sarah drew a fortifying breath and turned to Lisa, who waited apprehensively. "Mrs. Prince, in the neighborhood where the settlement house is located, there is a group of criminals that calls itself the Black Hand. They are engaged in several different illegal activities, and one of them is kidnapping children and sometimes women and holding them for ransom."

Sarah waited and watched as Lisa Prince absorbed this information and slowly, reluctantly, made the connection. "Jane, did you . . . ? Oh dear heaven, no wonder you're . . . How awful! I'm so sorry, my dear. Whatever can I do for you?"

"Nothing," Jane said, still angry. "I'm fine now. I escaped." She turned back to Sarah. "I heard one of them got killed."

Sarah blinked in surprise. How had she heard that? Sarah thought she'd left the settlement house before news of the murder had spread. "Yes, Nunzio Esposito."

"Do they know what happened? Do they know who did it?"

Why was she asking about this? She would have no reason to unless . . . Yes, it must be true. She must be the woman who had been held in that flat as Esposito's prisoner, just as they had feared. The poor girl, no wonder she was now so withdrawn and moody. It was a wonder she could function at all. "No, they don't know who killed him yet."

This only made her angrier. "But they must have some idea. Someone must have seen something. In that neighborhood, they know everything that happens."

They'd certainly known about the blond woman Esposito was keeping there. Should she mention that? Why not? "They say that Esposito was holding a woman in the apartment where he was killed, but she had left in the morning, and he was killed late that night."

Jane drew a deep breath, still holding her chin very high and glaring furiously at Sarah. "Then she couldn't have killed him."

"No," Sarah said quickly. Had Jane been concerned that she would be accused? How awful for her. "We think . . . That is, my husband is looking into it. He thinks perhaps one of Esposito's men killed him so he could take Esposito's place."

"That seems logical," Mrs. Prince said, obviously eager to solve the mystery and change the subject to one less horrifying.

"Is that what *you* think?" Jane asked Sarah.

Sarah frowned. Why did Jane care what she thought? But of course if Esposito had kidnapped and assaulted Jane, she'd be anxious for vengeance, perhaps even be a bit bloodthirsty, wanting to know every detail and eager to know whom she had to thank for taking her revenge. "As I said, we don't really know, but we have to consider the families of the kidnap victims. One of them might have taken advantage of knowing Esposito was alone in that building."

"Family members, yes," Jane said, nodding as if she'd

just reached a conclusion. "A family member could have done it. Someone who hated him."

Sarah thought of the final possibility they had considered. Should she mention it to Jane? But if Jane really was the woman in the flat, did that mean she'd gotten Mrs. Esposito's diamond? Sarah couldn't imagine a captive receiving a valuable gift. Had Mrs. Esposito been wrong about that? Was there another woman they didn't know about? "And someone saw Esposito's wife at the flat the night he was killed," she offered, allowing no trace of emotion into her voice.

"His *wife*? Why would she have been there?"

What an odd question. Sarah hesitated a moment and then stretched the truth a bit. "Rumor said that Esposito had a new mistress. Maybe she went to see for herself."

Jane was clearly shocked. "What kind of a woman does a thing like that?"

"I can't imagine," Lisa Prince said, obviously just as shocked. "Does the woman have no pride?"

"She did say she didn't actually care that he had a mistress," Sarah said, watching Jane's reaction closely.

"Didn't care?" Lisa exclaimed, outraged. "How could she not care?"

No one answered her.

"Why would she go there, then?" Jane demanded, apparently not convinced she had.

"She said Esposito had taken something of hers, something very valuable, and given it to this woman. She went to get it back."

"That's ridiculous," Lisa insisted. "What could be that valuable?"

"A diamond ring, I think," Sarah said, still watching Jane. Jane's face contorted. "A ring?" she echoed, then shook her head as if to clear it. "Is that what she said? That it was a ring?"

"Well, no. She didn't actually say, but she had bragged about a diamond her husband had given her, so I guessed it was a ring."

"She killed him, then," Jane said with certainty. "She was jealous and she couldn't bear to think he had another woman."

Which was exactly why they'd considered Mrs. Esposito a suspect in the first place. No one had anything to add to Jane's theory.

"How do you know all this?" Mrs. Prince asked after a long silence.

"I spoke with Mrs. Esposito."

"You're a busy bee, aren't you?" Jane said acidly.

"Jane, don't be rude," Lisa chided. "Mrs. Malloy is trying to help."

"I don't feel that she has helped. She has just upset me."

"I'm sorry for that," Sarah said, still trying to make sense of Jane's reactions. "I hope Mrs. Prince will be able to sympathize with you now that she understands what happened, though."

"Oh yes," Lisa said. "I'm afraid I haven't been very sympathetic, Jane. I had no idea. I thought you'd just been offended by the poor manners of the people at the settlement or something. I can't believe what you've been through."

"No one can," Jane said bitterly.

Sarah hated to upset Jane any more, but she couldn't leave without at least trying to verify whether she had been the woman in the flat with Esposito. If she wasn't, then they needed to find that woman. "I've been wondering, Jane, if you remembered anything else about the place where you were held when you were kidnapped," Sarah said. "It could help us locate the kidnappers and stop them."

She rolled her eyes. "I told you. It was in a tenement, but I have no idea where it was."

"And have you remembered anything that might help us identify your kidnappers?"

"No. I'm going back to my room now. I'm very tired." She got up and left without another word.

"I'm so sorry, Mrs. Malloy," Mrs. Prince said. "I wouldn't ordinarily try to excuse such rudeness, but I think under the circumstances . . ."

"Yes of course. I'm not offended. I don't think we can ever understand what she's been through." And perhaps they would never really know.

"At least I know what happened now. I suppose I can understand why she didn't want to go home to her parents. They would have been even more upset than Jane, and I can imagine them berating her for going to the city in the first place. No one wants to hear that when they're already upset and hurt."

"No, they don't. She'll have to go home eventually, though, and I'm sure she knows it. Perhaps in a few days, you can suggest that, and between the two of you, figure out something to tell her parents that would explain Jane's eagerness to leave the settlement without actually revealing the truth."

"Oh, I see. Yes, that's probably a good idea. They can't lecture her if they don't know how much danger she was really in."

"No, and I think she can just say that she wasn't suited to life in the settlement. Not many people are, I'm sure."

"I know I wouldn't be. Thank you for coming, Mrs.

Malloy. I'm not happy to have learned what happened to Jane, but I think it's for the best that I did. At least now I won't be irritated with her for being so reclusive."

"I'm sure she will appreciate your support, and feel free to call on me again if you think I can be of help."

After leaving Lisa Prince, Sarah started walking in the direction of Catherine's school. She mentally replayed her conversation with Jane Harding, trying once again to figure out what emotions lay behind her words and reactions. Naturally, she'd be angry about being kidnapped and traumatized from being assaulted, if that had indeed happened, but Jane's pain had seemed different than Sarah had expected. But people did react differently to these things, and she probably shouldn't judge.

KATE WESTROP PROVED JUST AS FRIENDLY AS TEO HAD promised. As soon as they were alone, Kate said, "So you and Jane were friends at school."

Maeve heard the unmistakable hint of disapproval in Kate's voice. She was not an admirer of Jane Harding. "Well, I may have exaggerated that a bit. I knew her, but we weren't really friends. I heard she was going to marry the head resident here, so I thought if I reminded her that we'd been at school together . . ." Maeve shrugged helplessly.

"It's just as well she's not here, then, because I doubt if she'd help you out. Jane is very much concerned about herself and no one else. I'm not at all surprised that she left the settlement."

"Do you think she's gone for good?"

Kate made a face. "I hope so. She made poor Mr. McWilliam so miserable."

"But I thought they were in love."

"*He* was in love, although I'll never know what he saw in her."

"She's very pretty," Maeve said as innocently as she could. "For some men, that's enough."

Kate gave a little snort. "Beauty is as beauty does, as my grandmother used to say. Come on, I'll show you around."

Kate led Maeve back inside, and they toured some of the classrooms, observing a few minutes of each of the lessons being taught. Maeve was impressed in spite of herself. The earnest expressions of the students, who were all adults, as they struggled with a new language or new ideas told her how important it was to them to become Americans.

Kate eventually took her to the large kitchen, where residents conducted cooking classes but also where they prepared their own meals. A few residents were gathered there, chatting, and Kate introduced her as a visitor. Finally, Kate took her into the last town house in the row, which housed the female residents.

"The male residents live at the other end, for the sake of propriety. I'll show you my room so you can see how we live. This is the parlor that we all share. We don't have very much free time, but when we do, we like to gather here."

Kate led her upstairs and showed her the spartan room where she slept. No wonder Jane Harding had been unhappy here, if she liked nice things.

"Did Jane stay here, too?" Maeve asked in a tone that said she didn't believe it for a minute.

"Yes, that's her room. Or it was." She indicated the room across the hall from hers. The door was open and Maeve wandered over to look. The room had an abandoned air to it and the bed had been stripped.

"It doesn't look as if she's coming back," Maeve said.

"I hope not. She was . . . Well, she just wasn't like the rest of us."

"What do you mean?"

"I mean she didn't like the people who come here and didn't want to talk to them. She also didn't like working. She just wasn't a nice person. But maybe you already know that."

Maeve wrinkled her nose in distaste. "I do."

"She liked to pretend she was better than the rest of us, too. She was always bringing things back with her when she went out, like a bunch of flowers or some trinket she'd picked up from a peddler."

"Why would she do that?"

"We don't get a salary, so I think she was trying to make everyone think she had more money than the rest of us. Like I said, she just didn't fit in."

"Still, she's only been here a few weeks. I can't believe she'd just walk out like that."

"She didn't just walk out. In fact, it was the strangest thing." Kate looked around as if to make sure they were alone, although they were the only two people in this building at the moment. "At first she just disappeared for a couple days."

"What do you mean, disappeared?"

"I mean she left to visit some new people or something and never came back. All her things were still here, but she wasn't. Mr. McWilliam told us she'd gone home. Some family emergency, he said. But he wasn't fooling anyone. She would have at least packed a bag if she'd really done that. And then she just turns up again one morning. She waltzes in and locks herself in her room and won't let anyone in."

"Where had she been?"

"No one knew, or if they did, they weren't saying. Mr. McWilliam said she wasn't feeling well and would be staying in her room for a few days. I had to get her meals and bring them to her. She didn't even thank me, not once." Plainly, Kate was still bitter about this.

"And then she really left?"

"Yes. The next day. It was quite a to-do. This woman shows up in a big fancy carriage. She was Jane's cousin, she said. Jane wasn't happy to see her, I can tell you. She was all upset because she hadn't had a chance to pack her things, although why she'd be upset about that, I have no idea. But she couldn't find her bag and she took mine and I'll probably never see it again. I was glad to see the back of her, I can tell you, even if she never does return my bag."

"Did you say she locked herself in her room after she got back?"

"Yes. She only opened the door when I brought her meals. Sometimes she didn't even open it at all and I had to leave the tray on the floor outside her door."

"And she never left the building again, at least not until her cousin came for her?"

"Not that I . . . Say, why are you so interested in Jane? I thought you didn't like her?"

"I don't, and it's such a fascinating story. Where do you think she was when she went missing? The other residents must have had some theories."

"I shouldn't gossip about another resident," Kate said without the slightest conviction.

"But Jane isn't a resident anymore."

"You're right, she isn't. And she never really was, if you want to know the truth. She never cared about this place or the work we do, like I said. The only thing she was interested in was who in the neighborhood had money."

"*What?*"

"I know. It seems strange, doesn't it? But I took her around the neighborhood when she first arrived, to show her where everything was, and she was very interested in who lived in the nicest houses."

"Who does live in them?"

"The businessmen who've been here awhile and done well for themselves. If they're immigrants, they build their houses here because nobody wants them on Fifth Avenue."

"I'm sure they don't. Was she interested in anybody in particular?"

Kate giggled and covered her mouth, as if she'd just remembered a delicious secret. "She was very interested in one of the men. He's got the biggest house in the neighborhood."

"Who was it?"

"It doesn't matter now. He was murdered a few days ago."

X

THEY HAD TO WAIT UNTIL THE CHILDREN WERE IN BED that evening before they could discuss what they had learned that day. Frank was still marveling over Sarah's success at questioning Jane Harding when he'd been certain they'd never have another chance to do so.

"So I didn't really learn very much from her," Sarah demurred when she'd finished her tale. They were all gathered in the parlor with Frank's mother knitting in her corner. She really enjoyed the electric lights that made it possible for her to see well even after the sun set. Frank had to admit he enjoyed them, too.

"You found out Jane still won't tell you anything helpful about where she was when she was supposedly kidnapped," Maeve said. "That's very strange if she really was kidnapped."

"And not strange at all if she wasn't being held against her will," Gino added.

"And it's quite possible that she wasn't," Maeve said.

"I don't know about that, but why do you think so?" Sarah asked.

"Because Kate Westrop told me that when she was first showing Jane around the neighborhood, the thing she was most interested in was who lived in the big fancy houses, and the person who lived in the biggest of them all was Nunzio Esposito."

"Maybe she's just nosey," Frank's mother said, reminding them all that she was there.

"Lisa Prince did say that Jane was very jealous of all the rich people who spent the summers in Saratoga Springs," Sarah recalled. "She also seemed to think that Jane really had no intention of marrying Mr. McWilliam. She thought the only reason Jane had come to the settlement house was to get herself to New York."

"Why would she want to do that?" Frank's mother asked.

"Perhaps to meet a rich man like her cousin did," Maeve said.

"But Lisa met Joe Prince in Saratoga Springs," Gino said.

"Then why didn't she stay there?" Maeve countered.

"Because she has no chance whatsoever of meeting a rich man there," Sarah said.

"Now I'm very confused," Maeve said. "Lots of rich men go there, and if her cousin met one, then why . . . ?"

"It's very simple to understand, if you're a member of society. You see, one way the people in society keep out climbers—"

"What's a climber?" Gino asked.

"I know that," Frank said with a grin, "because I am one. A social climber is somebody who is the first person in his family to ever get rich—people already in society have had money for generations—and he doesn't know any other rich people yet, so he tries to get invited to their parties and be accepted into society."

"But the people already in society absolutely refuse to know climbers," Sarah added. "So they don't invite them to their parties and their children never meet the climbers' children and society remains exclusive."

"But Lisa met Joe Prince," Maeve said.

"By accident, apparently. Even though Lisa's family was well off and part of the Saratoga Springs society, they weren't considered *top drawer* enough for the New Yorkers. One of the girls invited her to a party, though, which is one thing society hostesses guard against, because if you allow your sons to see these lovely, interesting girls, sooner or later they'll want to marry one."

"And that's what happened with Joe and Lisa Prince," Maeve said, obviously delighted by such a romantic tale.

"But it would never happen for Jane Harding, because her family wasn't well off at all, from what Lisa told me, and she'd never be invited under any circumstances."

"So she had to come to the city and find her own rich man," Gino concluded with a frown. "Do you think she could have chosen Nunzio Esposito?"

For a long moment they all considered that disturbing possibility.

"But why choose Esposito?" Maeve said finally. "He's old and he's married."

"And she's hardly likely to settle for being someone's mistress, no matter how rich he is," Sarah said. "She also didn't seem to know anything about the missing diamond ring, which probably means she didn't receive it as a gift."

"Oh dear," Maeve said in mock dismay. "That's the reason he'd supposedly taken it from his wife, to give it to his paramour."

"So if she didn't even know about it, that means she wasn't his *paramour*," Gino confirmed, adding a mocking emphasis to the final word.

"I think you're right," Sarah said. "If she really was the woman in Esposito's flat, she wasn't there willingly."

"Then why won't she admit it?" Gino asked.

"Because," Maeve said grimly, "being kidnapped is scandalous enough. If people knew she'd been locked away alone with Esposito for days . . ."

"Oh." They all pretended not to notice Gino was blushing.

"But it looks like she was," Maeve added.

"Yes, it does," Sarah said. "That poor girl."

"I did make sure to ask Kate Westrop if Jane ever left the settlement after she came back, and Kate didn't think she had," Maeve said. "She made quite a lot of work for Kate, who had to bring her meals to her because she wouldn't even leave her room."

"She did come out at least once, to speak to McWilliam, but that was long before Esposito was killed, so I guess we can cross Jane Harding off our list. I don't think Balducci killed Esposito either," Frank said.

"How can you be sure?" Gino scoffed.

"I can't of course, but he made a pretty good case for himself." Frank went through the logic of it for them, just as Balducci had done.

"My goodness, who would have guessed that being a gangster was so complicated?" Sarah marveled.

"He also said he and his men aren't interested in taking revenge on Gino. They know he didn't kill Esposito, and they know they didn't either, so they don't need to blame him."

"Did you believe him?" Maeve asked with a frown.

"No."

"Because that's exactly what he'd say if he wanted me to come out of hiding so they could kill me," Gino said sourly.

"So you're going to stay here until we do figure out who killed Esposito," Sarah said.

"And if we never do?" Gino asked just as sourly.

"We'll find out," Frank said.

THE NEXT MORNING, NO ONE COULD THINK OF A SINGLE thing they could do to find Esposito's killer. Even Maeve had to admit that going back to the settlement house in search of gossip was probably a waste of time. She took Catherine to school, as usual, and Frank headed for the office. Sarah decided to visit the maternity clinic, and Gino reconciled himself to a day spent tinkering with the motorcar.

Maeve arrived at the office just in time to greet a potential client, a man whose business partner had absconded with all their profits. He didn't want to report the theft to the police because if word of the crime became public, his clients would flee and take with them any hope of rebuilding the business. Frank listened with as much enthusiasm as he could muster under the circumstances. At least this was a case he had confidence he could solve. It was also a case Gino would have enjoyed, although Frank doubted the middle-aged Italian man Gino was now pretending to be would have much success.

When the new client left, Frank pulled up one of the chairs next to Maeve's desk. She'd been practicing her typing, and she stopped with a sigh, obviously grateful for the interruption.

"What are we going to do, Mr. Malloy? Gino can't hide forever."

"I guess we could let him show himself and see if anybody tries to kill him," Frank said in an attempt at humor.

"He'd love that, I'm sure," Maeve said, not seeing the humor at all. "He'd get to be a hero."

"Only if he survived."

"He wouldn't be able to imagine any other outcome, but I certainly can. Who do you think killed Esposito?"

"I wish I knew, but when I think about all the possible suspects, the only one who really has the nerve to confront a man like Esposito is—"

"—his wife," Maeve said with a knowing nod.

Frank blinked in surprise. "That's not what I was going to say."

"Really? What were you going to say?"

"I was going to say Balducci."

But Maeve frowned. "I thought you'd decided he didn't do it."

"He made a good argument, but who else would have the nerve? Everybody in the neighborhood was terrified of him."

"Not everybody or he wouldn't have needed a bodyguard."

Frank hadn't thought of it that way. "Maybe he used a bodyguard just so people would think he was important."

"Maybe, but they don't call them bodyguards for nothing."

"I suppose you're right. Now tell me why you think it's his wife."

"As you said, she's the only one who wasn't afraid to confront him."

"We don't know that," Frank said. "Maybe she was afraid of him. Maybe he used to beat her."

"Then why did she march right over to that tenement when she realized he'd stolen her diamond ring or whatever it was?"

Frank opened his mouth to reply, but he couldn't argue with her logic. "I see what you mean. That's not the way a woman acts if she's scared of her husband."

"She was probably furious and out for blood. *His* blood."

"And he told her he'd given the diamond to the other woman, so she wasn't going to get it back."

"What was it Mrs. Malloy told us? That he'd originally given it to his wife to sell if she ever fell on hard times."

"Something like that."

"Which sounds very thoughtful for a gangster," Maeve allowed. "Not many men worry about what will become of their widows."

"I'm sure a lot of men worry about that," Frank chided her. "It's just that not many of them can give their wives a diamond to sell."

"I suppose you could be right. At any rate, it's true that not many men could give their wives a diamond at all. Is that why engagement rings have become so popular?"

"I think they serve a different purpose."

"And what purpose is that?"

Frank smiled. "If a man jilts his fiancée, she can keep the ring instead of suing him for breach of promise."

"But a woman wouldn't have to support herself for the rest of her life over a broken engagement, would she? Not the way you would if your husband died and left you penniless."

"No, I guess not."

"So would a diamond be enough to support a widow? How much do diamond rings cost anyway?"

"I paid over a hundred dollars for Sarah's."

"That wouldn't keep her for the rest of her life," Maeve said.

"I see what you mean."

"So it would have to be a very big diamond."

"Or something else entirely," Frank mused.

"Something pretty valuable. Something valuable enough to go storming out late at night to confront your husband and demand that he give it back."

"And when he didn't have it . . ."

"And you found out another woman did have it, one who had disappeared or at least had left, that would make *me* mad enough to commit murder, and I imagine Mrs. Esposito felt the same way," Maeve concluded.

"Does that mean that Jane Harding could have this diamond thing after all?"

"Mrs. Malloy said she didn't seem to know anything about it."

Frank considered this. "What happened to it, then?"

"Let's see if we can figure it out. Apparently, he did take it from his wife," Maeve said, closing her eyes as she tried to imagine what had happened. Frank watched, controlling his amusement in case she really did come up with something. "Maybe he thought he could win Jane over with it somehow."

"A woman he'd kidnapped?" Frank scoffed.

"They say he was very charming. He was probably full of

himself, too. Men like that usually are. He kidnapped her because he wanted her, and he set out to win her heart."

"That sounds like a bad melodrama."

"I know, but men can be very stupid sometimes."

Frank couldn't argue with that. "All right. So maybe he's going to give her this diamond thing to impress her."

"That's exactly what I was thinking. But when he arrives at the flat, he discovers that she's escaped."

"Or just run away."

Maeve nodded. "Whatever it was, she's gone, so he can't give it to her. Then his wife shows up and demands it back, but he refuses. He's still thinking he can find Jane and win her over."

"He's really not very smart, is he?"

Maeve gave him a pitying look. "So he lies and tells his wife the girl took it, and the wife gets so angry, she stabs him."

"That makes sense, but what happened to the diamond thing?"

"The wife took it."

"But she didn't know he still had it. That's why she killed him."

"Maybe she searched him just to be sure and found it."

Frank sighed. "Or maybe whoever found his body took it."

"The bodyguard maybe. What was his name?"

"Dante. Or maybe Balducci or one of his other goons."

"Or the cop. What was his name?"

"Ogden," Frank said with another sigh. Cops always searched dead bodies they found and kept any valuables. It was a convenient way to supplement their income. "But if somebody found it, and it was worth as much as Mrs. Esposito seems to think, then that person will soon be throwing money around pretty freely."

"Then we should be able to find them easily. But that person didn't kill Esposito, so why do we care about him?"

"He might know something," Frank said.

"Well, I know something. I know Mrs. Esposito is probably the one who killed her husband, because she was the only one who could come at him with a knife like that."

"Another man could," Frank argued.

"Would Esposito really let himself get into a situation like that with another man?"

Frank was trying to picture it himself—he really needed to go to the theater more so he could see how these things were done—when the office telephone rang.

Maeve picked up the earpiece and spoke very professionally into the mouthpiece. "Yes," she said after identifying herself and waiting to hear what the caller had to say. "What? Say that again."

Her eyes grew large, and she gave Frank a look of astonishment. "Yes, yes. We'll meet you there."

"Who was that?" Frank demanded when she had hung up.

"It was Teo. She was using the telephone at the settlement house. Mrs. Esposito is dead."

THE ESPOSITO HOUSE WAS INDEED THE BIGGEST AND fanciest in the neighborhood. It resembled a stone castle with turrets and mullioned windows. Even Frank could see it was outrageous and bore the stigma of *new money*, but it probably succeeded in intimidating everyone in the neighborhood. He supposed that had been Esposito's intention in any case.

This time the police were still there, although they had already taken Mrs. Esposito's body away. Ogden stood guard at the front door, and he wasn't at all happy to see Frank join the crowd of onlookers. Frank wondered who would do the autopsy. Would they take her all the way down to Bellevue or give the body to a coroner nearby? And would that coroner know what he was doing, because many of them did not? But maybe someone had stabbed Mrs. Esposito, too, and the cause of death would be obvious even to the most incompetent medical man.

Teo was already there when Frank and Maeve arrived. She'd gone to the house as soon as she'd notified them, and she'd notified them the instant someone had brought the news to the settlement house, so she'd been there long enough to have heard all the gossip.

"Mrs. Esposito's maid found her this morning when she came to work," Teo reported, having drawn them aside from the crowd of onlookers so they wouldn't be overheard. "She'd been dead for a while."

"How did she die?" Frank asked.

"She was very sick. In the stomach. She made a lot of mess, according to the maid," Teo said gravely.

"What an awful way to die," Maeve sympathized.

Frank thought any way of dying was pretty awful, but women did hate making a mess. "If she was sick, why are the police here?"

"Because of her husband, I think," Teo said. "People think if he was murdered, maybe she was, too."

"Do the police think that?" Frank asked.

Teo shrugged. "They are here," she pointed out.

"Did the neighbors see anything? Or hear anything?" Frank asked. "You can't tell me they don't pay attention to this house, even with Esposito dead."

"You are right," Teo said. "They would watch for trouble,

if nothing else, but they will not say anything when the police are here."

Of course not. They didn't trust the police. "We'll have to come back later, after they're gone." Maybe Gino's middle-aged Italian man could find out something. "Is that Mr. Cassidi?" he added, trying to see through the crowd. He'd only gotten a glimpse, but he was pretty sure that was him.

"He lives on this street," Teo said, rising on tiptoe in an attempt to see over the crowd. "Yes, and his wife is with him."

Frank hadn't met Mrs. Cassidi of course, but she'd helped Sarah meet Mrs. Esposito and now Mrs. Esposito was dead.

"She probably won't want to see us," Maeve whispered to him, obviously thinking the same thing he was.

"I should speak to her," Teo said, oblivious to their hesitation. She knew nothing about the drama with Mrs. Esposito, and of course Mr. Cassidi employed Rinaldo. "Come, I will introduce you both."

Maeve cast Frank a desperate glance but followed Teo meekly. Left only with the option of appearing rude, Frank trailed along behind them as they made their way through the crowd that had spilled over the sidewalk and onto the street.

Teo greeted the Cassidis in Italian and had a brief, somber conversation with them as they obviously discussed the tragedy of Mrs. Esposito's death. Then she switched to English. "*Signor* Cassidi, I believe you know Mr. Malloy."

Cassidi frowned his displeasure, but his wife turned to Frank with interest. "Mr. Malloy, I know your wife, I think."

Frank managed not to wince. "Yes, you do."

Cassidi belatedly and grudgingly introduced them, and Teo introduced Maeve.

"We're very sorry to hear about Mrs. Esposito," Frank said.

Mrs. Cassidi pursed her lips and then said, "It is wrong to speak evil of the dead."

So much for Frank's concerns that she might be feeling guilty. "Did you happen to see anybody going to visit Mrs. Esposito?"

"Who would visit her?"

"Maybe the person who killed her."

Now he had the full attention of both of the Cassidis. "Do you think she was murdered?" Cassidi asked.

"If what they're saying is true, it's possible."

"They say she was very sick," Mrs. Cassidi said.

"Was she ever sick like that before?" Frank asked.

They all exchanged questioning glances. "Not that we heard," Teo admitted.

"I've seen people who were poisoned get sick like that very suddenly," Frank said.

"But who would do that? And why?" Mrs. Cassidi asked.

Frank almost said, "Maybe the person who killed her husband," but just in time he remembered he'd practically accused Cassidi of that at their meeting. Instead he said, "Maybe when we solve her husband's murder, we'll figure it out."

Cassidi glared at him, but Mrs. Cassidi nodded. Then she said, "Maybe you would like to know that a boy came home to his family last night. A boy who was kidnapped."

"Yes, I would like to know that," Frank said, forgetting all about Cassidi and his damaged feelings. "Do the police know? Have they spoken to him?"

"The police know nothing about it," Cassidi said, still annoyed but too passionate about this topic to let that stop him from talking to Frank. "The family did not tell the police he was taken."

"Then they must have paid the ransom," Frank said.

No one replied, telling Frank what he needed to know. "Do you think the family would talk to me? Or to Gino?" He turned to Mrs. Cassidi. "You said there were other children being held, too. If we could find them . . ."

She said something to her husband in Italian, and they had a brief argument that she apparently won. She turned back to Frank. "I will invite the boy and his mother to my house. The boy speaks English, and I think his mother would allow your wife to speak to him."

"Thank you, Mrs. Cassidi. Just let her know when to come."

Maeve tapped him on the shoulder. "Mr. Malloy, do you think that's a detective?"

Frank turned to see a man in a suit step out of the Esposito house and stop to speak to Ogden. This would be the precinct detective. Every precinct had one or two who investigated local crimes. If it was a big or important case, they would call in help from Police Headquarters, because the precinct detectives weren't the best ones on the force. This one looked like one of the worst of a bad lot.

Frank excused himself and went over to the wrought iron fence that surrounded the Espositos' small yard.

Ogden saw him and said something to the detective by way of warning, so he was ready for a fight by the time he reached the front gate.

Frank decided to pretend he hadn't noticed. "I'm Frank Malloy," he said, holding out his business card. "My partner, Gino Donatelli, is the one you charged with Esposito's murder."

The detective glanced over his shoulder at Ogden, who

was glowering at them both. "Ogden told me. I'm Sullivan." The two men shook hands. "Look, I know it was a put-up job with your partner, and I'm sorry he got caught up in it, but that's how things go in this neighborhood. You just have to bribe somebody and he's free, so what else do you need to worry about?"

"For one thing, I'm worried about who killed Mrs. Esposito."

"Who said anybody did?"

"It just seems strange she turns up dead right after her husband is murdered."

"She got sick. The coroner said gastric fever or something like that."

"In a perfectly healthy woman?"

"It happens all the time."

Unfortunately, it did. People got sick from bad water or spoiled food or something in the air. Who knew what caused all these illnesses? Still . . . "From what I heard, her symptoms could have been from arsenic poisoning."

"That's hard to believe, but maybe it's true. If it is, I'd say she committed suicide."

"A good Catholic lady like her? She went to Mass every day."

Sullivan shook his head. "Why are you so interested?"

"Because if she really was murdered and I can figure out why, maybe that will help me figure out who killed her husband. At least tell the coroner who does the autopsy that you suspect arsenic poisoning."

Sullivan smiled. "But I don't suspect arsenic poisoning."

"Then tell him I do."

Sullivan stared at him in wonder for a long moment. "I heard you used to be a cop yourself."

"Detective Sergeant Frank Malloy, at your service," Frank admitted.

"And you quit when you got rich."

"They made me quit."

"And now you amuse yourself by solving cases the police can't."

"Not exactly. I'm not amused by any of this, and I solve cases the police won't."

Sullivan sighed. "Well, I can tell you the police won't solve this one, because nobody cares that some dago gangster's widow died, even if she *was* murdered."

"Then you won't mind if I look into it, but I need to know if she really was poisoned."

"Don't you ever give up?" Sullivan asked in exasperation.

"Not often."

"All right. The coroner is Unger." He gave Frank the address.

"Is he any good?"

"How would I know? Now I'm going to see if I can find another crime to solve. This one is yours."

Frank didn't thank him.

Mrs. Esposito is dead," Maeve announced to Gino the moment she arrived home and had sent Catherine into the kitchen for an after-school snack and they were alone. They were in the hallway, so Gino drew her into the parlor where they were less likely to be overheard.

"What do you mean, she's dead?"

Maeve explained how Teo had telephoned the office and what they had learned since. "Mr. Malloy went to talk to the coroner and I had to get Catherine from school."

"Do you really think she was poisoned?"

"How likely is it that she just suddenly got sick and died several days after her husband?"

"You're right, that does sound suspicious."

"And the precinct detective told Mr. Malloy he's welcome to investigate, so that's exactly what he's going to do."

"He can't investigate in that neighborhood. He'll need my help."

"You'll have to talk to him about that. Oh, and we saw Mr. and Mrs. Cassidi, and they told us a kidnapped boy was just released last night."

"Petrosino will be happy to hear that."

"We can't tell him, or at least he can't investigate. The family didn't go to the police."

Gino muttered something that might have been a curse.

"But," Maeve continued doggedly, "Mrs. Cassidi is going to arrange for Mrs. Malloy to meet with the boy and his mother to see if he can tell us anything that will help locate the place where they hold the victims."

"Why Mrs. Malloy?"

"So no one will think they went to the police, I guess. The Black Hand could still take revenge, even though they returned the boy safely."

"You're right. But who would have killed Mrs. Esposito and why?"

"I have no idea, and I'm heartbroken."

"You didn't even know the woman," Gino reminded her.

"I know, but I'd just convinced Mr. Malloy that she was the one who killed her husband."

Gino thought that was hilarious.

"Don't laugh. It made perfect sense."

"I'm sure it did. Who did he think did it?"

"Balducci or one of his gang."

"Which makes a lot more sense. We'll have to find somebody who actually saw them do it and isn't afraid of the Black Hand in order to prove it, though."

"Which is why it would have been so nice if Mrs. Esposito had done it."

SARAH BLAMED HERSELF FOR MRS. ESPOSITO'S DEATH.

"Don't be silly," Malloy said. "We don't even know yet if she was murdered."

He'd waited until after supper to tell her the news, when Maeve had taken the children up to bed and Gino had mumbled something about needing to work on the motorcar and sneaked out to the garage. Neither of them wanted to be there when she found out, she realized.

"But you're pretty sure she was murdered, or you wouldn't have tracked down the coroner and bribed him to do an autopsy."

"All right, I am," he admitted sheepishly, "but you didn't kill her."

"But I involved her in all this."

"She was already involved. She was married to Esposito."

"You don't understand," Sarah said. "I drew attention to her by confronting her in the church. That must have frightened someone."

"Do you think she knew who killed her husband?"

Sarah frowned. Could she have? "She didn't seem to, and I think Mrs. Cassidi and I made it pretty clear we thought she'd done it. If she did know or even suspected, why wouldn't she have told us, if only to clear herself?"

"She surely would have, so she probably didn't know

then," Malloy said reasonably. "But maybe she figured it out later. Maybe she even said something to the real killer."

"And then invited him over for a visit so he could poison her." Sarah shook her head. "That doesn't make any sense at all."

"So you see, it's not your fault."

"I'm not sure how that proves it's not my fault. I think it just proves that Esposito's killer had no reason to kill *her*."

"No reason that we know of, at least not yet," he added.

"And now we'll never find out because she's dead."

"Maybe somebody saw whoever it was who killed her. Hardly anything happens in that neighborhood that at least a dozen people don't see."

"But will they tell you anything?"

"I'm going to take Gino in his disguise. He might be able to get something out of the neighbors."

"This case is impossible. Every time we think we have it figured out, we . . ." She gestured helplessly.

"A boy that the Black Hand had kidnapped came home last night," he said, probably to distract her.

He succeeded. "He did? That's wonderful."

"Especially because Mrs. Cassidi thinks she can get the boy to talk to us."

"Maybe he can give us more information about where he was held than Mrs. Cassidi did," Sarah said, warming to the thought. "Even if we could just stop these kidnappings, that would be something."

"Mrs. Cassidi didn't think it was a good idea for me to talk to him, though, in case the Black Hand gets wind of it. They might not be too happy if the boy is talking to the police."

"You're not the police."

"They probably wouldn't see much difference. But she thought the boy's mother might let him talk to you."

"Me? Oh, that's an excellent idea. I'm a nurse. I'll check him to make sure he's in good health."

"That's what I was thinking. You'll take your medical bag. Mrs. Cassidi will send you a message about when you can meet. And Sarah?"

"Yes?"

"None of this is your fault."

XI

WHILE SARAH WAITED AT HOME TO HEAR FROM MRS. Cassidi and Maeve dropped Catherine off at school on her way to the office, Frank and Gino—in his disguise—went to Italian Harlem to question the Espositos' neighbors. They found out very little, because even though Gino spoke Italian, they didn't know him and didn't trust him, but one of the neighbors did tell them where Mrs. Esposito's current maid lived. The Espositos, it seemed, had a difficult time keeping help, as more than one of the neighbors was only too happy to mention. No one would live at a gangster's house, so they had no live-in help, and the daily girls they did manage to hire often got frightened and left without notice.

Frank and Gino had to take the El back downtown to where the maid lived with her family. Because she was a Negro, she and her family lived in one of the worst tenements and paid higher rent than white people paid for better tenements. Landlords knew the Negroes didn't have many housing options, so they charged what they wanted and never did any upkeep on the buildings because their tenants couldn't leave.

Frank had to lie to get someone to tell them which flat Mary White lived in because the people there didn't trust him for the same reasons the people in Italian Harlem didn't trust him. To overcome their reluctance, he told them Mary hadn't received her salary, and he'd been tasked with delivering her final pay. That led them to a rear flat on the fourth floor. The older woman who opened the door looked terrified when she saw them.

"We paid the rent," she insisted, her gaze darting nervously between Frank and his odd companion.

"I'm not from the landlord. You see, well, Mrs. Esposito didn't give Mary her final pay. I'm delivering her salary to her," Frank lied, although he was perfectly willing to give Mary what was owed to her if that would motivate her to answer his questions. "Is Mary here?"

The woman looked shocked, but at least she seemed to believe Frank. "I . . . *Mary!*" she called.

A young woman came up behind her, obviously reluctant and just as frightened as the woman who must be her mother. Her eyes were wide and her lip was trembling. She looked as if she had been crying, which would be understandable considering the shock she'd had yesterday.

"Miss White," Frank said, pulling off his hat in the hope that a show of respect would put her at ease, at least a little. "I think Mrs. Esposito owed you some money, and of course you should be paid for yesterday, since you made the trip up. It wasn't your fault that Mrs. Esposito was . . . Well, it was a terrible thing, but not your fault, so you shouldn't have to suffer. May we come in?" Frank looked around meaningfully at the other doors in the corridor, which had opened during this brief exchange as the neighbors tried to hear what these white men had come to say.

The two women exchanged a glance. Mary shrugged, still looking uncertain, but her mother stood back so the two men could enter. Gino pulled off his hat as well and nodded to the two ladies as he walked by them into the flat. His disguise must have confused them, since he looked like he should be sitting in an Italian restaurant drinking grappa and gossiping with the other old men instead of accompanying someone who looked like a rich Irish cop.

Frank glanced around the kitchen, which was sparsely furnished but immaculate. If Mary kept Mrs. Esposito's house this clean, she'd been lucky to have her. "Can we sit down?" He gestured to the kitchen table with its four mismatched chairs.

"If you like," Mrs. White said, still frightened but now equally confused. She was a plump woman whose face showed a life of struggle. Her dress was faded but clean and pressed, her apron blindingly white.

Frank and Gino took two of the seats and waited while Mary and her mother took the other two.

"That must have been a shock when you found Mrs. Esposito yesterday, Mary," Frank said, using the gentle tone he always took with his daughter, Catherine.

"Yes, sir, it was," Mary said softly. She looked about eighteen, her face still smooth with the beauty of youth and innocence.

"Can you tell me where you found her and what you saw?"

Mary blinked in surprise. "Why do you want to know that?"

Her mother shot her a warning look. "You answer the man, Mary. He gonna pay you."

Mary straightened. "I found her in the . . ." She gave her mother a pained glance. "In the bathroom."

"I heard she'd been sick."

"Yes, sir. Real sick. I . . ." She lowered her gaze to where her hands were clenched on the table. "I was glad nobody told me to clean it up."

"Was she still dressed or in her nightclothes?"

Plainly, she found this a strange question, but she said, "Still dressed."

Frank nodded. "Did you notice anything else? Anything strange or out of the ordinary?"

Mary shifted uneasily in her chair. "The front door was open. When I got there, I mean. She always kept it locked, and I'd have to knock. But it was open just a little, like somebody went out and didn't close it all the way."

"So you just went in without knocking," Frank said.

"Oh no, sir. I knocked, but she didn't answer, so that's when I went in."

"And what did you see? Not Mrs. Esposito, at least not at first, I'd guess."

"No, sir. I saw . . . It was strange. I went in the kitchen and there was a tray with tea things on it."

"Tea things?"

"Yes, sir. A pot and two cups. They was used, like she'd had company and then brought the tray back in the kitchen for me to wash up the things later."

"And did you wash them?"

"Yes, sir, I did."

Frank managed not to sigh. So much for testing the cups for poison. "Then what did you do?"

"I started cleaning, like I always do, but when I got upstairs, I smelled . . ." She glanced at her mother again.

"I'm sure we all know what you smelled," Frank said gently. "So you went to investigate."

"I thought maybe the toilet was broke or something, but then I saw her on the floor and I was so scared. I ran out and went next door and somebody went for the police and . . ." She was crying again.

"That's all right, Miss White. Thank you for telling me."

Mrs. White reached over and patted her daughter's hands where they were still clenched on the table, but she shot Frank a dirty look. "Why'd you need to know all that for anyways? She don't like talking about it. It's a horrible thing, even if that lady was married to a crook."

"I'm sorry, but it was important to know exactly what happened."

"Important to who?"

"To me," Frank said with a small smile. "Miss White, how much did Mrs. Esposito owe you?"

Mary's head snapped up at that and she glanced at her mother for some kind of assistance.

"Tell the man, Mary," her mother said.

"She owed me a dollar from before."

"And for yesterday?"

"Fifty cents."

Frank thought that was criminal. He pulled out a five-dollar bill, a week's wages for a working man, and slid it across the table to her.

"I don't have no change, mister," she said in dismay.

"You don't need any. That's for your trouble. I'm sorry you were the one who found Mrs. Esposito."

Mary sniffed and snatched up the money before Frank could change his mind, stuffing it into her skirt pocket. "Thank you, sir."

"Who are you, mister?" the mother asked suspiciously. "You don't look Italian." She couldn't help glancing at Gino, who certainly did, even though he hadn't uttered a word.

"I'm Frank Malloy." He reached into his pocket and pulled out one of his business cards. One of the expensive, engraved ones. Mary White deserved that much. He laid it on the table, but neither woman made a move to pick it up.

"You work for Mr. Esposito?" the mother asked with another meaningful glance at Gino.

"No. I'm trying to figure out who killed him, though. I don't suppose either of you would have any ideas." Frank looked at Mary, who was focused on her hands again. "You didn't happen to hear Mrs. Esposito say anything about it, did you, Mary?"

Mary's eyes filled with fear again, and she shook her head. But maybe she was lying. Why would she be so afraid if she really hadn't heard anything?

Frank tried another tack. "People said Mrs. Esposito had a diamond ring or something like that, something valuable that her husband had given her. Did you ever see it?"

Mary shook her head again. "He had a safe. Mr. Esposito. It was big. I think he kept his money in it. If she had anything like that, she would've kept it in there, too, I guess."

"You never saw her wearing anything like that?"

"Mrs. Esposito, she didn't like to show off. She said the devil gets jealous or something like that. She was Catholic," she added, as if that explained a lot of strange behavior.

Frank nodded, thinking of his mother. "I guess you wouldn't know if Mrs. Esposito had any enemies."

Mary gave this a few moments' thought. "Nobody liked her, I know that. The neighbors wouldn't speak to her on the street. That's why I was surprised to see the tray. I couldn't think who would visit her."

"You shouldn't speak ill of the dead, girl," her mother said.

Mary just shrugged.

"I know what you mean, though," Frank said. "If we could figure out who it was, we'd know who killed her."

"She was killed?" Mrs. White echoed in horror. "Didn't nobody say that."

"We aren't sure, but I think she may have been poisoned," Frank said.

"I never poisoned her," Mary cried in renewed terror. "Please, sir, I wasn't even there!"

"I know that. Don't worry, Mary. No one is accusing you. I think whoever visited her the day before did it. That's why I was wondering if you had any idea who it was."

"None at all," she claimed, and Frank knew she wouldn't say, even if she did. She was too frightened of him and men like him.

Frank thanked them and they stood to leave. "Oh, Mary, one more thing. You said Mrs. Esposito was still dressed. Was she wearing a house dress or was she dressed up, like she'd been expecting company?"

"Just a house dress, mister."

Frank thanked her again, and they left. They pretended not to notice the eyes staring out of the partially opened doors as they descended the stairs. Mary and her mother would probably be visited by a lot of curious neighbors.

"So at least we know how Mrs. Esposito could have been poisoned," Gino remarked when they reached the sidewalk. "Assuming she really was poisoned."

"I'm going to visit the coroner tomorrow to see if he found anything. Over the phone, seemed to know what I was talking about when I mentioned testing for arsenic, although I wish I could've called in our old pal Jerusalem Moody. At least I know for sure that he knows what he's doing."

"Yes, too bad he's so far downtown from Italian Harlem."

"We'll just have to hope this Unger is at least half as good as Moody." Which they both knew wasn't likely, but they could still hope.

A FEW MORE DAYS LIKE THIS, WITH NOTHING TO DO BUT think, and Maeve's typing would be at the expert level. She pulled the sheet of paper, on which she had just typed hundreds of words copied from a book, out of the typewriter and tossed it into the wastepaper basket beside her desk. Not a single person had even walked down their hall, much less come in to consult with them that day. Maeve was very much afraid she would die of boredom soon. Why did everyone else have something important to do and she was just sitting here, typing nonsense onto paper she would throw away?

A day had passed since Mrs. Esposito's body had been found. Surely, rumors were swirling by now. Maybe Teo had heard something. Maybe someone at the settlement house had heard something. Would they think it strange if she showed up again, snooping around? Would anyone even talk to her now?

But she didn't have to snoop around, she realized. They had identified someone at the settlement who had a very good reason for wanting Nunzio Esposito dead—especially if Jane Harding had told him who had kidnapped her and why. If Jane had been the woman being held in the flat and McWilliam knew it, then he could have gone crazy and who would blame him? Mr. Malloy didn't think Esposito would have let a man get close enough to stab him, but he probably wouldn't have been afraid of someone like McWilliam, whom he would have considered weak and harmless.

Maeve couldn't think of a reason why he would have killed Mrs. Esposito, but she could certainly see the woman admitting him to her home. She would also have considered him harmless. Poison, they always said, was a woman's weapon, but a man who had been raised to revere women might hesitate to use violence against one. Poison would be a neat alternative.

Having convinced herself that it was a good idea, Maeve locked up the office and hurried out to catch the El for Italian Harlem.

SARAH ARRIVED AT MRS. CASSIDI'S HOUSE THAT AFTER-noon with her medical bag and a list of questions. The list of questions was in her head of course, so she wouldn't frighten the boy or his mother. Mrs. Cassidi answered her knock and admitted her to the house.

"How is the boy doing?" Sarah asked in a whisper after they had greeted each other.

"Children are so . . ." She gestured, trying in vain to find the right word. "Things do not bother them so much."

Or the children just didn't show it. Sarah didn't say that, though. Let Mrs. Cassidi think the boy was fine after his ordeal. Mrs. Cassidi took her into the parlor.

The drapes had been drawn, even though it was the middle of the day. Sarah thought perhaps the mother didn't want anyone to see her son. She'd naturally be protective.

Indeed, she was sitting beside him on the sofa with one arm draped around his shoulders, and she jumped to her feet the moment Sarah and Mrs. Cassidi entered the room.

"Mrs. Malloy, this is my friend, Mrs. Gallo, and her son, Fabio." Fabio was a handsome boy of about twelve, with large, dark eyes and curly black hair.

Sarah told them how happy she was to meet them and shook hands with Mrs. Gallo and the boy. Fabio thought shaking hands with a strange lady was amusing, and Sarah was happy to see he didn't seem too upset, at least at the moment.

"I explained to Mrs. Gallo that you are a nurse and that you examined me after I came home to make sure I was in good health," Mrs. Cassidi said, although they both knew Sarah had done nothing more than give Mrs. Cassidi a sympathetic ear.

"Do you speak English, Mrs. Gallo?" Sarah asked.

But Mrs. Gallo shook her head and gave her apology in Italian.

"Mama can't speak English," Fabio said without a trace of an accent, "but I can tell her what you say if you need to talk to her."

"Thank you, Fabio, but I mostly just need to talk to you. Have you ever been examined by a doctor before?"

"No," he said in wonder. "Are you a doctor?"

"No, I'm a nurse, but I can check the same things a doc-tor would. Is that all right? I'll explain everything I'm going to do."

The boy nodded, obviously intrigued. Sarah opened her medical bag, the one that had belonged to her first husband, Tom, who really had been a physician. The boy and his mother and even Mrs. Cassidi watched with avid interest as she pulled out the implements she would use.

"This is a stethoscope. I'm going to use it to listen to your heart." Sarah showed him how the curved parts fit into her ears and how she would press the bell at the other end to his chest. "When I'm finished, I'll let you listen, too."

Fabio and the two women watched closely, with Mrs. Gallo obviously ready to snatch her son away if Sarah tried anything untoward. She listened to the boy's heart and then had him turn around so she could hold the bell to his back to check his lungs. Then she let him hear his own heart and he insisted that his mother listen as well. Having completed this part of the exam without incident, Sarah could see Mrs. Gallo had relaxed a bit.

Sarah started rummaging in the bag for the next instru-ment and said as casually as she could, "I understand you had quite an adventure, Fabio."

"You mean when I was kidnapped?" he said with an odd note of pride.

"Yes, that's what I mean. It must have been hard, being away from your family all that time."

"I missed them," he admitted, "but there were other boys there to play with."

"Do you remember their names?"

"Yes. Tony and Alberto and Caesar."

Oh dear. "Did you know any of them already?"

"No, but we are friends now."

"And they stayed behind when you left?"

"Except Tony. He had already gone home."

Sarah nodded. "You see this? It's an otoscope. I'm going to use it to look in your ears, but first I'm going to put this on my head." She showed him the round mirror with a hole in the middle that was attached to a leather strap. Everyone watched, fascinated, as she fastened the strap around her head.

"What is that for?" Fabio asked in wonder.

"We'll go over to the window and I'll try to catch the light with the mirror and shine it into your ear. Come along, I'll show you."

Sarah chose the window that faced the side of the house, in case Mrs. Gallo was worried they'd be seen from the street. Mrs. Gallo followed them anxiously but made no attempt to interfere. Sarah moved the mirror over her eye, so she could see through the hole, and demonstrated how the light could be reflected from the window. "That will let me see inside your ear." Then she showed him, checking both his ears. They repeated the exercise after Sarah fetched the metal tongue depressor from her bag and checked Fabio's throat.

She let him play with the otoscope for a few minutes. "Do you remember the place where you stayed when you were on your adventure?"

"Sure."

"What was it like?"

"It was an old house. We were upstairs. We each had a cot, and there were two more cots that were empty."

"What could you see when you looked out the windows?"

He peered at her through the otoscope. "We couldn't see out the windows. They were painted black."

"You couldn't see anything at all?" Sarah asked.

Fabio grinned. "We could see a little. We scraped some of the paint away with our fingernails."

Sarah grinned back. "What did you see?"

"A tree. A really big tree, taller than the windows and right beside the house. We could've reached the branches and climbed down it if we could've gotten the window open."

"Was it locked?"

"No, they nailed it shut. You could see the nails. We tried to open it but it wouldn't move."

"That was very clever of you to at least try."

"We all wanted to go home."

"I don't blame you." Sarah pulled a small hammer out of her bag. "Now I'm going to test your reflexes."

"What are reflexes?"

"Sit down on this chair and I'll show you." Sarah took him to a wooden chair that sat against the wall. She tapped his knee and he laughed out loud when his foot automatically kicked out.

"How did you do that?" he marveled.

"Like this." She tapped his other knee and his other foot kicked out. Even the women laughed that time.

Sarah had to explain how reflexes work and demonstrate on both of the ladies as well, much to everyone's delight.

"Did someone watch over you when you were at the house?"

"Some men."

"Would you recognize them if you saw them again?"

"We never saw their faces. They always wore masks."

"What about their voices? If you heard them again, would you know them?"

The boy shrugged. "Maybe."

"Can you remember anything else about the house? Did you hear any strange sounds?"

Fabio's nose wrinkled as he tried to remember. "A train sometimes, but it was mostly quiet. Not like here."

Just as Mrs. Cassidi had said. They exchanged a knowing glance.

"Fabio," Sarah said, "you can tell your mother that you are in good health."

His mother smiled gratefully when he had translated Sarah's message.

"*Grazie*," she said with heartfelt thanks.

But Sarah couldn't help thinking about the two boys who were still being held and any other children who might have joined them. How on earth would they ever find them?

On the ride uptown, Maeve had considered how best to approach McWilliam. He'd never met her and would have no idea of her connection to the Donatellis or the Malloys, so she could be whomever she wanted to be. She decided to be Jane Harding's friend again.

Maeve glanced around when she entered the settlement, glad to see the entrance hall was practically deserted. Classes were in session and most everyone seemed to be occupied. Maeve hurried up the stairs before anyone could notice her, fingers crossed in hope of finding Christopher McWilliam in his office.

The door was open and she saw him at his desk, his back to the door. She watched him for a moment and noticed he seemed to be just staring out the window, which overlooked the street. Maeve rapped sharply on the door jamb, startling him.

He jumped a little and turned, rising to his feet when he saw her in the doorway. "May I help you?"

"Are you Mr. McWilliam?"

"Yes, I am." He looked distracted and oddly haggard. Guilty conscience?

"I'm Maeve Smith. I'm sorry to bother you, but . . . Well, I had a friend at school who told me about the work you're doing here, and I'm interested in volunteering. I was wondering if you had a few minutes to answer some questions for me."

He forced himself to smile, which she could see took some effort. "I'm pleased to meet you, Miss Smith. Please have a seat."

Maeve sat down on the worn sofa at the other end of the room from his desk, and he dragged his chair over and set it down so he could face her. Now that she'd had a chance to study him more closely, she realized his shirt looked like he'd slept in it and his suit was wrinkled. He looked like a man who had given up. "Who was the friend who told you about our work?"

"Jane Harding."

He winced at that, a spasm of pain contorting his otherwise handsome face. "I see."

"Yes, I came by the other day to see her, but they told me she wasn't here."

"Uh, no. She left, I'm afraid."

"That's what the girl I spoke to said. Miss Westrop was her name."

He smiled weakly. "You said you had some questions."

"Yes, I do. Miss Westrop said I would need to apply if I wanted to volunteer, and that I would need references."

"That's right. We require three references as to your character."

"Could Jane be one of them? I thought she would be especially good since she works here."

"She doesn't . . . That is, she's gone . . ." To Maeve's horror, his voice broke and he looked as if he might actually weep. He quickly pulled out a handkerchief and blew his nose. Obviously, he was still devastated by Jane Harding's desertion.

How wonderful!

"Mr. McWilliam, are you all right?" she asked, not even having to feign her concern. "Can I get someone for you?"

He shook his head, unable to speak, and Maeve jumped up and closed the door. He wouldn't want anyone to see him like this, she was sure, and she didn't want anyone to interrupt them. She cast about for something to do to help and she saw a carafe of water on his desk with a glass next to it. She poured some water into the glass and took it to him.

"Here, drink this," she said, holding out the glass.

He looked up in surprise, his red-rimmed eyes squinting in confusion until he saw the glass she was offering. He accepted it obediently and drank it down. She took the empty glass from him and set it on the floor, then resumed her seat opposite him.

"Something has happened to Jane, hasn't it? Please tell me. Maybe I can help."

He tucked away his handkerchief and gave her a sheepish look before lowering his gaze again. "I'm terribly sorry. I don't know what came over me."

"It must be something awful, and I know it concerns Jane. You can trust me, Mr. McWilliam. If anything has happened to her . . ."

"She's fine," he said without much conviction. "I mean, she . . . she went to stay with her cousin."

"With Lisa?" Maeve marveled, thus proving she knew Jane well indeed. "It really must be something bad if she's with Lisa. They don't get along at all, do they?"

He blinked in surprise. "They . . . I believe they have made up their differences."

Maeve frowned skeptically. "Was that even possible? And why didn't Jane just go home? Oh my, is she sick? Or hurt?"

"No, not at all . . . That is . . ."

"Please tell me! It can't be as bad as I'm imagining."

"She was . . . kidnapped."

"*Kidnapped?*" Maeve echoed in amazement. "But she's not . . . I thought that only happened to millionaires who could pay ransoms."

"This was . . . different."

"How was it different?"

McWilliam rubbed his forehead as if it ached, and it probably did, because obviously he knew who had really kidnapped Jane and why. Had Jane told him or someone else? But who else even knew?

"Mr. McWilliam, if Jane was mistreated in some way . . . Well, I'd like to help, if I can."

He just shook his head.

Maeve cast about for some other way to get through to him, and then she found it. "Mr. McWilliam, I know about you and Jane. That is, I know she was in love with you and that you two hoped to marry."

He looked up in surprise. "She told you that?"

"Oh, I know you weren't engaged yet, but—"

"No, I mean she told you she was *in love* with me?"

Maeve knew she had him then. She smiled with as much

tenderness as she could manage. "Yes. I don't think anything else could have brought her to New York."

"She seemed genuinely excited about working at the settlement house, at least at first," he said sadly.

"Why did she change her mind . . . ? Oh, I see. After she got kidnapped, I suppose she was afraid to stay here."

"Yes, she . . . That's what she said."

Maeve could see he was lying, or at least not telling the whole truth. "But surely she . . . Oh, now it all makes sense. Miss Westrop told me that Jane had disappeared from the settlement house for a few days. That must have been when she was kidnapped."

McWilliam blanched. "Is that what people are saying? That she disappeared?"

"I can't remember exactly what Miss Westrop said, but she knew Jane was gone for a few days and hadn't taken anything with her."

"We were so careful not to tell anyone about the kidnapping. I shouldn't have even told you."

"Don't worry, I won't tell a soul, and how kind of you to keep it a secret, or at least try to. No lady wants people to know she was taken away by gangsters and held against her will." Maeve managed to shiver with horror at the very thought.

"You mustn't say a word to anyone, Miss Smith. Swear to me," he said, almost desperate.

"Of course. I wouldn't want to hurt Jane, although I imagine you want to hurt whoever did this to her."

His eyes widened. "Yes, well, I do but . . ."

"But what? Do you actually know who did it?" she asked, amazed again.

"Yes, I do, but . . . he's dead."

"Dead?" Maeve hoped she looked suitably horrified. "He deserves it of course, and . . . Oh my, is it the man Miss Westrop was telling me about? The fellow from the Black Hand?"

McWilliam gasped. "She told you about him?"

"She said he . . . Well, she mentioned that Jane had admired his house or something like that and then he was murdered."

"What else did she say?" he asked, leaning forward to impress upon her the urgency of his question.

"Oh dear, I'm afraid it was some scandalous gossip," Maeve hedged, trying to look dismayed at the prospect of relating it.

"*What did she say?*" he insisted.

"That he was murdered in the apartment where he kept his mistress," she confessed.

McWilliam reared back as if she'd struck him. "She wasn't his *mistress*. She was his *captive*. She hated him. She told me!"

"Now, now, you mustn't upset yourself. What does it matter in any case? You can't possibly care . . ." She stopped herself as she pretended to consider what he'd said. "Was Jane the mistress? I mean the captive he held there?" she quickly corrected herself. "Of course she was! The poor thing. How will she ever stand the shame of it?"

"That's why you must never tell anyone," he said. "Swear it to me, Miss Smith. We have to do whatever we can to protect Jane."

"You're right. I'll never breathe a word of it, but . . ."

"But what?" he demanded when she pressed her fingers to her lips as if to hold back what she had been about to say.

"Nothing."

"No, tell me. What were you going to say?"

"I . . . I'm sorry, Mr. McWilliam. I know how much you care for Jane, and this can only hurt you."

"Nothing can hurt me now. What were you going to say?"

Maeve sighed in despair. "Miss Westrop told me that people are saying the mistress—because that's what they think she was—that the mistress is the one who killed this gangster."

"No," he said, shaking his head.

"I'm sure Jane couldn't have done that. In fact, Miss Westrop said Jane locked herself in her room when she got back."

"Yes, yes, that's right, she did."

"Then if she was locked in her room, she couldn't possibly have killed him, could she?"

"No, she couldn't," he confirmed.

"But someone did. I wonder who it could have been."

McWilliam straightened in his chair, his face white, his eyes bloodshot, and his expression suddenly suspicious. "I can't imagine why it would matter to you, Miss Smith."

Maeve tried a placating smile. "It's just that . . . well, people are saying the woman killed him, and I can certainly understand why she would want to, and Miss Westrop did mention that Jane didn't even answer her door at least once when she knocked, almost like she wasn't there. Maybe she did leave her room, which would mean that she might have—"

"Who are you?" he demanded, suddenly angry. "Why are you here?"

Maeve sighed in defeat. "I'm Maeve Smith, like I said. I work for Frank Malloy."

He reared back again, this time in fear. For a moment, she thought he might actually bolt, but instead he stared at her for what seemed an age before straightening his shoulders and schooling his expression to appear calm. "I see. And you think Jane Harding killed Esposito. Well, you're wrong, Miss Smith, because I did. I'm the one who killed Esposito."

XII

Sarah had hoped to catch up with Malloy and Gino as they were making the rounds of the neighborhood, but Mrs. Cassidi told her they'd finished up before she arrived.

"Thank you for arranging for me to meet with Mrs. Gallo and Fabio," Sarah told her when those two had left.

"I happy to do it. You were very good with the boy. His mother told me he would not speak with her about his time away."

"He probably didn't want to frighten her. Children can be oddly protective of their parents. But he knew she couldn't understand what he said to me. Did what he said help you remember anything else?"

"No, but the tree was a good thing to know. We do not have many large trees still growing in the city. Farmers cut them down first, and then the rest went when they started building tenements."

"But you think you were out in the country."

"Even still, not many of the houses have big trees like that right next to them. It must be an old house, and the tree grew up beside it."

"You're right. I didn't think of that. That should make it a little easier to find."

"Are you going to look for it, then?"

"You heard Fabio. At least two boys are still being held there, and if we can find the house, maybe we can also find the kidnappers."

Mrs. Cassidi shook her head. "Even if you find them and lock them away, someone will take their place."

Sarah was very much afraid she was right.

She thought she would be the first to arrive back home, but Malloy and Gino were already there. The three of them had just finished sharing what they had learned from Fabio Gallo and Mary White when Maeve arrived home with Catherine.

Sarah could see at once that something was wrong. Maeve looked as if she had lost her best friend. Sarah quickly ushered Catherine into the kitchen for a snack, knowing their cook would look after her. Mrs. Malloy and Brian came in a few minutes later, and Sarah asked her mother-in-law to take charge of the children for a while so she could speak with Maeve.

She found Maeve in the parlor with Malloy and Gino, all of them looking glum.

"We know something happened," Malloy said, going over to close the parlor door. "But she wouldn't tell us anything until you got here."

"I did something really stupid," Maeve said.

"Don't tell us you're the one who stabbed Esposito," Gino said in an awkward attempt at humor.

No one laughed, and Maeve didn't even give him a dirty look.

"Just tell us," Sarah said. "Maybe it's not as bad as you think."

"Oh yes, it is. I went to the settlement house this afternoon to see Christopher McWilliam."

No one spoke for a long moment while they all took that in and tried to think why it was so terrible.

"What made you do that?" Malloy finally asked.

"Because I was in the office, typing, and I was thinking about all the people we thought had a reason to kill Esposito, especially to kill him in that apartment that night. We'd talked about McWilliam, but nobody had ever really questioned him."

"I did," Malloy reminded her.

"But that was before we decided that Jane Harding was really the woman Esposito was keeping there," Maeve said.

"Even if she was, how would McWilliam know that for sure if we just figured it out ourselves?" Sarah asked.

"He'd know it if she told him," Maeve said.

Which was something none of them had considered.

"Why would she tell him, though?" Sarah asked. "Surely, she wouldn't want anyone to know, least of all the man who wanted to marry her."

"But maybe she did," Maeve said. "Maybe she wanted to be rid of McWilliam and his righteous cause so much that she decided to tell him, thinking he would be so disgusted, he'd stop wanting her and let her go without an argument."

"But if he really loved her," Malloy said, "it wouldn't matter to him."

Sarah had thought she couldn't love him any more than she already did, but she had been wrong. "Oh, Malloy, how sweet you are."

"*Sweet?*" he echoed incredulously. "No one ever accused me of that before."

"It *is* very nice," Maeve agreed, "and I'm afraid most men wouldn't feel that way, but I think McWilliam would agree with Mr. Malloy, if Jane had given him a chance."

"But she didn't," Gino said. "She just left."

"And did McWilliam tell you he knew about Jane and Esposito?" Malloy asked.

"Yes. When I called the woman Esposito's *mistress*, he informed me that she was his *captive*, and then he actually broke down and almost cried right in front of me."

Malloy and Gino looked suitably appalled at such unmanly behavior.

"Which means he had a very good reason to kill Esposito," Sarah said.

"Do you think he did it?" Gino asked Maeve.

Maeve sighed and looked even more miserable than she had before. "Well, he did confess."

"What?" Malloy nearly shouted, and Gino actually jumped to his feet.

"He *confessed*?" Gino repeated in amazement.

"I was giving him all the reasons why Jane might have done it, hoping to get him to reveal something, and I guess that was too much for him. He couldn't stand having her get blamed, so he told me he did it."

"We need to tell someone," Gino said, obviously realizing

this would mean the Black Hand would no longer have a reason to pin the murder on him.

"Yes, we'll have to think this through," Malloy said. "We want to make sure the right people know so he's charged and the charges against Gino are dropped. McWilliam probably isn't going to confess to anyone else, and Ogden and Sullivan might not even want to investigate, so we have to make sure that—"

"There's no need," Maeve said, still grim. "Before I could even ask him anything else, he told me he was going to tell the police and he left."

"He left? Of his own free will?" Malloy marveled.

"He seemed very determined, but of course I didn't think he really would. I thought maybe he was going to run away instead, so I went after him. But he went right to the precinct house and got himself arrested."

Gino gave a whoop of triumph. "I need to tell Mr. Nicholson so he can get the charges against me dropped. Should we send Balducci an announcement, too?"

Sarah wanted to share Gino's joy, but she could see that Maeve was not joyful at all. "What is it, Maeve? Isn't this good news?"

"It could be," she said, "but I don't think he did it."

They all stared at her in astonishment, and Gino plopped back down into his chair.

"Why not?" Gino demanded. "Why would he say he did if he didn't?"

Maeve sighed and gave him an apologetic smile. "Because he's just as nice as Mr. Malloy and he loves Jane Harding and he wants to protect her. I think I convinced him that she did it, so he's going to take the blame for her."

"That's crazy," Gino insisted.

"But it could be true," Malloy said.

"Jane couldn't have killed Esposito," Sarah reminded them. "She was locked up in the settlement house."

"I might have hinted that she could have snuck out," Maeve said sheepishly.

"How did you do that?" Sarah asked.

"Kate Westrop told me Jane didn't always answer her door when Kate knocked, so I suggested that maybe she wasn't there the whole time."

"That's possible, I guess," Sarah said, "but why would Jane have gone back to the flat after she escaped?"

"To kill Esposito," Gino said.

Maeve gave an unladylike snort of derision.

"Let's think this through," Sarah said. "Would a sheltered young woman, raised in a respectable home to be a lady, really go out into the city, late at night, all alone, to murder a man whom she knew to be a gangster who might be capable of anything?"

"A man who had kidnapped her and raped her over a period of days?" Maeve added. "Even when I was suggesting it to McWilliam, I didn't really believe it."

"But she might've been with him because she wanted to be," Gino reminded them.

"Even if she was, she'd already left him for some reason," Maeve said.

"And she was very upset," Sarah reminded them. "I saw that myself. I just can't picture her going back to confront him or something. What would be the reason?"

"To kill him," Gino pointed out reasonably.

"And that brings us back to explaining how a gently bred

young lady would decide to murder a gangster who terrifies most of the people in Italian Harlem," Maeve said.

"Which means," Malloy reminded them all, "that if McWilliam is confessing to protect Jane Harding, he's making a very unnecessary sacrifice."

"And the real killer is still going free," Sarah added.

"But maybe Maeve is wrong, and McWilliam really did kill Esposito," Gino said.

"I'd feel a lot better if he did," Maeve said. "But even if he did, why on earth would he kill *Mrs.* Esposito?"

"So I guess I'm going down to the Tombs tomorrow to pay him a visit," Malloy said.

Before he could go to the Tombs the next morning, however, Frank had to go uptown to see Unger, the coroner who was doing Mrs. Esposito's autopsy. Frank figured he'd had enough time by now to run whatever tests he needed to run to find out if she'd been poisoned.

Unger's office was in a storefront on 99th Street. The place was as dismal and depressing and smelly as one would expect of a place that processed dead bodies. Unger came out into the tiny front office at the sound of the bell over the door. He wore a large rubber apron, dark with stains, and was wiping his hands on a rag that was even dirtier than he was.

"Oh, it's you," he said by way of greeting.

"Did you find anything?"

Unger sighed, and Frank's expectations dropped accordingly. "Arsenic is hard to find."

"I told you about the tests—"

"Yeah, I know, but she died too quick. If it takes a long

time for somebody to die, it leaves traces. From arsenic poisoning, I mean. But she only lasted an hour, maybe two. Whoever dosed her gave her a lot."

"Then you think she really was poisoned."

"There's things to look for. Her esophagus was inflamed. That's her . . ." He gestured to his throat.

"I know, it goes to her stomach." Years of reading autopsy reports had given Frank a rudimentary knowledge of human anatomy.

"That means she ate or drank something harsh. Her stomach was pretty empty, except for some tea, and that's where I got lucky."

Frank's hopes rose once again. "Lucky?"

"It wasn't much, mind you, but just enough. It was arsenic all right."

"You're sure? You'd testify to that in court?"

"You didn't say nothing about court."

Frank gave him a look.

"All right. I can testify if it comes to that. Do you know who did it?"

"Not yet. Not for sure, anyway."

"Too bad. Her husband was a rat, but she didn't deserve this. Arsenic is a bad way to go."

THE TOMBS WAS JUST AS SQUALID AS FRANK remembered from his last visit here, a sojourn that had been mercifully brief after he was arrested for murder. The stench of mold and rot permeated the building, adding to the general air of despair. The city had announced it was going to build a new jail, but Tammany Hall was involved, so heaven only knew when it might actually be finished.

Christopher McWilliam hadn't been bailed out yet, so Frank found him in his cell, sitting on his filthy bunk and looking as despondent as a man should look locked in the Tombs for a crime he hadn't committed.

"What are you doing here, McWilliam?"

He smiled wanly. "I could ask you the same question."

"I'm visiting you, which I thought was pretty obvious. The real question is, why did you put yourself in here and why haven't you bailed yourself out?"

"Surely you've heard. I killed Esposito."

"Did you, now?"

McWilliam frowned in confusion. "Don't you believe me?"

"Let's just say I'm having a hard time of it. Why did you kill him?"

Something like alarm flickered across his face. "Because he was an evil man. He didn't deserve to live."

"Why did you go to that particular tenement to kill him?"

"What?"

"You heard me. How did you know he'd even be there?"

"I . . . I took a chance."

"All right. You took a chance, but how did you even know about that place? You said you'd never heard of it until after Esposito died, and that's not where he lived, after all."

"He . . . I heard a rumor."

"I thought you didn't listen to rumors."

"I listened to that one."

"All right, a rumor about what?"

McWilliam winced at that. "They said he was keeping a woman there."

"So you decided, for no particular reason, to go to the place where he kept his mistress and murder him right in front of her."

"She wasn't there."

"And did you know she wouldn't be there?"

"Of course I . . . Wait a minute. Why do you care about any of this? Usually when a man confesses to a murder, people just believe him."

"Some people do, and some people don't particularly care if he's guilty or not, but I do. I'm just trying to be sure."

"You can be sure."

"Can I? Because I'm worried that you might be trying to protect someone else."

"Who would I be protecting?" he scoffed with credible outrage.

"Miss Harding."

Anger flared in his bloodshot eyes and he jumped to his feet. "Do you think a lady like Jane Harding is capable of murder?"

"I think anyone is capable of murder, given the right circumstances, but I think it's unlikely she killed Esposito."

That left him gaping for a moment, but he collected himself quickly. "I'm relieved to hear it."

"So if she didn't do it, then you're a fool to take the blame if you didn't do it either."

"I would be, wouldn't I? So we must conclude that I did kill Esposito."

Frank decided to try a different approach. "All right. I guess you wouldn't say it if it wasn't true. Just one thing I don't understand. Why did you kill Mrs. Esposito?"

"What are you talking about?"

"I just spoke with the coroner this morning, the one doing the autopsy on her body. He told me she was poisoned."

McWilliam blinked in surprise. "I . . . I thought she was sick. They said she died of gastric fever."

"The symptoms of arsenic poisoning are very much the same."

McWilliam had to think about this for a long moment. "I don't know anything about it."

"I was afraid of that."

"But I did kill Esposito. That part is true. Maybe . . . maybe his wife committed suicide after he died."

"Because she was so sad, I guess." Frank pretended to consider this. "Except she was a good Catholic. She went to church every day. Catholics believe that suicides go to hell."

"Oh."

"Yes, well, maybe somebody else killed her, if you say you didn't."

"I didn't. I swear it."

"But you did kill Esposito."

"Yes."

"How did it happen? I mean, what made you go there that night?"

"I told you. I heard he had a . . . a place. I thought it would be a good chance to catch him alone."

"So you knew his mistress wouldn't be there."

McWilliam shook his head as if to clear it. "You're confusing me."

"Am I? Sorry. I was trying to help you remember. How did you know his mistress wouldn't be there?"

Pain twisted McWilliam's face. "You must know. If that girl, that Miss Smith . . . She said she works for you. If she knows, you do, too."

"Knows what?"

"About Jane. That she was the woman he was keeping

there. He kidnapped her and he . . . he *used* her." McWilliam might have been willing to marry Jane in spite of her despoiling, but he wasn't willing to forgive her rapist.

"So she told you what happened to her."

"Yes. She was so ashamed. She thought I couldn't possibly love her anymore, and that's why she left the settlement house. She'd escaped him, but she would never be able to escape what he'd done to her."

That did make sense, and it did give McWilliam an excellent reason to kill Esposito. Frank just had to be sure. "But you couldn't have gone there intending to kill him."

"Why not?" He seemed genuinely baffled.

"Because . . . How did you intend to kill him? With your bare hands?"

"I . . . I hadn't thought about it."

"Because you couldn't count on finding a weapon at the apartment, and you didn't take a weapon with you, did you?"

"I told you, I hadn't planned."

"How did it happen, then?"

"What do you mean?"

"How did you come to kill him? Did you knock on the door and he just let you in?"

"He didn't know it was me. He opened the door and I forced my way inside."

"And then what?"

"Then I told him what I thought of him, what an evil man he was and how he didn't deserve to live."

"And he just stood there and listened?"

"Yes, he did. It made me furious, and when I thought of what he'd done to Jane, I . . . And then I saw the knife."

"Where was it?"

"What do you mean?"

"You said you saw it. Where was it?"

"It was . . . on the table. I picked it up and stabbed him."

"How did you do it? Show me."

"Show you what?"

"How you did it. Pretend you're holding the knife and show me how you did it."

"I . . ." He looked at his hands for a moment, then closed his right one into a fist, holding the imaginary knife. "Like this." He raised his arm and pretended to stab Frank in the chest.

"Thank you, Mr. McWilliam. That was very informative."

"I can't imagine how."

Frank just smiled. "Now tell me why you haven't bailed yourself out of jail yet."

"I . . . I didn't think I deserved to be out of jail."

"Do you have any money? I know they don't pay you much at the settlement house. What I mean is, can you afford to pay your bail?"

"I . . . I suppose."

"What about your family? Could they help you?"

He winced. "I haven't told them yet."

"They'll find out, Mr. McWilliam. They'll have to live with the shame of having a son who is a murderer."

His face twisted in pain. "I didn't think of that."

"Well, think of it. I'll speak to an attorney I know, and if you need help paying your bail, let me know." He handed McWilliam his card and left him gaping in surprise.

WHEN HE GOT BACK HOME, FRANK FOUND GINO IN THE garage, working on the motorcar. Frank wondered, not for the first time, if the machine really needed so much attention or if Gino just enjoyed taking it apart and putting it back together.

"How is McWillliam doing?" Gino asked when he saw Frank in the doorway.

"Not well. He didn't think he deserved to get bailed out, but I went to Nicholson's office and they said they'd take care of it."

"They probably won't be too happy to have a confessed killer back at the settlement house."

"I'm sure you're right, but after talking to him, I agree with Maeve. I don't think he did it either."

"Why not? If he knew what Esposito had done to Jane . . ."

"He did. He admitted it, but . . . You saw Esposito's body. Where was he stabbed?"

"In the stomach." Gino laid down the part he'd been inserting into the engine and demonstrated being stabbed in the soft part of his upper abdomen, just below the ribs.

"That's what I thought, but that's not what McWilliam said. He claims he stabbed Esposito like this." Frank demonstrated an overhand thrust. "I didn't think to ask if they'd done an autopsy, but I'm guessing the knife hit that big vein that runs down from the heart. I forget what they call it. I've seen people stabbed like that before, though. You don't last long if that vein gets cut."

Gino nodded. "What did he say about Mrs. Esposito?"

"That he didn't kill her. He didn't even know she was murdered."

"That's interesting."

"Yes, it is. If the same person who killed Esposito didn't kill his wife, then who did and why?"

"And why did they kill his wife at all? She must've known something or seen something when she went to the flat the night Esposito was killed."

Frank sighed. "Too bad she didn't tell Sarah about it when she had the chance. But at least we know she was definitely murdered. That coroner said she was poisoned, and you don't serve yourself tea in two cups and make it look like you had a guest if you're going to kill yourself."

"Do we think she would have invited Balducci or one of those other thugs in for tea?"

"I doubt it, and besides, Balducci doesn't seem like the type to use poison. Why wouldn't he just shoot her or stab her or choke her?"

"But why would *anybody* poison her? Or kill her at all, for that matter?"

"If we can answer that question, I think we'll know who killed both of them."

SARAH WAS JUST COMING DOWN THE STAIRS WHEN MALloy came into the foyer. He'd obviously entered the house through the back door. "You're back."

"Yes, I saw the coroner and then I went to visit McWilliam at the Tombs."

"What did the coroner have to say?"

"Arsenic."

Sarah winced. "That poor woman."

"And since her maid found the tray with the tea things, I think we can be pretty sure she didn't kill herself."

"Yes, I think we can. What about McWilliam?"

"I was just telling Gino I don't think he's our killer. He didn't even know how Esposito was stabbed."

"Oh dear, that's awful. Didn't you tell him that we don't think Jane Harding could have done it?"

"I tried, but he still wouldn't budge. He seems determined to accept the blame regardless." He looked her up and down approvingly. "Where are you going?"

He'd noticed she was dressed for a formal visit. "To see Lisa Prince. She sent me a note asking me to call on her at my earliest convenience."

"Do you suppose Jane heard that McWilliam had confessed?"

"It's possible, I suppose, although I doubt Mrs. Prince hears much gossip from Italian Harlem."

"Maybe someone from the settlement house sent word to Jane."

"That could explain it. Everyone there seemed to know about their relationship, even though they thought it was a secret. It would be natural for them to think she'd want to know. But we can only guess. I'll find out for sure when I get there."

"Will you tell Jane about McWilliam if she doesn't already know?"

"Of course. I also intend to encourage her to visit him and assure him that she's innocent, so he doesn't have to sacrifice himself to save her."

"I hope she has better luck than I did."

LISA PRINCE WAS WAITING FOR SARAH IN HER PARLOR and she welcomed her warmly. Sarah was a little surprised to see that she was alone. She'd been sure the invitation to visit had been made on Jane's behalf.

"Thank you for coming, Mrs. Malloy," Mrs. Prince said when she had instructed her maid to bring them tea.

"I was glad for the invitation, although I'm surprised not to see Miss Harding. Is she still with you?"

"Yes, she is."

When she didn't offer anything else, Sarah asked, "Has she had any news from the settlement house?"

"Not that I know of. Has there been some?"

"Yes, although I'm afraid it isn't very good news."

A worried frown marred Mrs. Prince's lovely face. "Will it be upsetting, do you think?"

Sarah really had no idea, so she said, "It might be."

"You will think me terribly inhospitable, but Jane is still, well, not exactly good company, although she still hasn't done anything that would justify putting her out. Joe is rapidly losing patience with her, I'm afraid. I've thought about writing to her parents, but she hasn't even told them that she left the settlement yet, so that feels a bit like tattling."

"I can see your dilemma. Hasn't she said anything about her future plans?"

"No, she hasn't. At least she's started going out, although not on actual visits. She only goes for walks in the park and shopping trips where she doesn't buy anything. I know she doesn't have a lot of spending money, but I'd be happy to supply her with whatever she might need."

"That's very generous of you."

Mrs. Prince waved away the compliment. "This news you have for Jane, may I ask what it is?"

Sarah hesitated, not exactly sure how to approach the subject, but Mrs. Prince misunderstood her hesitation.

"I'm not asking you to betray her confidence, of course. If it's some kind of secret that I shouldn't know, then by all means, don't tell me, but . . . Well, Jane can be rather volatile, and if it's something that will upset her, perhaps it would be better if she didn't know at all."

"I'm actually not sure how she will take this news, Mrs. Prince. Perhaps I really should tell you first so you can be the judge."

Lisa Prince squared her shoulders, as if bracing for a blow. "All right."

"You'll remember when I was here before, I told you that the man who was the head of the Black Hand, the gang that was kidnapping people, had been killed."

"Yes, I remember it very well. You and Jane were trying to decide who might have killed him. You thought his wife might have done it, or maybe it was Jane who thought that."

"Yes, we did think that, but . . . Well, his wife is dead now, too."

"Dead? How did that happen?"

"Someone poisoned her."

Mrs. Prince gasped. "Poisoned! How awful."

"It is awful, and now we don't think she killed her husband at all. We suspect that she may have figured out who did kill him and that person decided to make sure she never told anyone else."

"And that's what you wanted to tell Jane?"

"No, not at all. What I need to tell Jane is that Christopher McWilliam has confessed to killing Nunzio Esposito, the man who was the leader of the Black Hand."

"Christopher?" she echoed, horrified. "Why on earth would he do a thing like that?"

"That's just it. We don't think he did."

"Who doesn't think so?"

"My husband and his partner and I."

"But not the police?"

"The police tend to believe people when they confess to murder."

"I suppose they would. I really don't know much about these things, I'm happy to say."

Sarah tried a reassuring smile. "There's no reason why you should, and I sincerely hope you never have to learn more. In any case, we are very much afraid that Mr. McWilliam suspects that Jane Harding is the one who killed Esposito."

"Jane?" she echoed, only this time she didn't seem at all shocked or horrified. "Why would Jane have killed him? Or anyone, for that matter?"

"Because Esposito is the man who, uh, had Miss Harding kidnapped." Which was all Lisa Prince really needed to know about that terrible episode.

Mrs. Prince considered this. "I can see why Jane might have had a reason to hate this man, but . . . Why would Christopher think she was the one who killed him?"

"I don't really know, and quite frankly, we aren't absolutely sure that is why he confessed, but we are very sure he is innocent, and Miss Harding is the only person we can imagine him making such a sacrifice for."

Before Mrs. Prince could react, a knock at the door told them the maid had arrived with their tea. Mrs. Prince allowed the girl to pour and serve it while she was obviously still trying to make sense of all Sarah had told her.

When the maid had finally left, she drew a deep breath,

as if gathering her courage. "Let me guess, you want to tell Jane all of this and ask her to convince Christopher he doesn't have to make this terrible sacrifice for her."

Sarah frowned. "I have a feeling you don't think this is a very good idea, Mrs. Prince."

Lisa Prince leaned back in her chair and bit her lip. Obviously, she had something important to say, and just as obviously, she was loath to say it.

"Perhaps if you tell me the reason you wanted me to call on you today, that would help," Sarah said.

Sarah had learned from Malloy that the best thing to do, when someone was reluctant to speak, was to simply wait. People hated silence and they would often betray even the strictest confidences to fill it. So she waited, although it seemed to take forever for Mrs. Prince to make up her mind.

Finally, she surrendered. "When you were here before, you told Jane that this woman, this gangster's wife . . . What was her name?"

"Mrs. Esposito."

"That she had a diamond of some kind."

"I think I said a diamond ring, although that was a guess."

"And that her husband had taken it and given it to his . . . to some woman."

"Mrs. Esposito apparently believed he was going to give it to her, yes."

Lisa Prince drew another breath, although this one was unsteady. Plainly, she hated this. She hated all of it, particularly what she was going to say next, and Sarah tried to set her face so she wouldn't react too strongly to whatever it was and frighten her.

"Mrs. Malloy, I think I told you that Jane's family was never well-to-do and that she never had nice things."

"Yes, you did tell me that."

"You will understand my surprise then, when my maid informed me that Jane has secreted in her dresser a diamond necklace."

XIII

Sarah's mind was racing. What did this mean? What did it prove? A diamond necklace. No wonder Olympia Esposito had been so incensed over its loss. Something like that would indeed provide a woman with security if she should be left widowed. She could even sell off the diamonds one by one, if it came to that.

But what did it mean that Jane had it? Where and when had she gotten it? Did Esposito give it to her? Did she take it from him after he was dead? But how would she have done that if she really was hiding away in her room at the settlement house all night?

Even more disturbing was the question of *why* she had it. If Esposito had given it to her, did that mean that he thought of her as his mistress and not as his captive? A man might delude himself that a woman he ravished had welcomed his attentions, but would a man as worldly as

Esposito be deluded enough to believe she loved him? Enough to believe she was going to stay with him voluntarily? Enough to give her something so valuable?

None of this made sense.

"Could this necklace be the thing this man's wife said he took from her?" Lisa Prince asked when Sarah didn't respond.

"I think it's very likely." What should she do now? Ask more questions, of course, but what would Malloy want to know? Nothing that Sarah felt comfortable asking Jane Harding outright, for fear of how she might react. But could she get her to admit something accidentally? Perhaps that was the best course for now. "Mrs. Prince, you mustn't say anything to Jane about the necklace."

"I wouldn't know what to say. I didn't want her to think the maid was going through her things. She was just putting away the underclothes she had washed for Jane. When she saw it, she thought she should tell me, since something so valuable should be locked up."

"I understand completely, and I also understand that you don't want to upset Jane. That's why you shouldn't mention it, and tell your maid not to mention it either."

"But where did she get it? I mean, obviously from that Italian woman or her husband but . . ."

"Don't try to figure it out. Don't worry about it at all. I'll speak to my husband and we'll decide what to do."

"I wish I *could* stop worrying. I don't think I want Jane in my house anymore, if she was involved with this awful man."

"Remember she was kidnapped. She was an innocent victim," Sarah tried.

"Kidnapped people don't receive diamond necklaces, Mrs. Malloy."

Which was only too true. How could she handle this without revealing to Jane that they knew about the necklace? Because if Jane was volatile, that would certainly set her off, and if Jane wasn't an innocent victim, she might be a killer.

"I think I know how to handle this, Mrs. Prince. I just need for you to sit there looking concerned and not saying anything. Whatever you do, don't mention the necklace, now or after I leave."

"I understand. What are you going to do?"

Sarah told her and Mrs. Prince seemed somewhat relieved. When Sarah had answered all of her questions, she sent for Jane.

"You're like a bad penny, aren't you?" Jane said when she saw Sarah.

"Jane, is that any way to treat a guest?" Lisa Prince chastened her.

"She's your guest, not mine. If you've come to ask me more questions, I haven't remembered anything else."

"Please sit down, Jane," Mrs. Prince said. "Mrs. Malloy has some news for you."

"I hope it's good news," Jane said, taking a seat as far from the other two women as she could.

"I'm afraid it isn't," Sarah said. "You see, Mr. McWilliam has confessed to killing Nunzio Esposito."

As Sarah had expected, Jane was genuinely surprised. "He has?"

"Yes. He went to the police and they have charged him with the murder. He is locked up in the Tombs."

"The *tombs*? He's not dead, is he?"

Sarah had forgotten Jane wasn't a native New Yorker. "No, that's what we call the city jail. Because . . . Well, it doesn't matter. We're hoping he can be released on bail until we can get everything straightened out."

"What do you need to get straightened out?"

"The fact that Mr. McWilliam is innocent. We are very certain that he didn't kill Mr. Esposito."

Jane considered this for a moment and her eyes narrowed. "Why would he say he did, then?"

"That really is difficult to understand, isn't it? But knowing Mr. McWilliam as you do, I'm sure you can believe that he might have confessed in order to protect someone whom he loves very much."

Jane didn't need any more information than that. "Do you think Christopher is protecting *me*?" she scoffed. "Does he think *I* killed that man?"

"We don't know what he thinks because he won't admit it, but as strange as it sounds, we think he does believe he is protecting you."

Several emotions flickered across her face, fear and alarm and near panic, but she finally settled on anger. "That's ridiculous."

"Of course it is," Sarah agreed, quite reasonably. "But you can see how tragic this is for Mr. McWilliam if he confesses to a murder he didn't commit in order to keep you from being punished for a murder you didn't commit either."

If Sarah had expected to see empathy from Jane Harding, she was disappointed. "Christopher is a fool, and a stupid fool at that."

"And yet he's also a good man who loves you."

Jane sighed. "I suppose you expect me to do something, but I'm certainly not going to confess to killing that man just to save Christopher."

"I doubt the police would believe you in any case," Sarah

said with more truth than she wanted to admit. "But if you can convince Mr. McWilliam that you are innocent, then he will no longer feel the need to protect you."

Plainly, Jane had no enthusiasm for this suggestion at all. "How am I supposed to do that? You can't expect me to go visit him in this tombs place, I hope."

"As I said, we are trying to get him out on bail. Perhaps he could call on you here and—"

"Heavens no," Jane said with feigned horror. "We can't have an accused murderer paying calls at my respectable cousin's house. What would people say?"

"No one would know he's an accused murderer, Jane," Mrs. Prince said gently, breaking her promise not to speak.

"Well, I won't see him here," Jane insisted. "He's such a stupid man, he deserves to be locked up. I'm not sure I can forgive him for thinking I'm a murderer either."

"But Jane, he'll go to prison. He might even be executed," Mrs. Prince argued.

"It's his own fault, isn't it? No one asked him to do such a stupid thing."

"But Miss Harding," Sarah said, "do you really want *any-one* thinking you're a murderer?"

"It's such a simple thing, Jane," Mrs. Prince said. "And people who know Christopher will find it hard to believe he could do such a thing. They may guess his motives just as Mrs. Malloy and her husband did and blame you."

Jane turned her anger on her cousin. "And if they don't guess, I'm sure you'll be happy to tell them, Lisa."

"Of course I wouldn't," Mrs. Prince insisted, but Jane had already jumped to her feet.

"All right," she said furiously. "I'll tell him, if it will even do any good, but I'm not going to the jail and he's not coming here. Arrange something suitable, Mrs. Malloy, and let me know. If I'm still feeling charitable by then, I'll speak to him."

With that, she turned and left the room, slamming the door behind her.

"I see what you mean about her being volatile," Sarah said.

Mrs. Prince was rubbing her head. "When I tell Joe all this, he'll want her gone, I know, and I can't keep it from him."

"No, you can't, and I won't blame him at all. I'll try to arrange for her to meet with Mr. McWilliam, but now I'm not even sure she will do it when the time comes."

"I can't understand what's gotten into her. Why would she refuse to save Christopher from making such a terrible mistake?"

Should she tell Mrs. Prince what she was now almost positive was true? That Jane Harding had not been an innocent victim and that she might even be a killer? But no, knowing that would only put Mrs. Prince in danger. "You should probably write to her parents at once and ask them to take her home."

"But if she needs to meet with Christopher—"

"He can go to Saratoga, if necessary. You don't need to feel guilty about sending her home. You've done far more than anyone could expect."

"I suppose you're right."

"I'm sorry to have gotten you involved in all this. I never would have delivered that note in the first place if I'd had any idea—"

"Please, don't blame yourself, Mrs. Malloy. Jane would simply have mailed the note and I would still have felt obligated to take her in."

"Don't wait," Sarah said. "Write the letter to Jane's parents as soon as I'm gone. That way you can tell your husband you've already taken steps to be rid of her."

"Yes, that should placate him. Quite frankly, we'll both be glad when she's gone."

Sarah couldn't help thinking they would also both be safer.

WHEN SARAH RETURNED HOME, MALLOY HAD ALREADY gone to the office, and for the first time in a week, Gino went with him. With Christopher McWilliam charged with killing Esposito, the Black Hand couldn't possibly be interested in him anymore. The children had come home from school, so she spent the rest of the afternoon with them. After her encounter with Jane Harding and realizing all that it meant, she needed to spend some time with people who were still truly innocent.

Brian, Malloy's son from his first wife and Sarah's son by adoption, was signing so quickly now that Sarah could hardly keep up. Thank heaven Catherine could understand most of what he said and could help Sarah if she missed something. Her own signing skills were still rudimentary, but Brian was patient and would show her if she didn't know the sign for something.

"Nobody at Miss Spence's School knows how to sign except me," Catherine informed her. She was also signing for Brian's sake, and from his smile, Sarah knew this was something they had previously discussed.

"Maybe you could teach them," Sarah said.

Catherine grinned mischievously. "I'm thinking about

starting a secret club. We could sign to each other and nobody else would know what we are talking about."

"Would that be nice to the other girls?"

Catherine gave this some thought. "They could learn if they wanted."

"Maybe you could teach all the girls," Sarah suggested.

Catherine smiled beatifically. "That would be wonderful. Then the teachers wouldn't know what we were saying!"

SARAH HAD PUT OFF TELLING ANYONE WHAT SHE HAD learned at Lisa Prince's house until they could speak uninterrupted. After the children were in bed, the adults gathered in the parlor, as usual. Gino had already told them he was planning to move back home the next day, since he probably wasn't in danger anymore, so this would be their last evening together like this. Sarah deeply regretted having to ruin it.

"What did Mrs. Prince want to see you about?" Malloy asked when they had taken their places around the cold fireplace. The electric lights cast a warm glow in the twilight gloom, making the room she had furnished so carefully seem even cozier.

"I actually thought that perhaps Jane Harding was the one who wanted to see me, to ask me about Christopher McWilliam's arrest, but she wasn't even in the room when I arrived. I asked Mrs. Prince if Jane had received any word from the settlement house, and she had not, so I had to tell her about McWilliam. She was shocked, as you can imagine. She has known Mr. McWilliam for most of her life, I gather, and she couldn't believe him guilty of murder."

"That makes several of us," Malloy said.

"Did she agree that McWilliam might be protecting Jane?" Maeve asked.

"She did think it likely, although she was as reluctant to believe Jane could be guilty as we were."

"*Were?*" Malloy knew her too well to miss that hint.

"Yes. Mrs. Prince had asked me to come because she had something very important to tell me. You see, her maid discovered that Jane is hiding something in her room."

"A bloody butcher knife?" Maeve guessed slyly.

"No," Gino said. "She left that sticking out of Esposito's stomach."

"Children, behave," Mrs. Malloy snapped from her corner, reminding them she was there.

Maeve and Gino exchanged a chagrined glance and turned back to Sarah expectantly.

"Jane Harding is hiding a diamond necklace in her room."

That elicited just as much shock as Sarah had felt herself this afternoon.

"It's a *necklace*," Maeve said. "No wonder the wife was so mad!"

"How did she get it?" Gino wanted to know. "Did Esposito give it to her after all?"

Maeve gave him a pitying look. "Men can be pretty stupid where women are concerned, but I can't imagine a man giving such an extravagant gift to a woman in hopes that she'd forget he'd kidnapped and abused her."

"I can't either, Maeve," Malloy said with an approving nod.

"Think about it," Sarah said. "To whom does a man give something as expensive as a diamond necklace?"

"To his wife," Gino said, "because we know he did."

"Or to his mistress," Maeve added, "in appreciation for her, uh, favors."

"Not to win her," Malloy said, "but because he has already won her."

"And perhaps in Jane's case, in order to keep her," Sarah said. "Jane has spent her entire life being jealous of rich girls who had pretty things that she could never have."

"That still doesn't mean she killed Esposito, though," Gino reminded them. "She was at the settlement house that night. Besides, why would she kill a man who had given her a diamond necklace? He would probably give her lots of other nice things as well."

"Gino's right," Maeve said. "Also don't forget, she'd left him by then, of her own accord."

Sarah sighed. "You didn't see Jane's reaction when I told her McWilliam had confessed, though. She was surprised but not nearly as dismayed as I had expected when I suggested that he might believe he was protecting her. In fact, she didn't seem eager at all to convince him to recant his confession if he had made it on her behalf."

"Maybe she's just a selfish witch who enjoys seeing other people suffer," Maeve suggested.

"Or maybe she's mad because she thinks he really did kill Esposito and she was still hoping to get more nice things from him," Gino said.

"And maybe we need to find out exactly what McWilliam knows, and why he really confessed to the murder," Malloy mused.

"I thought we decided he did it to protect Jane," Gino said.

"That's what we *decided*, but what convinced him she needed protection?" Malloy asked.

"I did," Maeve said. "Remember, I was telling him all the reasons why she might have done it."

"But all those reasons didn't convince *us* that she did it," Gino said.

"No, they didn't," Malloy said, "so I think I need to pay Mr. McWilliam another visit to see if he has a reason we don't know about."

FRANK HAD TO MAKE SOME TELEPHONE CALLS THE NEXT morning to locate Christopher McWilliam. Nicholson's office informed him that they had successfully bailed him out last evening, but they had no idea where he had gone. Someone at the settlement had no knowledge of McWilliam's whereabouts either, but promised to get back to him. After waiting an hour, Frank tried again. This time he was informed tersely that McWilliam was there but would be leaving soon. Apparently, the settlement house staff didn't want him there, as Frank and his crew had theorized.

Gino was only too happy to drive Frank up to Italian Harlem. They arrived just as McWilliam was leaving the building with his suitcase in hand.

"Where are you off to, McWilliam?" Frank called.

McWilliam did not seem happy to see them. "None of your business."

"Make it my business and we'll give you a lift."

McWilliam stood there for a long moment, obviously undecided.

"I may have some good news for you," Frank tried. "Come along. What have you got to lose?"

Plainly, he realized he had nothing left to lose and trudged over to the motorcar. Gino hopped out and opened the door to the back seat, which was a good foot higher than the front seat and had its own doors. McWilliam hefted his suitcase into it and climbed in without giving Gino so much as a glance.

"Where are we going?" Frank asked amiably.

"I have no idea," McWilliam said grimly.

"Let's take him home," Frank told Gino.

"I can't go home. My parents know nothing of this," McWilliam protested.

"I meant *my* home," Frank said. "We can talk privately there."

McWilliam offered no word of protest, so Gino drove on.

"Why are you doing this?" McWilliam shouted from the back seat after a while. Conversing in the motorcar over the noise of the engine was challenging.

"Because I'm a nosey do-gooder," Frank said. "Like you."

McWilliam had nothing else to say, so they made the trip back to Greenwich Village in silence.

Frank and Gino escorted McWilliam into the house and Sarah came to meet them. Maeve, it appeared, had gone on to the office after taking Catherine to school.

"Mr. McWilliam was no longer welcome at the settlement house," Frank explained.

"I'm sorry to intrude, Mrs. Malloy, but your husband insisted," McWilliam said with little grace.

"I'm sure he did. You'll stay for luncheon, of course. I'll tell my cook and I'll have some lemonade brought in for you. You must be parched." After giving Frank a knowing glance, Sarah retreated, leaving them to it.

Frank led McWilliam into the parlor, where he sank wearily into the chair Frank indicated. The man looked even worse today than he had in the Tombs, even though his clothes were now clean and pressed. His face was gray and his eyes sunken.

They waited for Hattie, the maid, to bring in the lemonade, and then Frank and Gino took their seats. Frank said, "McWilliam, my partner and I are baffled by your behavior."

"Why should you be?" he asked, apparently confused.

"Because we know you didn't kill Esposito, so naturally we can't understand why you are claiming that you did."

"What makes you think I didn't kill him?"

"For one thing, because people who know you can't imagine you doing such a thing, but mostly because you don't even know how he was killed."

"He was stabbed. I told you, I stabbed him."

"But the way you told me you stabbed him is not the way he was killed. I can understand," Frank hurried on when McWilliam would have argued, "that you hated Esposito after what he did to Miss Harding. You must have been filled with rage by what she told you."

"I was!"

"Of course you were. Any man would be. But you didn't go out that night, full of hate, and attack an unarmed man and murder him, did you?"

"Yes, I did. I confessed! Why would I say I did if I didn't?"

"Because you're protecting Miss Harding."

McWilliam stiffened in his chair. "That's . . . ridiculous."

"Is it? My assistant, Miss Smith, believes that she convinced you that Miss Harding was the real killer and that's why you decided to confess instead."

"No, I . . . That's not why," he protested weakly.

"Then why?"

"I just . . . When Miss Smith said those things about

Jane, I realized she might be blamed, so I decided I had to admit I had done it."

"But Miss Harding was locked in her room at the settlement house that night. No one even thought she could have done it. Miss Smith was just baiting you."

Frank waited, but McWilliam had nothing to say to that. Nothing at all. His desperate glance darted from him to Gino and back again.

"But you know something else, don't you? Something we don't," Gino said. The boy was learning. "You must, because *we* didn't really think she could have done it. Why would a respectable young lady leave the safety of the settlement house and return to the place where she had been held and assaulted to face the very man who had assaulted her?"

"You're right, she wouldn't," McWilliam said with false confidence.

"And yet she did go back there," Frank guessed. "She went back there and you knew it somehow."

"No, that's crazy," he tried.

"It's not crazy at all," Frank said. "Well, maybe her going back there seemed crazy to you, but you knew she did. That's why you confessed, because you knew she did. How did you know she went back there?"

"I didn't, I swear!" he cried, but he wasn't very convincing.

"Did you see her somehow?" Gino asked. "Did you see her leaving the settlement house?"

"Of course he did," Frank said. "His desk overlooks the street. He would've been sitting there late that night, trying to work because he couldn't sleep. He was still too upset after his conversation with Miss Harding and what she'd told him."

"No," he protested weakly, but all the color had drained from his face.

"What did you think when you saw her leaving?" Frank asked brutally. "Did you know where she was going?"

"I thought she was running away," he cried in despair. "She had a bag with her, a Gladstone bag. I thought she'd packed her things and was going home."

"And you just let her leave?" Gino scoffed.

"No, of course not! I went after her. It wasn't safe for her to be out alone that late. I tried to catch up to her, but then I realized she wasn't going to the train station. She was going the wrong way, so I just followed her."

"To protect her," Frank suggested.

He nodded. "Yes, to protect her."

"What did you think when she went into that tenement?" Gino asked.

"I thought she must know someone there, a friend she could stay with."

"And did you follow her in?" Frank asked.

"Of course. I had to be sure she was safe. What if her friend wasn't home? What if they turned her away?"

"And did you hear anything? Or see anything?"

His face twisted in anguish.

"You did, didn't you?" Gino said. "What was it? An argument?"

"Just Jane's voice. Not the words, but she was . . . angry."

Gino cast Frank a look of disgust. "None of the neighbors would admit to me that they heard anything that night."

"Didn't you go up to see what was happening?" Frank asked McWilliam.

"I started to, but then Jane came running out of the flat.

I was still downstairs and she ran right past me. She didn't even see me in the dark."

He covered his face with both hands, and they waited while he composed himself.

"Did you go upstairs to see what had happened?" Frank asked as gently as he could.

"No, why should I? All I knew was Jane had argued with someone and left. I went after her. I told you, it wasn't safe for her, alone in the streets. I saw that she made it back to the settlement house. I had no idea what had happened at that flat until the next day."

"But you suspected Jane was the one who had stabbed Esposito," Gino guessed.

"I . . . I knew it was *possible*, but no one else knew Jane had been there. If the police found out, they'd believe she killed him, and I didn't think she should be blamed for it, not after what he'd done to her. He deserved that and more, so I didn't tell anyone."

"And then Maeve let you know that we suspected her," Gino said.

Now McWilliam was desperate in a different way, desperate to make them understand what he had to do. "I couldn't let her be accused. It would ruin her life if it became known what had happened to her, even if she wasn't prosecuted for murder. The shame of it, she would never be able to hold her head up again. I couldn't allow it."

"So you decided to sacrifice yourself," Gino said. His tone said how foolish he thought that decision had been.

"And I haven't changed my mind. If you tell anyone what I said today, I'll call you a liar."

The three men sat in silence while McWilliam thought he had settled everything, Gino waited to see how Frank would convince him otherwise, and Frank chose his next words very carefully.

"Mr. McWilliam, did you know that Esposito had given Jane a diamond necklace?" Frank asked.

From the look on his face, he hadn't. "Who told you that?" he demanded.

"It doesn't matter. He did, and we know she still has it. Men don't give diamonds to women they kidnap."

"What are you saying? I won't sit here and listen to you insult Miss Harding."

"You're right, it's not easy to hear, is it?"

"And I won't hear it. It's a vicious lie."

"Her cousin Lisa told my wife about the necklace."

McWilliam shook his head but there was no force behind it.

"We think Miss Harding went to Esposito in the first place of her own free will," Gino said, "and that she was never kidnapped."

"But she ran away from him," McWilliam said. "She was . . . devastated. And she said . . . she told me . . ." He gestured helplessly.

"She told you what she wanted people to believe," Frank said. "We don't know what happened between them or why she left him. Lovers' quarrel, maybe."

"Don't say that!"

Frank shrugged in apology. "We also don't know why she went back the next night, but she wouldn't have gone back to a man she feared, would she?"

McWilliam shook his head again, this time in despair.

"Mr. McWilliam," Frank said as firmly as he could, "you need to reconsider this noble gesture you are making on

Miss Harding's behalf, because it is entirely possible that she doesn't deserve it."

Sarah, who had probably been listening and must have realized McWilliam was at the end of his tether, chose this moment to appear in the doorway and invite them in to lunch.

McWilliam followed them meekly and ate hardly a bite. Conversation was limited to the weather and the upcoming Republican National Convention in Philadelphia. McWilliam apparently had no opinion on who should be nominated and no one pressed him. President McKinley would certainly be the party's choice for a second term, but the current vice president had died recently and rather unexpectedly, so speculation was running high about who would be chosen for that position. Frank and Gino and even Sarah managed to make the discussion last through the end of the meal.

"Thank you for your hospitality, Mrs. Malloy," McWilliam said as they rose from the table. "I shouldn't impose on you any longer, however."

"But where will you go, Mr. McWilliam?" Sarah said with obvious concern. She probably really did care, too.

"I . . . I'm sure I can find a hotel."

"You aren't in any condition to be on your own. Why don't you stay with us for a day or two, until you've had time to make some plans?"

"I couldn't possibly . . ."

"Of course you can. Gino has been staying with us for a week, and he's decided to move back home today. You can have the room he's been using. In fact, Gino, why don't you take him up there now. He looks like he could use some rest.

He's been through quite a lot the past few days. Just make yourself comfortable, Mr. McWilliam. We'll call you when it's time for dinner."

Before he could protest, Gino had collected McWilliam's suitcase from the front hall and started up the stairs. It only took a little more encouragement for him to follow.

"That poor man," Sarah said when they were out of sight.

"He has a lot to consider, but I think we convinced him he's been wrong about Jane Harding."

"Do you think so? I'm just worried he'll be so devastated by her betrayal that he won't even want to clear his name. Maybe the thought of going to prison is appealing to him right now."

"I suppose I should mention that he might end up in the electric chair instead," Frank said, only half joking. "That would probably convince him."

"What do we do about the charges against him, though? Even if we convince Mr. McWilliam to tell the truth, that he saw Jane leave the settlement house and followed her to Pleasant Avenue, he didn't actually see her kill Esposito. He doesn't know for sure that Esposito was dead when she left, and we don't have any proof she was even there except for his word. All she has to do is deny the whole thing and say he's lying to protect himself."

"You're right, it doesn't seem likely that the district attorney will drop the charges against him just because he changed his story. And what about Mrs. Esposito? Did Jane kill her, too? And why?"

"At least Jane is someone Mrs. Esposito might have admitted to her home," Sarah said with a frown.

"And served tea to," Frank added.

"And poison is a woman's weapon, as they say."

"I don't know. If we could only get Jane to confess . . ."

"She did agree to speak with Mr. McWilliam, or at least I think she did. Maybe if he tells her he followed her that night, she'll be frightened and admit what she did."

"Or at least tell us what really happened," Frank said. "It's worth a try, I suppose."

"She said she wouldn't see him if he went to the Princes' home, though, and she won't go back to the settlement house, but maybe she'll come here."

"If we tell McWilliam that she's coming here to see him, he'll probably stay."

"I'll send Lisa Prince a telegram. This isn't something I want to arrange on the telephone."

Frank nodded. "Good. Maybe when McWilliam sees Jane again, knowing what he now knows, he'll come to his senses."

XIV

Gino had brought down his own bag after showing McWilliam to his room, and he decided to use the motorcar to return to his parents' house that afternoon and inform them he was moving back in.

"I hope they haven't rented out my bed while I was gone," he joked.

"I'm sure your mother will be thrilled to have you back," Sarah said, "although it will be strange not having you here with us all the time."

"I know," he agreed. "I'll miss Maeve and her, uh, nightly lectures."

"She'll miss giving them to you, I'm sure," Sarah said knowingly.

Malloy decided to go along with Gino since there was nothing more to be done on the case until they heard back from Mrs. Prince. They sent Sarah's telegram to Lisa Prince on the way.

Sarah stayed home in case Mr. McWilliam needed anything or decided again that he should leave and needed to be talked out of it once more. But she heard nothing from him. She hoped he was sleeping or at least resting. He looked as if he hadn't done much of either recently.

After a quiet afternoon, Maeve returned with Catherine, and Mrs. Malloy returned with Brian.

"I'm afraid Gino is going home," Sarah told them, signing the words for Brian's benefit. Everyone groaned in disappointment except Maeve, who just frowned. "He and Papa took Gino's things over in the motorcar, but they'll be back for supper. And we have a new guest."

"Who is it?" Maeve demanded in amazement.

"Mr. McWilliam," Sarah replied, enjoying her and Mother Malloy's surprise. "He, uh, had to leave the settlement house and didn't really have anywhere else to go."

"Won't his parents take him in?" Mother Malloy asked with obvious disapproval.

Sarah smiled, so the children wouldn't be alarmed. "They don't yet know about his current situation, so Malloy invited him to stay with us for a few days, until he can make other arrangements."

"Or until we can clear up his *current situation*," Maeve said with a grin. "Come along and let's get a snack," she added to the children, making the sign for "cookie."

They were only too happy to race her to the kitchen.

"I suppose you'll want me to watch the children while you talk to Maeve," Mother Malloy said.

"If you don't mind," Sarah said. "There are some new

developments she should know about with Mr. McWilliam in the house."

"Did that hussy kill the gangster after all?"

"It's looking more and more likely, although we may never prove it."

"That would be a shame."

It certainly would, if Mr. McWilliam ended up taking the blame.

Mother Malloy removed her hat and gloves and followed the children into the kitchen. A few minutes later Maeve returned.

"What on earth happened?"

"Malloy found out Mr. McWilliam had gotten out on bail and returned to the settlement, so they . . . Well, it's a long story. Come into the parlor where the children can't hear us."

They settled in and Sarah told her everything she could remember about their conversation with McWilliam.

"Why didn't he go up to the flat?" Maeve lamented. "If he'd seen Esposito dead, then he would've known she did it."

"And he probably would have confessed sooner and we never would have known Jane did it at all."

"And Mrs. Esposito would still be alive, although I still can't see any reason for her to be killed by anyone."

"I know. The more we learn about this, the more confusing it becomes."

They both looked up when they heard the front door open.

"We're in the parlor," Sarah called, and Malloy and Gino came in.

"I thought you went home," Maeve said to Gino as the two men took seats.

"That's a fine greeting. I did go home, but I had to bring the motor back."

She frowned at Malloy. "I thought you were going to learn how to drive that thing, too."

"I can drive it," he claimed.

"If he has to," Sarah said.

"And as long as Gino is around, I don't have to. Has Sarah told you everything we found out today?"

"I think I did," Sarah said.

"What I still don't understand is why Jane went back to the flat that night," Maeve said.

"I don't understand that either," Sarah said. "If Esposito had somehow convinced her to join him at the flat in the first place—"

"Seduced her, you mean," Maeve said.

"Yes, seduced her to come and stay with him there—"

"To become his mistress, in other words," Malloy said.

"Yes, then that explains why she was there originally, but obviously something happened that upset her and caused her to leave him. She was definitely in a state when she returned to the settlement house."

"So upset that we believed she had been kidnapped and escaped," Maeve reminded them.

"That's right," Sarah said. "So maybe she had some sort of argument with Esposito and changed her mind about him."

"Whatever happened, she returned to the settlement, probably because she didn't know where else to go," Maeve said.

"Then I went to her room and got her to open the door," Sarah said.

"And she told you she'd been kidnapped and—"

"*Wait a minute.*"

Everyone turned to Sarah in surprise.

"What is it?" Malloy asked.

"I'm trying to remember exactly what she did say."

They waited while she thought. Finally, she said, "I think I was the one who said she'd been kidnapped."

"What?" they all cried in unison.

"It's true. I just realized. She was very upset and didn't want to speak to anyone and wouldn't open her door. I thought . . . Well, we all thought she was just upset from her ordeal and too embarrassed to show her face, so I wanted to reassure her. I told her no one knew she'd been kidnapped, that Mr. McWilliam had kept it a secret to protect her reputation. I don't remember exactly what I said, but something like that, so she'd open the door and talk to me."

"So she never claimed she was kidnapped?" Gino marveled.

"Not that I remember, but she didn't contradict me either."

"Of course she didn't," Maeve said. "She'd run off with a man and she had no idea how she was going to explain her absence and then you gave her the perfect excuse."

"I certainly didn't mean to," Sarah said, "but Maeve is probably right."

"I love being right," Maeve informed them. Gino made a rude noise.

"So then what happened after you told her you knew about the kidnapping?" Malloy asked.

"She said she couldn't stay at the settlement any longer. I wasn't surprised, I have to admit, and she said she was going to ask her cousin Lisa to take her in for a few days. She asked me to mail the letter to Lisa."

"But you delivered it in person instead," Malloy said.

"That's right, so Lisa Prince went to get Jane the very next day."

"And in the meantime, she told McWilliam that she had been kidnapped and assaulted and could never marry him and she was leaving the settlement to stay with Lisa," Malloy said.

"Why would she tell him all that, though?" Gino asked. "Wasn't just being kidnapped enough?"

"I think she wanted to make sure he wouldn't want her anymore," Sarah said. "She never wanted to marry him, and this was a chance to cool his desire for her once and for all."

"Except it didn't, because he's such a good man," Maeve said. "But that still doesn't explain why she left the settlement house that night and went back to the flat."

"McWilliam thought at first that she was just going home," Gino said.

"Why did he think that?" Maeve asked.

"Because she was carrying a bag. Obviously, she'd packed up her clothes and was going someplace. He thought it was back to Saratoga Springs."

"But she was actually going back to the flat, so why did she pack a bag for that?" Maeve asked. "Did she plan to make up with Esposito and stay, so she was taking all her clothes with her this time?"

"She certainly hadn't taken anything with her the first time," Sarah said. "That's what made everyone think she'd been kidnapped."

"Even if she was going back to him, she didn't need to take her clothes with her," Malloy said.

"Why not?" Maeve asked.

"Because Esposito had bought her all new clothes."

"He had? How do you know?" Sarah asked.

"Remember when Teo and I searched the flat after Esposito died? I told you we found a bunch of women's clothes there, all expensive and *brand new*, according to Teo."

"That's right," Sarah said. "We wondered then if he'd been trying to win her over with them. Wasn't there a silver dresser set, too?"

"Yes, and one set of clothes that were old, like she'd left them behind and worn something new when she left," Malloy said.

"And Jane had that fancy new suit when she returned from her supposed kidnapping," Sarah recalled. "I'd assumed it was hers, although I'd wondered why she would have dressed so well for working in the neighborhood. So all those clothes were apparently for her."

"So if Jane had all those clothes at the flat and didn't need to take her old clothes with her from the settlement house when she went back there, why was she carrying a bag?" Gino asked.

Maeve jerked in her chair. "I know! She wasn't taking her old clothes with her. She was going to get the new clothes and bring them back with her to the settlement!"

"Of course!" Sarah cried. "Because how could a girl who loved nice things leave all those lovely clothes behind? Why didn't we think of that before?"

"Because we didn't know about the bag before," Gino said.

Even Malloy was nodding. "Teo and I even talked about how the woman might have wanted to take the rest of the clothes with her, but she must not have had anything to carry them in. But then we found an empty Gladstone bag in the flat, so we decided she must not have intended to leave for good."

"Could that have been Jane's bag that you found?" Sarah asked. "Did Mr. McWilliam mention if she still had it with her when she ran out?"

"She couldn't have," Maeve said. "I just remembered. Kate Westrop, the woman who showed me around the settlement, told me Jane threw a hissy fit the morning that Lisa Prince came to get her. Jane couldn't find her Gladstone bag to pack her things, and she ended up taking Kate's."

"There," Gino said in triumph. "That's proof that Jane went back to the flat that night."

But was it? Sarah wondered. Was it enough to prove Jane Harding killed both Esposito and his wife? "It's enough for us, but probably not for a court of law."

Before anyone could argue, someone started pounding on their front door.

"What on earth?" Sarah said, going to the parlor door. Malloy was close behind her.

Their maid had already reached it and opened it to a well-dressed man who appeared to be in a fury. "Is this the Malloy house?" he demanded.

"Mr. Prince," Sarah said, hurrying out into the entrance hall. "What on earth is wrong?"

He pushed past Hattie, stopping short when Frank stepped up beside Sarah. "Are you Malloy?"

"Yes, I am, and you must be Joe Prince," Malloy said, holding his own temper with difficulty at this rude invasion of his home.

"That's right, and I've come to tell you to leave my wife alone."

"Has something happened?" Sarah asked.

"Yes. She told me last night about your visit yesterday, Mrs. Malloy. I must say, I do not appreciate your interference in what is a sensitive family matter. Lisa is extremely upset."

"I know she is, but I urged her to write to Jane Harding's parents immediately and ask them to come and get her."

Mr. Prince made a visible effort to calm himself. "So my wife told me. She had already written the letter, which I mailed myself this morning, but then your telegram came and . . . Well, she's worried herself into a state and made herself ill, so I must ask that you stop trying to involve our family in this very sordid business."

"Did you say your wife is ill, Mr. Prince?" Sarah asked in alarm.

"Yes, she's made herself physically ill with worry and—"

"May I ask what is wrong with her? What her symptoms are?"

"That's really none of your business, Mrs. Malloy," he said stiffly, which confirmed Sarah's worst fears.

"Have you sent for a doctor?"

"No, it's just a stomach upset—"

"I must see her immediately, Mr. Prince. I'm a nurse. How did you come here?"

Her obvious alarm had alarmed him, too. "I . . . I got a cab . . ."

"Gino," she called unnecessarily, since Gino and Maeve had also come into the hall. "Bring the motor around." Gino ran out the still-opened door.

"I'm going with you," Malloy said.

"What is it?" Prince asked, truly frightened now.

"We'll explain on the way," Sarah said.

* * *

JOE PRINCE GAVE MAEVE HIS DOCTOR'S NAME SO SHE could telephone and have him go to their house at once. Sarah sat in the back seat with Joe and told him what she could over the roar of the engine. By the time they arrived at the Prince house, he was completely terrified for his wife.

Gino had barely stopped the motorcar in front of his house before Prince had thrown open the door and jumped down. By the time he had unlocked the front door, Sarah had caught up with him, and Malloy was right behind her.

Prince ran up the stairs with Sarah following. On the third floor, he reached one of the doors and pushed it open. He froze there for a moment, and Sarah could see past him into the room. Lisa was sitting up in the bed, and Jane was handing her a teacup. They had both looked up in surprise at the interruption.

"Stop!" Sarah cried. "Don't drink that!"

Joe charged into the room, around the bed, and knocked Jane to the floor.

Sarah ran to the other side of the bed and snatched the cup from Lisa's fingers.

"What in heaven's name . . . ?" she cried. "Joe, what are you doing?"

"We have to save the tea," Sarah said, carefully cradling the cup. "So it can be tested."

"Tested for what?" Lisa asked, completely bewildered.

"Arsenic," Prince said between clenched teeth as he glared down at where Jane lay on the floor, glaring up at him. "She was poisoning you."

"What?" Lisa cried, staring down in horror at Jane. "Why would she poison me?"

"I only gave her a little," Jane said, glaring back at Lisa with hate-filled eyes. "If she was sick, she'd let me stay to take care of her instead of sending me back home. I won't go back there, Lisa. You should know that."

They all stared at her in horror for a long moment. Then Prince turned to Sarah. "What shall we do with her?"

"Is there someplace you can lock her up? We'll need to get the police."

"The police?" Lisa echoed in amazement.

"She tried to kill you, darling," Prince said. He grabbed Jane's arm and hauled her to her feet.

"You're hurting me," Jane cried.

"Good," Prince said, force-marching her out of the room.

Lisa looked up at Sarah. "Did she really try to poison me?"

Sarah glanced at the cup she was still cradling. "We'll soon find out, but yes, from what your husband told me, I'm sure she was. That's how she killed Mrs. Esposito."

"Sarah, what's going on?" Malloy's voice called from downstairs.

"I'll be right back," Sarah said, and hurried out.

Joe Prince was returning from having locked Jane in her room. "Will Lisa be all right?" he asked her anxiously.

"The doctor should be on his way. Meanwhile, I'll get her some milk to drink. That binds the arsenic." Sarah didn't like to think how she'd learned this sad fact. "Go in and sit with her."

He nodded and hurried back into the bedroom. Sarah walked carefully so she wouldn't spill the tea and found Malloy waiting for her at the bottom of the stairs. He knew better than to go barging upstairs and into a lady's bedroom.

"How is she?" Malloy said.

"I don't really know. Jane was giving her this tea when we arrived, so we'll need to get it tested."

He took the cup from her, and they both went in search of the kitchen. Sarah got a maid to take some milk up to Mrs. Prince while Malloy asked for a container into which he could pour the tea.

Sarah went back upstairs and sent the maid down with the teapot as well, in case Jane had poisoned it, too. "How are you feeling?" she asked Lisa.

"I . . . I hardly know." She turned to her husband, who had pulled a chair up beside the bed and was holding her hand.

"When did you first start feeling sick?"

"Right after supper last night. I'd told Joe everything when he came home, and I was very upset. Jane kept asking me what was wrong, and I finally told her I thought it was time for her to return to Saratoga."

"Oh dear."

"Yes, I knew it was a mistake as soon as I said it. She was very angry of course. She was concerned that I would tell her parents she'd been abducted and others would find out and she would be ruined. I promised her that I wouldn't, and then she seemed to calm down a little. In fact, she started being very nice. She even brought me some tea . . . Oh!"

"And it was after you drank it that you felt sick," Sarah guessed.

"But why would she want to kill you, darling?" Joe Prince said. "What would that gain her?"

"Maybe she was telling the truth," Sarah said. "Maybe she just intended to make Mrs. Prince ill. Then she could convince you that you needed her help."

The doorbell rang and Prince said with some relief, "That must be the doctor."

"I'll go down and tell him what we know," Sarah said.

The doctor was appalled, and Sarah got the impression he didn't quite believe her wild tale of an evil cousin and poisoned tea, but he'd seen enough accidental arsenic poisonings that he knew just what to do. She left him to it.

She found Malloy and Gino waiting in the parlor. "Have you sent for the police?"

The two men exchanged a glance. Malloy said, "I'm not sure if the Princes would thank us for that. It will mean publicity and scandal."

"But we can't just let Jane go. She's killed two people and tried to kill a third."

"Yes, but unless she confesses, I don't think we can prove any of it."

"We'll have the poisoned tea, but she'll certainly claim to know nothing about it," Sarah sighed. "So why don't I try to get her to confess?"

In the end, Malloy only consented when Sarah agreed that he should wait outside Jane's bedroom door in case she tried anything untoward.

Sarah knocked on Jane's bedroom door, realizing too late the irony of that courteous gesture since the door was locked. "Jane, I'd like to speak with you a moment," she said, turning the key and opening the door.

The room was pleasant, decorated with delicately carved furniture, light green drapes, and a matching satin coverlet on the bed. The wallpaper featured spring flowers. Quite a contrast from the spartan quarters at the settlement house.

Jane had pulled the chair from her dressing table over so she could sit and look out the window. She didn't even turn when Sarah came in. "It's too far to jump. I already checked."

The room had no other chair, so Sarah sat down on the edge of the bed nearest to where Jane was. She let the silence stretch a bit, in case Jane had anything else to say, but she didn't speak. Finally, Sarah said, "How did you come to know Nunzio Esposito?"

She turned to Sarah with a sly smile. "That's a mystery, isn't it? How could a respectable young lady like me know a man like that?"

"It is very hard to believe."

"I could hardly believe it myself," she said a bit smugly. "It was like a fairy tale. He fell in love with me at first sight. He saw me the very first day I was in the city. That girl Kate was showing me around the neighborhood. It was my hair that he noticed first, he said." She touched her golden hair tenderly. "He'd never known a woman so beautiful."

Or so blond, Sarah thought. Only women from Northern Italy had blond hair, and they would be untouchable for a man from Southern Italy, like Esposito. "That's very romantic," Sarah lied.

"He arranged to encounter me when I was visiting some of the neighborhood women. He gave me a nosegay the first time." A nosegay. Of course. Kate Westrop had told Maeve how Jane had often returned with flowers. "Do you know society girls get bouquets from their admirers before they go to a party? They take them to the party, pinned to long ribbons if they have a lot of them, to show how popular they are."

Sarah did know that. She'd received her share of bouquets in her day. "I'm sure you were very popular."

"No, I wasn't. I was never invited to the parties," she countered bitterly. "Because we didn't have any money. But Nunzio didn't care about that, and he had lots of money. He said he adored me. He said I would have everything I ever wanted."

"So he took you to a flat in a tenement?" Sarah asked, genuinely baffled.

"He couldn't take me to his house. We weren't married yet," she informed Sarah haughtily. "He made a place for me to stay, though, and it was lovely. And he bought me clothes. Beautiful clothes, silks and satins."

Sarah somehow managed to keep her voice neutral. "That was very nice of him."

"He loved me," she said almost defensively. "He gave me a diamond necklace to prove it. I'd never seen anything like it."

When Sarah had no reply for that, Jane turned to face her defiantly. "He put it around my neck, and then he undressed me, until all I was wearing was the diamond necklace. He *worshipped* me. I didn't know what it could be like when a man worshipped you like that. It was . . . *amazing.*"

Sarah had to swallow down her disgust. "What went wrong, Jane? Why did you leave him?"

Her lovely face crumpled into despair. "He was married!" she cried in anguish. "He never told me, not until after. Not until I'd spent two nights with him, and we'd done such things . . . things that could never be undone. I asked him how soon we could be married and he said he already had a wife but I would be his *queen*. But he's not really a king, is he, Mrs. Malloy? What would I have been a queen of?"

"You must have been very angry."

"I was furious, but I couldn't let him see, could I? He was a dangerous man. Everyone said so. And at first I didn't understand. I told him he could get a divorce. People do, don't they? Even the Vanderbilts get divorced."

"But he was Catholic," Sarah said.

Jane huffed in disgust. "He said his wife would never agree. We could never marry. He wanted me to be his *mistress*. Can you imagine? The shame of it! People would turn up their noses and laugh at me and I would never be accepted anywhere!"

"So you left him."

"I didn't know what else to do. I saw my life, what it would be. I couldn't bear it, so I ran back to the settlement house."

"And I gave you the perfect story to tell, didn't I?"

Jane smiled again, and the sight of it made Sarah's skin crawl. "Yes, you did. I might have thought of it myself, but I didn't have to. You made it so easy for me."

"But you couldn't forget all the beautiful things you'd left behind at the flat, could you?" Sarah prodded.

"Yes, all those lovely clothes. I'd never had clothes so fine, and they were mine, really. Nunzio had them made especially for me. All I had to do was go back to get them."

"But you couldn't go in the daytime when someone might see you."

"No, I couldn't, but it wasn't far. I could be there and back before anyone even knew I was gone."

"Christopher McWilliam knew you were gone."

If her expression was any indication, she hadn't known that. "Did he?"

"Yes, he was at his desk, and he saw you leaving. You had your Gladstone bag with you, didn't you?"

"Yes, to carry the clothes. It wouldn't hold all of them, I knew, but I could wear one outfit and take as many as would fit."

"Weren't you afraid of seeing Esposito?"

"No. Why would he be there once he realized I was gone?"

"But he *was* there, wasn't he? Waiting for you."

"I couldn't believe it. He had no idea I had left him, and he didn't even understand when I told him I'd never be his mistress. He told me that I had no choice, that I already was!"

"Is that why you stabbed him?"

Her face twisted with rage. "I hated him then. He wasn't even worried. He was sure I couldn't leave him. He didn't realize why I was looking in the kitchen cabinets. Maybe he thought I was going to make him supper," she said with a strange smile. "He wasn't even concerned when I pulled out the butcher knife. He was still smiling when I stuck it in him."

Somehow Sarah didn't shudder. "Do you realize you just confessed to murder?"

"No one saw me, and if you tell anyone, I'll call you a liar. Nunzio kidnapped me and I escaped. If anyone does accuse me of murder, I'll say I was just defending myself against another assault."

"Did Mrs. Esposito assault you, too?"

Jane's face contorted again. How could she be so lovely one minute and so ugly the next? "That was your fault."

Sarah had feared as much. "I didn't kill her."

"But you . . . She told you about the necklace. Nunzio said he bought it just for me, but it was hers first, wasn't it? She wanted it back, too, because he'd told her she could use it to support herself if anything happened to him. I know he did, because he told me the same thing when he put it around my neck."

"But you had the necklace. Why did you need to kill her?"

"I didn't know she'd gone to the flat that night until you told me. I had to be sure she didn't see me there."

"Did she know who you were when you knocked on her door?"

Jane's smile was almost feral. "I told her, but she wasn't jealous. I expected her to be jealous, but she was only inter-ested in the necklace. I found out she had no idea I'd killed him, but it was too late by then. I'd already put the arsenic in her tea."

"Where did you get it?"

"From here. Every well-run home in New York has some on hand to kill rats. You should know that."

She did know that. "So Mrs. Esposito didn't see you at the flat?"

This time Jane's smile was sweet. "No. She got there after he was dead and she never even knew I was there. I asked her."

Why had Mrs. Esposito lied about finding him alive? Probably to cast suspicion away from herself. Sarah sighed again, wearily this time. "Mrs. Esposito may not have seen you that night, but Christopher McWilliam did."

"How could he?" Jane scoffed. "He wasn't there. You said yourself he was in his office when he saw me leave."

"He also followed you. He was worried about your safety."

"You're lying!"

"No, I'm not. He followed you to the tenement on Pleas-ant Avenue. He was in the stairwell when you argued with Esposito and stabbed him, and he saw you running out."

Jane frowned as she considered this. "Then why did he say he'd killed Nunzio?"

"Like I told you, to protect you."

"Stupid fool. Well, there's nothing I can do about that. If he wants people to think he did it, I can't stop him."

There was plenty she could do, and she knew it, but Sarah also knew she wouldn't. "No, but I can stop him. I already told him that you weren't kidnapped and that you'd gone with Esposito willingly. He also knows you killed Mrs. Esposito and now I can tell him why, and you also tried to kill your cousin, Lisa."

"I told you, I wasn't going to kill her," Jane protested.

"The police may see things differently. We've sent for them, Miss Harding," Sarah said, rising from her seat on the bed.

"No!" Jane cried in anguish. "That's not fair!"

Sarah started walking to the door, and Jane began to scream. She flung herself at Sarah, nearly knocking her down, but Malloy had been listening and he was there in a trice, helping Sarah wrestle the girl away. Sarah's cheek burned where Jane had scratched her as she staggered back, out of Jane's reach.

"Get out," Malloy told her, holding Jane's hands so she couldn't reach Sarah.

Jane was sobbing now, great heaving gulps, and when Malloy released her hands, she sank to the floor in a heap.

He followed Sarah out into the hall and locked the door

behind them. Joe Prince had come out into the hall to see what was happening.

"She's crazy," he said, listening to Jane, who now was wailing incoherently.

"Yes," Sarah said. "I'm very much afraid she is."

XV

"WHAT WILL HAPPEN TO THE GIRL NOW?" MRS. ELLS-
worth said when Sarah had told her the whole story of Jane
Harding. The two women were sitting in Sarah's breakfast
room, enjoying a cup of coffee.

Several weeks had passed since that awful day at the
Prince home, and Sarah's neighbor had come over early on
this morning to borrow some sugar and ended up staying for
a visit. Mrs. Ellsworth had somewhat of a reputation for
knowing everything that happened in the neighborhood,
although having a new daughter-in-law living with her had
proven somewhat of a distraction, so she was a bit behind
the times.

"What would happen to Jane was a big concern, as you
can imagine. Mr. Prince insisted that the police arrest her
for trying to poison his wife. The tea did contain arsenic,
and while Jane might have only intended to make Lisa sick,

she certainly wasn't experienced at that, and she'd put in more than enough to kill her."

"How awful! I hope she's all right now."

"She hadn't drunk any of that batch yet, thank heaven, and Jane really hadn't put too much arsenic in the tea she had given her the night before. Lisa recovered quickly and it seems she has recovered completely."

"She was very lucky her husband came to chasten you," Mrs. Ellsworth said. "But you were going to tell me what happened to Jane."

"Yes, well, Lisa and Joe Prince had to notify Jane's parents, who were naturally distraught. In spite of everything she'd done, the very idea of a young woman like Jane Harding going to prison was unthinkable, particularly when she was obviously no longer in her right mind, or at least she was giving every indication of it."

"Do you think she was just pretending?" Mrs. Ellsworth asked.

"She was quite hysterical the last time I saw her, and I'm sure she was terrified when they put her in the Tombs, which would probably have caused even more hysteria. In any event, they couldn't let her go free either, after she poisoned her own cousin. Who knows what she might have done if her parents took her home with them to the town she'd fought so hard to escape? So the parents compromised and put her in an asylum."

"Somehow I can't help thinking that would be worse than a prison."

"If you really were in your right mind, I think you're right, but who knows? At least Jane won't be able to hurt anyone else."

"What do you think of my new hat?" Maeve asked,

coming into the breakfast room to model it. She turned slowly so they could get the full effect.

"It's very nice, dear," Mrs. Ellsworth said a little hesitantly.

Sarah understood. Something wasn't quite right. "Do you have it on backward?"

Maeve reached up to touch it, as if she could tell by feel if it was right or not, and Mrs. Ellsworth gasped.

"What's wrong?" Sarah asked, hoping her dear friend hadn't suddenly been taken ill.

She should have known better. "It's very bad luck to wear your hat backward, Maeve dear," Mrs. Ellsworth said. As Sarah had learned, Mrs. Ellsworth seemingly had a superstition for every occasion.

Maeve quickly removed the hat pin and pulled it off her head. "I don't need any bad luck today, not when I'm spending it with Gino's family."

At Mrs. Ellsworth's surprised look, Sarah said, "Gino has invited Maeve to the feast of Our Lady of Mount Carmel in East Harlem."

"It's not really a feast," Maeve said, examining her hat with a critical eye to determine where the front really was. "It's a festival, with a parade and lots of food and games and that sort of thing."

"With Gino's family?" Mrs. Ellsworth said archly.

"Just his oldest brother and sister-in-law," Maeve said, still studying her hat.

"Although Maeve did recently meet Gino's parents," Sarah said with a wink.

"Which did not go well," Maeve said, "so you can save your matchmaking superstitions. They want Gino to marry a Catholic girl."

"And here you are, going to a Catholic festival," Mrs. Ellsworth said, winking back at Sarah.

"Only because I like Teo and Rinaldo," Maeve said, "and the food. Does this look right?" She set the hat gingerly on her head so as not to mess up her carefully pinned hair.

"Yes, much better," Sarah said. "Have a wonderful time."

Maeve rolled her eyes and was gone.

"And speaking of bad luck," Mrs. Ellsworth said when Maeve was gone. "What does Mr. Malloy think of Governor Roosevelt being nominated for vice president?"

"He's disappointed because he thinks Theodore is doing a fine job as governor, and Theodore isn't best pleased either. My mother told me that he believes certain people pushed for him to be nominated because they didn't like his efforts to clean up corruption in New York state."

"He didn't have to take the nomination, did he?"

"He felt he had to, I think. His nomination was approved unanimously, but everyone knows the vice presidency isn't a very important job. If McKinley is re-elected, poor Theodore will be stuck in Washington for the next four years with nothing much to do."

"Unless the president dies," Mrs. Ellsworth said.

"McKinley is a relatively young man and in good health, so I don't think that's very likely, and we'll have lost Theodore as governor and his efforts at reforming New York."

"You're right. Poor Mr. Roosevelt."

MAEVE HAD TO ADMIT THE FESTIVAL WAS MORE FUN than she had expected. The streets had been decorated with gold bunting, and electric lights had been strung everywhere. The parade was noisy and they were mostly carrying a statue of the Virgin Mary, whom Maeve had learned was the real Lady of Mount Carmel. What Mount Carmel had to do with anything, Maeve wasn't sure, but she wasn't interested enough to ask.

Teo and Rinaldo seemed thrilled to have her there, though, and they didn't even tease her very much about coming with Gino. Enzo and several of Gino's younger brothers and cousins had also come up from Little Italy for the festival, and they *had* done a lot of teasing. Fortunately, it was all in Italian, so she didn't even have to pretend not to understand.

As the day wore on, the wine flowed more freely and people laughed a lot more. Maeve noticed men making donations at the statue of Mary, dropping money into a basket at her feet and not even trying to hide how much they were giving. One man in particular stepped up to the statue and paused, making sure everyone was looking before making his donation. He was wearing an expensive suit and a diamond stick pin that glittered in the bright July sun. When he had everyone's attention, he dropped in an enormous wad of greenbacks. The gasps from the crowd were his reward as he smiled beneficently at everyone and then made his way slowly through the crowd to wherever he was going.

"Balducci," Gino whispered to Maeve. "Trying to be a big man in front of all these people."

"Is that what Esposito would have done?" she asked.

"Probably. But his gift isn't so generous when you realize that it was extorted from all the people here."

Maeve glanced at the faces of those watching Balducci leave, and she didn't see admiration or respect. She saw only fear and hatred. How many of them had paid a ransom for a kidnapped family member? How many had paid money for protection from the very men who were collecting it?

Some of Gino's younger brothers and cousins came running up and started jabbering at him, obviously trying to get him to do something.

"He's very good at darts," one of them told her in English. "We want him to win us a prize over there." He pointed to the area where the game booths had been set up.

Gino was shaking his head and making excuses, but Teo said, "Go on. Maeve and I will look around here. They have some beautiful things in the stalls that she might want to buy."

Maeve happily agreed and the boys dragged Gino away.

"If you are looking at lady things, we will go find some *vino*," Rinaldo said cheerfully, and he led Enzo and some of the older cousins on a quest for wine.

Maeve and Teo started examining the goods for sale at various stalls, brightly colored fabrics and elaborately embroidered linens and delicately carved statues of saints.

"What do you think?" Teo asked, holding up a bolt of fabric.

"Beautiful."

"I think I will buy some. I will need new clothes soon. I am going to get very fat," she said with a twinkle, lightly touching her stomach.

Maeve needed only a moment to figure out what she meant. "Oh, Teo, that's wonderful. When are you due?"

"In February, I think."

"Does Rinaldo know?"

"Yes, but not his family. We have not told anyone yet. Only you."

"I'm honored, but why did you tell me?"

Teo smiled. "Because I think you will be part of our family soon."

Oh no, was this the bad fortune Mrs. Ellsworth had predicted? Maeve's face felt as if it were on fire, and she shook her head as fast as she could, but that only made Teo laugh.

"Gino and I are just friends," Maeve protested.

"We will see," Teo said, and turned to the vendor to ask her to cut a length of the fabric for her.

They wandered out of that booth and on to the next, but Maeve hardly saw the goods that were on display. Was this what Gino's family was expecting? Did Gino know? Surely he didn't or he never would have brought her here today.

"Teo! Teo!"

The shout caught their attention, and both women stepped out of the stall to see who was calling her. At the sight of them, a young boy came running over to them. Maeve recognized him as one of Gino's younger brothers. Or was he a cousin? She wasn't even sure. There were so many of them to keep straight.

Teo said something to him in Italian, and he answered in a rapid patter of words and many wild gestures that told Maeve something truly bad had happened. Teo's eyes were terrified when she turned to Maeve. "Someone has taken Gino."

"What do you mean, *taken*?"

"Kidnapped, I think, from what Alonzo says. They were taking turns, throwing darts to win a prize. Gino stepped back to let the other boys have their turns, and when they looked for him again, he was gone and there was a letter on the ground where he was standing."

"What kind of letter?"

"A letter, in an envelope," Alonzo said. He obviously

spoke English as well as Teo when he wanted to. "It has a black hand on it."

This was the bad fortune Mrs. Ellsworth was talking about.

Teo made a distressed sound and crossed herself. "Where is this letter? Who has it?"

"Come," Alonzo said. "Rinaldo said you should come."

The women followed him, making their way through the crowds with agonizing slowness.

They found the Donatelli men and boys gathered in a cluster, all looking furious and frustrated.

"What does the letter say?" Maeve demanded of Rinaldo, who held a white envelope as gingerly as if he expected it to explode at any minute.

"I don't know. It has Mr. Malloy's name on it."

Maeve snatched it from his hand. It did indeed have a crude drawing of a hand in heavy black ink and *Frank Malloy* written across it in uneven block letters. Without hesitation, she tore it open. The Donatelli men and boys gasped in unison at her boldness, but she didn't care. She wasn't going to wait for Mr. Malloy to find out what it said.

What it said was very simple. They would release Gino if Mr. Malloy paid fifty thousand dollars in ransom. Teo was reading over Maeve's shoulder.

"They want *fifty thousand dollars* in ransom," she told the others.

This caused more than a gasp. An angry murmur quickly became shouted imprecations, mostly in Italian. Finally, Rinaldo hushed them. "Why do they want so much? They must know we cannot pay."

"Mr. Malloy can pay," Maeve said, holding on to her temper with difficulty. Getting angry wouldn't help Gino. She had to keep her head. "They must have found out he's rich, and they want some revenge because Gino and Mr. Malloy embarrassed Balducci."

"Will he pay it?" Enzo asked.

Maeve turned all the strength of her fury on him. "No, he will not, because we are going to find Gino and bring him back today and put an end to this nonsense once and for all."

It was an empty promise and an impossible task, but the males in their group didn't think of that. The older ones had been drinking enough to feel invincible and the younger ones still thought they were.

"How will we find him?" Rinaldo asked.

"They have a house where they take the people they kidnap," Maeve said. "It's not in the city, but it's not far away either."

"Where is it?"

Maeve's mind was racing. How could they find it? She and Gino had been driving the motorcar out in the country off and on for weeks now, looking and looking, and hadn't located it. She knew who could tell them, though. They had just never had the ability to ask before. "Someone at Esposito's saloon will know, and if enough of you demand it, he will tell us."

Rinaldo's eyes lit with understanding, and he nodded. He explained the plan to everyone in Italian, and all the brothers and cousins agreed with shouts.

"You'll probably need more men," Maeve said. "They'll need to see that the whole community is turning against them. Who else will help?"

"Mr. Cassidi," Rinaldo said with confidence.

"I just saw his wife a few minutes ago in one of the stalls," Teo said.

"Go find her," Maeve said. "He'll help, and tell him to bring everyone he can find."

"All the men who work for Mr. Cassidi will come, too, and men whose businesses have to pay protection," Rinaldo said, then switched to Italian to issue orders to his motley crew. Men and boys instantly scattered in all directions to find reinforcements. Rinaldo turned to Maeve. "I told them where to meet and to bring what weapons they can find."

"Balducci's men will have guns," Maeve said.

"They probably won't shoot in their own saloon, and even if they do, they can't kill us all."

Maeve had no reply for such bravado.

They saw Teo and Mrs. Cassidi making their way back to them, and Rinaldo raced toward them, with Maeve in his wake.

"Teo told me what happened," Mrs. Cassidi said. "I will find my husband. He will bring more men."

Rinaldo told her where they would be meeting, and Mrs. Cassidi hurried off.

"Teo, you should not be involved in this," Rinaldo said with a concerned frown. Naturally, he would be worried about her condition.

"No, she shouldn't," Maeve agreed, ignoring Teo's sputtered protests. "But you can do something very important, Teo. Go to the settlement house and tell Mr. McWilliam what happened. Then telephone Mr. Malloy. He won't be in his office today, and I think he and Mrs. Malloy were taking the children out, but you can telephone his house and leave a message. Then you will have to wait for him to get home and telephone you to find out what is happening."

"Will he come?"

"I don't think anything could stop him from coming, but

he'll be too late, I'm sure. I hope we'll have Gino back by the time he gets here."

Teo hurried away, leaving Maeve and Rinaldo alone in the milling crowd of people.

"Thank you for making her safe," Rinaldo said.

"It's an important task," Maeve said, shrugging off his gratitude. "Go ahead and help your brothers gather up more men."

"What will you do?"

"I'll go get the motorcar."

"Mr. Malloy's motorcar?"

"Yes, Gino drove it up here today. We'll need some way to get to him when we find out where he's being held."

"But who will drive it?"

Maeve said the one thing she knew, out of all that had happened today, would terrify him the most: "I will."

MAEVE DROVE SLOWLY AND CAREFULLY. SHE HADN'T yet driven in the city, although Gino had let her spend hours behind the wheel when they were out in the country, looking for the kidnappers' house. She pulled up to the curb near the saloon, and she couldn't believe how many men had gathered in the appointed meeting spot, far more than would fit in the motor. She saw all the Donatellis of course, Mr. Cassidi, and even Christopher McWilliam, but dozens more had joined them. They carried pieces of pipe and cord wood and boards obviously broken off packing crates or taken from construction sites. All of them were armed with something, but none of them carried a gun that she could see. She hoped that would be enough.

She sat there for a long moment, allowing herself to

really think of Gino for the first time. She'd been so busy
planning his rescue, she hadn't let herself even remember
that he was being held prisoner, that he might also have
been injured, because she knew he wouldn't have gone willingly. He might be hurt or even dying, and regardless of
what they said about kidnappers not wanting to hurt their
captives, people did sometimes die. Balducci certainly had
no love for Gino or Mr. Malloy. He might see this as an opportunity to take Mr. Malloy's money and Gino's life in
exchange for his own pride.

Her eyes burned, but she refused to cry. There would be
time for that later, if she needed to cry. For now she would
only think about how to save him.

Rinaldo had seen her, and he came running over, unable
to disguise his amazement that she had really driven the
motorcar. "I sent some of the men for wagons, too. There are
too many to go in this."

"I can see that. You should let everyone else in the saloon
go, but be sure you catch everyone who's in the Black Hand.
I'm sure everybody knows who they are. But be careful because they might have guns."

"We will take them away," Rinaldo assured her.

"Then knock them around a bit so that they're really
scared, but you don't need to hurt them badly. When they're
good and scared, ask Balducci where they've taken Gino. If
he resists, start beating on his men some more until one of
them talks."

Rinaldo smiled, which made him look so much like
Gino, she thought her heart would break. "Gino will be
proud of you."

With that, he hurried back to rejoin the group that was
quickly becoming a mob.

She saw several open wagons had pulled up along the street. She only hoped they would soon have someplace to go. At someone's command, the mob of men surged forward. Two men in front carried a beer barrel between them, and when they reached the saloon, they heaved it through the plate glass window.

Breaking glass, Maeve observed, was one of the most distressing sounds on earth, and the roar of surprise and terror that followed proved it. Men came pouring out of the saloon, some bleeding and all of them stumbling and cursing and screaming. The mob caught and held a few of them and let the rest go. When the saloon had emptied, the mob surged inside, taking their captives with them.

An eerie silence fell on the street as the terrified saloon patrons fled and the curious stood mute, waiting to see what would happen next. Even the mob had stilled as they went about their work inside. It didn't take them long. Soon the mob emerged, pouring out of the saloon like one giant entity with a vital purpose. Maeve saw they had Balducci. He was bleeding from a cut on his head and his eyes were crazed with terror. Rinaldo threw him down into the street. He came up on his knees, seeming to beg.

"If my brother is not there, we will come back here and burn this place to the ground with you in it," Rinaldo told him.

Balducci said something Maeve couldn't hear, and then Rinaldo, Enzo, and the older cousins were heading for the motorcar while the rest of the mob separated and piled into the various wagons.

Maeve realized that at some point she had risen to her feet, so she quickly sat back down, ready to drive when her passengers arrived. That was when she discovered Mrs. Cassidi was sitting beside her.

"There will be children there," she said at Maeve's surprised look. "I can help."

Enzo was leading a man whose head was also bleeding and who was obviously not coming willingly.

"He knows where the house is," Rinaldo explained, squeezing into the front seat beside Mrs. Cassidi.

Enzo and some of the cousins started to push their captive into the back seat, but he balked and started shouting in Italian, pointing at Maeve.

Rinaldo grinned. "He's more afraid of you driving this thing than he is of us."

Someone gave him a whack, and he finally allowed himself to be shoved into the back seat.

More men than she would have imagined managed to squeeze into the motor, and a couple even clung to the sides. Enzo translated the captive's directions into English for Maeve, and she drove north, out of the city, across the Harlem River, and into the country she and Gino had already explored so thoroughly. She drove slowly so the wagons could keep pace.

Maeve had been right—it wasn't far—but no wonder they hadn't found it. The house was probably over a hundred years old and surrounded by enormous trees, so it was practically invisible from the road. It looked deserted, with its blackened windows and overgrown yard.

By the time they reached it, the men's anger had cooled to grim determination. They climbed out of the motor and the wagons and gathered in the road.

"They may have guns," Rinaldo said.

"They will be too shocked to use them if we surprise them," Mr. Cassidi said. "They will not be expecting trouble."

No, they wouldn't be. No one had ever challenged them before.

The men started silently, spreading out so they could surround the house. Mrs. Cassidi grabbed Maeve's arm. Maeve looked up in surprise and saw the fear on her face. Of course she was afraid. This was where she had been a prisoner for weeks.

"Are you all right?" Maeve whispered.

"I will be," she replied.

Someone shouted a command in Italian and then all the men roared out their fury. Smashing wood and shattering glass and a single gunshot made Maeve and Mrs. Cassidi instinctively cling to each other, but the cacophony did not last long. Soon an eerie silence fell, and Mr. Cassidi emerged from the broken front door and gestured them to come.

Mrs. Cassidi did not hesitate. She strode forward as if in triumph, leaving Maeve to scurry behind. Mr. Cassidi said something to her in Italian, but she didn't even look at him. She kept walking into the house. Maeve followed and they found two men kneeling in the front room, surrounded by the army of angry Italians. The two men had their hands raised in surrender, their expressions terrified.

Both men obviously recognized Mrs. Cassidi, and their terror only increased when she spoke to them. One of the men replied in a wheedling tone, apparently begging for mercy. Mrs. Cassidi smiled with satisfaction and turned to her husband. Some silent communication occurred between them, and he strode forward without hesitation, raised the length of pipe he held, and crushed the man's skull.

Maeve cried out in surprise, but no one else made a sound except the other man being held. He started begging and pleading, but no one even looked at him. Plainly, Mr. Cassidi had avenged his wife.

But where was Gino? Maeve couldn't forget the single gunshot. Would they have killed him when they realized they had been discovered? Then she saw Rinaldo waving to her from the other side of the room. She skirted the body that now lay crumpled and the sobbing man still begging for his life and pushed through the crowd of rescuers to find a hallway leading to the rest of the downstairs.

"Gino?" she asked.

"He's all right," Rinaldo said, pointing to an open door.

Maeve hurried in, her heart pounding. He was sitting on a cot, rubbing his wrists while Enzo untied a rope from around his ankles. "Gino!"

He looked up in surprise. "Maeve, what are you doing here?"

His hair was a mess and one eye was turning purple and his good suit was filthy and torn at the shoulder. "I could ask you the same question," she said, and then burst into tears.

"*Dio mio*," Enzo muttered, shaking his head.

Maeve didn't care. She went to Gino, who tried to stand up but Enzo pushed him back down because he wasn't finished untying the ropes, so Maeve could only throw her arms awkwardly around Gino's shoulders and rest her cheek on his head and say, "Thank heaven you're all right."

"Ouch," he replied, jerking his head away because she'd pressed his swollen eye to her bosom.

"*Are* you all right?" she asked through her tears. Why on earth was she crying *now*? "Except for that, I mean?" She gestured toward his bad eye.

"And a splitting headache, yes, I'm fine. What on earth are you doing here, though?"

"She drove us here in Mr. Malloy's motorcar," Enzo informed him happily. "She's a pretty good driver for a girl."

Maeve cuffed him on the shoulder, making him laugh.

At last he pulled the ropes free. "Do you think you can walk?" Enzo asked.

"Give me a minute." He looked up at Maeve. "There are children upstairs. I could hear them."

"Mrs. Cassidi came with us. She'll look after them. Are you sure you aren't hurt? How did they get you away from the festival?"

"They sapped me." He rubbed the back of his head gingerly. "I wasn't completely out, but I couldn't fight them, and two of them just dragged me away. People probably thought I was just drunk."

Of course they did.

"How did you find me?" Gino finally thought to ask.

Enzo glanced at Maeve and grinned. "*Your girl* suggested that we mob Esposito's saloon and beat up Balducci's men until one of them told us where you were."

Gino gazed up at Maeve for a long moment with a look of wonder on his face. Maeve thoroughly enjoyed it until he finally said, "What took you so long?"

THE QUICK BROWN FOX JUMPS OVER THE LAZY DOG," Maeve whispered to herself as she hit each key. She was definitely getting faster at this. How many more hours would she have to practice before she got really good? Maeve wasn't sure she wanted to find out.

She heard footsteps in the hall outside the office and

looked up expectantly, ready to greet a prospective client. But the person who stepped through the door wasn't a client.

"Gino," she said in surprise. "Are you . . . How are you feeling?" Mr. Malloy had told him to take all the time he needed to recover from his ordeal, but it had been only two days.

His black eye had turned several ugly shades of yellow and green, but he was still very handsome. He'd paused awkwardly half-in and half-out of the door, as if uncertain of his welcome. "Where's Mr. Malloy?"

"He's out on a case."

Gino frowned. "Without me?"

"It was an easy one."

He nodded. Then he came all the way into the office, and she saw he had simply been concealing a bouquet of flowers he held in his other hand.

"I, uh, brought you these." He held out the flowers.

"That's nice," she said uncertainly. She got up and walked around her desk to take them. "What is the occasion?"

He made a face. "To thank you for . . . well, you know, what you did."

She pretended to be surprised. "Did you think I'd let somebody kidnap you and not do anything?"

Gino sighed. "Enzo and Rinaldo both told me how the whole thing was your idea."

"Not the *whole* thing," she demurred. "It wasn't my idea to burn down the house." The rescuers had decided to show the Black Hand their opinion of the kidnappings by setting fire to the house once they'd freed the kidnapped children. They'd left the dead body of the man Mr. Cassidi had executed inside as a further warning. No one, they knew, would be interested in investigating either the killing or the fire.

"Maybe not, but my brothers were even afraid to open the envelope. Without you . . ."

He was right of course, but Maeve didn't need to embarrass his brothers any more. "They were just in shock. As soon as I realized they could get a bunch of angry Donatellis together, it was obvious they could do what nobody had been able to do before. I just had to mention that somebody in that saloon would know where you were. They did the rest."

Gino shook his head. "My mother can't believe they let a girl drive a motorcar."

Maeve grinned at that. "She *was* awfully surprised when I dropped you and your bothers and cousins off at the house. I still can't believe your brothers rode with me."

"They'll be telling their grandchildren about it."

Maeve thought about Teo's baby and wondered if Gino knew yet. "Are you really all right?"

"My head still aches a little, but Mr. Malloy sent a doctor to look me over and I'm fine. The only thing that might not recover is my pride."

"What are you talking about?"

He pulled another face. "Being rescued by a girl."

She didn't have to pretend to be annoyed. "I didn't do anything you wouldn't have done for me."

"Yes, but—"

"But nothing, and the men did all the rescuing."

"You just told them what to do. Rinaldo said you were as brave as a man."

"I wasn't brave at all. I was scared spitless when I realized they'd taken you. They wanted fifty thousand dollars! How do you even carry that much money? I was sure they just planned to kill you out of revenge."

"And that scared you?" he said with a little too much interest.

"Of course it did! You're my . . . *friend*. I don't want anything to happen to you."

"Is that all I am, a *friend*?"

"I . . ." Suddenly, Maeve couldn't seem to catch her breath.

"Maeve?" He reached up and gently cupped her face in his hands.

"Wait!" she cried.

"Wait for what?"

"If you kiss me, we can never go back."

"Go back where?"

Was he an idiot? "Back to being friends!"

He smiled at that. "I don't want to go back there. Do you?"

She wanted to laugh and cry at the same time. "I'm not Italian and I'm not Catholic and your mother hates me."

"Forget all that. Do you just want to be *friends*?" he demanded.

"No, I don't," she said with a sigh.

Author's Note

As the grandchild of Italian immigrants, I really love researching and writing about the Italian-American experience. I've also been anxious to "meet" more members of Gino's family and to advance Maeve and Gino's relationship, at least a bit. Fans have been nagging me about them for a while now, so I thought it was time. This book is the result of all that.

I learned some interesting things while researching this book. I was a little surprised to discover that the Black Hand was not part of the Mafia or, as I originally believed, the forerunner of the Mafia. It was, in fact, a completely separate group, operated by Calabrians, that challenged the Mafia, which was run by Sicilians. The Black Hand did sell protection and kidnap women and children, as I described here. It was finally ended by Postal Inspector Frank Oldfield, a member of the most powerful federal law enforcement agency at that time. Who knew that about postal inspectors? He took down train robbers, murderers, and embezzlers, and in 1909, he finally was able to take down sixteen members of a Black Hand organization, resulting in the first international organized crime conviction in America.

Joseph Petrosino was a real police officer in New York City, one of the first Italian officers on the force and a pioneer in the fight against organized crime until he was assassinated in 1909 while in Sicily on a secret mission.

Settlement houses were an early attempt to meet the needs of the poor in a practical way. Perhaps the most famous of these was Jane Addams's Hull-House in Chicago, but many existed in other cities as well. In 1895, the Union Theological Seminary Alumni Club started a settlement house in East Harlem. I based the Harlem Settlement House on this one, although I located it in a different place and changed many details.

The Church of Our Lady of Mount Carmel is a real church in East Harlem. They still hold the annual festival I describe, although now it is held in August instead of July. They did not add the dancing Giglio until 1909, which broke my heart because I wanted to include it in this story, but it was too historically inaccurate to "fudge." Maybe I can use it in another story.

Please let me know how you enjoyed this book. You can follow me on Facebook at Victoria.Thompson.Author, on Twitter @gaslightvt, or email me through my website, victoriathompson.com. If you email me, I'll put you on my mailing list and let you know whenever I have a new book coming out.

Keep reading for a special preview of
the next Gaslight mystery

MURDER ON WALL STREET

Coming soon from Berkley Prime Crime!

THE BABY SEEMS TO BE IN THE RIGHT POSITION, BUT YOU haven't dropped yet, so I think you have a while still to go."

Sarah Malloy managed a smile. No woman in the last month of her pregnancy wanted to hear she still had a while to go, especially in July.

"How long is a *while*?" Jocelyn Robinson asked crossly as she sat up in her bed and rearranged her clothing after Sarah's examination. They were in Jocelyn's bedroom, which she had obviously newly decorated with the most stylish furnishings.

"No one can say for certain. Babies come when they're ready."

"But . . . I thought it would be easy to figure out since I know exactly when . . . when the baby got started," Jocelyn said with a frown.

By which Jocelyn meant that she knew the exact day when she had been raped by a young man whom she'd had no reason to suspect would dream of doing such a thing.

Sarah's reassuring smile held. "That does make it easier, but even still, we can't predict exactly when the baby will come. You could give birth tomorrow and prove I have no idea what I'm talking about."

"I don't want to insult you," Jocelyn said with a rueful grin, "but I'd be very happy to give birth tomorrow. Or even today." She wrinkled her nose hopefully. "Don't you know some midwife trick to hurry things along?"

Sarah laughed at that. "I know a dozen, but none of them really work. About all they accomplish is giving the expectant mother something to do while she's waiting."

Jocelyn sighed and reached out in a silent request for Sarah to help her up from the bed. When she was on her feet, after some effort from both women, Jocelyn invited Sarah to join her downstairs for some cool lemonade.

The parlor—like the bedroom and most of the rest of the house—had been redecorated since Jocelyn had married Jack Robinson in January. The dark, heavy velvet furnishings favored by the house's original owner—and left undisturbed after Jack had acquired the house—had been replaced by lighter, more fashionable damask, showing Jocelyn's excellent taste. Today the parlor windows were open to what little breeze was available, and the lemonade was a welcome treat.

When the maid who had served them withdrew, Sarah said, "How are things going with you and Jack?"

Jocelyn sighed, making Sarah a little fearful of what her answer would be. Sarah had, after all, played matchmaker for the couple, who hadn't even known each other until a few weeks before they wed. "I can't believe how kind Jack has been to me. From the very first day, he's been so thoughtful about everything."

"I noticed that you are sharing the bedroom," Sarah said. The little signs of Jack's presence had been everywhere.

Jocelyn smiled shyly at that, and the color blossomed in her cheeks. "Yes, we have been, almost from the beginning. Jack is . . ." She gestured helplessly.

Sarah was sure she understood. Jack had set out to completely charm his bride, and he had obviously succeeded. "So that part of your marriage is good," Sarah guessed.

Jocelyn sighed again. "Better than good."

"But something isn't right," Sarah guessed again, wondering if she dared offer advice or even if she would have any to give.

"Not really. It's just that . . ." Sarah waited, giving Jocelyn time to choose her words. "I can't help wondering if Jack will be able to accept the baby."

"Has he said anything to make you think he won't?"

"No, he hasn't, but he doesn't speak of the baby much at all. Neither do I, come to that. I think we're both a little . . . self-conscious about it."

"He did understand that the baby is part of the bargain you made with him when you chose to marry," Sarah said. "I know some people think Jack Robinson is an immoral man because of the way he made his living, but he does have his own moral code. Keeping his word is important to him."

"Oh, I know he'll keep his word, but providing for a child and accepting it as your own are two very different things."

"Ah yes, I see what you mean. I can't speak for Jack, of course, but I do know that it's very possible to come to love someone else's child as much as you would your own."

"How could you know that?" Jocelyn scoffed.

"Because neither of my children is mine by birth."

"What?" Jocelyn asked, thoroughly shocked. "What do you mean?"

"Brian is Malloy's son with his first wife. She died when . . . when he was a baby." No sense telling a pregnant woman that Malloy's first wife had died in childbirth. "And Catherine was a foundling. I took her in, and when Malloy and I married, we adopted her. I adopted Brian at the same time."

"And you . . . you love them?"

"As if they were my own flesh and blood. Malloy already loved Brian, of course, but he's come to love Catherine just as much. So you see, families can be made as well as born, and let's not forget we're talking about a baby here. Nothing is cuter or easier to love than an infant."

"Even for a man?" Jocelyn asked with a worried frown.

"Especially for a man," Sarah said with a knowing smile, "because he doesn't have to get up with it in the middle of the night or change its diapers or do all the unpleasant parts of parenting."

Jocelyn finally smiled at that. "I see what you mean. I hadn't thought of that."

"Just give Jack a chance. If you expect him to accept the baby, he probably will. He might not be as excited as he would be if he were the baby's father, but let him know you expect him to be the father in every way from now on, and he will probably rise to the occasion."

Jocelyn's sigh was more relief than worry this time, and she rubbed her rounded stomach possessively.

"Do you feel a little better now?" Sarah asked.

"A little. I'll just be glad when the baby is born and I know how he's going to react."

"Speaking of knowing, have you spoken to your parents?"

"Oh my, didn't I tell you? Well, I think I did tell you that I wrote to them right after the wedding so they would know where I was and why I'd left the clinic." When they originally found out she was pregnant, Jocelyn's parents had sent her to the maternity clinic that Sarah had opened on the Lower East Side. They had wanted to keep her out of sight so she could give birth in secret, put the baby up for adoption, and resume her place in society.

"Yes, you told me that. I'm sure they were quite surprised."

"They always assumed I'd been lying about being raped, of course. When I married Jack, they decided that I'd just been ashamed of being seduced by a gangster and made up the whole rape story."

"That's probably just as well, since that's what you and Jack expected people to believe anyway."

"Yes, well . . . It hurt when they didn't believe me, and I don't think I can ever forgive them for that, but seeing their faces when they met Jack almost made up for it."

"They've met him then?" Sarah asked in delight.

"Oh yes. I had invited them to dinner. They didn't respond at first, not for months in fact. I wasn't surprised. They must have been thoroughly shocked that I would dare defy them like that and marry without getting their permission, much less without them even knowing. Then, about a month ago, my mother wrote me a note saying they would be happy to meet my new husband. We had put an announcement in the newspapers, of course, and we had already entertained some of my friends who were also anxious to meet my notorious new husband. I guess my parents' friends were asking all sorts of questions about their new son-in-law, and how could they admit they'd never met him?"

"That would be difficult. Even if you'd eloped against their wishes, they'd eventually be reconciled."

"And so they were. I'd done all the redecorating of the house by then. Jack was so generous. He told me to buy whatever I wanted."

"And you did a marvelous job."

"Thank you," Jocelyn said with a modest smile. "My parents were shocked, though. I don't know if they expected to find me living in a hovel or what, but they were obviously impressed by the house. And they were terrified of Jack!"

"Terrified? Why?" Sarah asked, amazed.

"His reputation, I suppose. And I'd also like to think they felt at least a little guilty for sending me to the clinic."

"Maybe they thought Jack would want revenge or something," Sarah said.

"Maybe," Jocelyn agreed. She was really smiling now. "Anyway, they were so nervous, they could hardly have a conversation. I have to admit, my mother did seem to have been worried about me. She told me privately that she'd wanted to visit me right away, but Father wouldn't let her come."

"How did Jack treat them?"

"That's the really funny part. Even though they were obviously frightened of him, he treated them with complete respect. I think that upset them more than anything."

"Because they'd been expecting him to be angry, I suppose."

"Or uncouth. Jack said he was nervous about meeting

them, but you never would have known. He was the perfect host."

"I'm sure Jack has been in much more stressful situations. Your parents probably weren't carrying weapons, for example," she said with a grin. "Have they invited you to dine with them in return?"

"Yes, but I'm too far along to be out in public, so I had to decline."

"Are you serious?" Sarah asked.

"Oh yes. Jack doesn't want me to leave the house for fear I'll go into labor, and even if I wanted to defy him, my *servants* wouldn't permit it."

"And by *servants*, I assume you mean Tom and Marie O'Day," Sarah said with an amused smile. Sarah knew Jocelyn's butler and cook well from a case she and Malloy had worked on. Jack Robinson had hired the O'Days to help him with his new, respectable persona.

"Exactly. Marie has been making sure I eat well every single day, and Tom guards me like I was some rare treasure entrusted to his care. They only relax their vigilance when Jack is at home."

"And is he frequently at home?"

"More so of late. He has been divesting himself of almost all his illegal businesses. He said they kept him out in the evenings when he preferred to be home with me." Jocelyn gave her another modest smile.

"How very sweet of him."

"I thought so."

"What business is he in now?"

"He's buying real estate, or so he says. He calls it investing."

"How respectable."

"That's what I told him. He seems quite pleased with himself, although I do worry about him. Businessmen can be rather unscrupulous. I hope no one is taking advantage of him."

"Oh Jocelyn," Sarah said, shaking her head. "If I were you, I'd worry about Jack taking advantage of other people. That's far more likely!"

THE NEXT MORNING, FRANK LOOKED UP WITH PLEASURE when Jack Robinson entered the modest offices of *Frank Malloy, Confidential Inquiries*. Maeve Smith, his part-time secretary who also served as nanny to his children, was at home taking care of the children this summer morning, and his partner was still recuperating from a particularly troublesome case, so Frank was holding down the fort alone.

After the two men had greeted each other and observed the usual pleasantries—Jocelyn was doing well, as Sarah had already reported to Frank at dinner last night—and Frank had escorted Jack into his private office, the men settled back into their chairs. Frank said, "Now tell me what brings you here."

"Hayden Norcross is dead."

Frank frowned as he tried to remember where he had heard the name. "Is that the fellow who was shot in his Wall Street office the other day?"

"The very one."

Frank considered this information for a moment and found nothing of interest in it. "I saw it in the newspapers, but why do you care?"

"Don't you know who Norcross is?" Jack asked, a bit puzzled.

"Some rich society fellow who made his living by cheating other rich society fellows, I'd guess."

"He's . . ." Jack looked away, and for the first time in the year since Frank had known Jack Robinson, he looked disturbed. But only for a moment. When he turned back to Frank, he was resolute again. "He's the man who . . . attacked Jocelyn."

By which he meant Norcross was the erstwhile suitor who had raped Jocelyn and gotten her with child. Then he had denied it and refused to marry her. Jack must hate Norcross with a passion, and he certainly had good reason to want him dead, and now Norcross really was dead. "I see," Frank said, afraid that he saw all too clearly. "And you need to hire a private investigator to help you."

NATIONAL BESTSELLING AUTHOR

VICTORIA THOMPSON

"Victoria Thompson shines."

—Tamar Myers, national bestselling author
of *Tea with Jam and Dread*

For a complete list of titles,
please visit prh.com/victoriathompson